MORAY I
THE CASE OF AL.

KATHERINE DALTON RENOIR ('Moray Dalton') was born in Hammersmith, London in 1881, the only child of a Canadian father and English mother.

The author wrote two well-received early novels, *Olive in Italy* (1909), and *The Sword of Love* (1920). However, her career in crime fiction did not begin until 1924, after which Moray Dalton published twenty-nine mysteries, the last in 1951. The majority of these feature her recurring sleuths, Scotland Yard inspector Hugh Collier and private inquiry agent Hermann Glide.

Moray Dalton married Louis Jean Renoir in 1921, and the couple had a son a year later. The author lived on the south coast of England for the majority of her life following the marriage. She died in Worthing, West Sussex, in 1963.

MORAY DALTON MYSTERIES
Available from Dean Street Press

MORAY DALTON

THE CASE OF ALAN COPELAND

With an introduction by Curtis Evans

DEAN STREET PRESS

Published by Dean Street Press 2020

Copyright © 1937 Moray Dalton

Introduction Copyright © 2020 Curtis Evans

All Rights Reserved

Published by licence, issued under the UK Orphan Works
Licensing Scheme.

First published in 1937 by Sampson Low

Cover by DSP

ISBN 978 1 913054 83 0

www.deanstreetpress.co.uk

LOST GOLD FROM A GOLDEN AGE

The Detective Fiction of Moray Dalton (Katherine Mary Deville Dalton Renoir, 1881-1963)

"GOLD" COMES in many forms. For literal-minded people gold may be merely a precious metal, physically stripped from the earth. For fans of Golden Age detective fiction, however, gold can be artfully spun out of the human brain, in the form not of bricks but books. While the father of Katherine Mary Deville Dalton Renoir may have derived the Dalton family fortune from nuggets of metallic ore, the riches which she herself produced were made from far humbler, though arguably ultimately mightier, materials: paper and ink. As the mystery writer Moray Dalton, Katherine Dalton Renoir published twenty-nine crime novels between 1924 and 1951, the majority of which feature her recurring sleuths, Scotland Yard inspector Hugh Collier and private inquiry agent Hermann Glide. Although the Moray Dalton mysteries are finely polished examples of criminally scintillating Golden Age art, the books unjustifiably fell into neglect for decades. For most fans of vintage mystery they long remained, like the fabled Lost Dutchman's mine, tantalizingly elusive treasure. Happily the crime fiction of Moray Dalton has been unearthed for modern readers by those industrious miners of vintage mystery at Dean Street Press.

Born in Hammersmith, London on May 6, 1881, Katherine was the only child of Joseph Dixon Dalton and Laura Back Dalton. Like the parents of that admittedly more famous mistress of mystery, Agatha Christie, Katherine's parents hailed from different nations, separated by the Atlantic Ocean. While both authors had British mothers, Christie's father was American and Dalton's father Canadian.

Laura Back Dalton, who at the time of her marriage in 1879 was twenty-six years old, about fifteen years younger than her husband, was the daughter of Alfred and Catherine Mary Back. In her early childhood years Laura Back resided at Valley House, a lovely regency villa built around 1825 in Stratford St. Mary, Suffolk, in the heart of so-called "Constable Country" (so named for the fact that the great Suffolk landscape artist John Constable painted many of his works in and around Stratford). Alfred Back was a wealthy miller who with his brother Octavius, a corn merchant, owned and operated a steam-powered six-story mill right across the River Stour from Valley House. In 1820 John Constable, himself the son of a miller, executed a painting of fishers on the River Stour which partly included the earlier, more modest incarnation (complete with water wheel) of the Back family's mill. (This piece Constable later repainted under the title *The Young Waltonians*, one of his best known works.) After Alfred Back's death in 1860, his widow moved with her daughters to Brondesbury Villas in Maida Vale, London, where Laura in the 1870s met Joseph Dixon Dalton, an eligible Canadian-born bachelor and retired gold miner of about forty years of age who lived in nearby Kew.

Joseph Dixon Dalton was born around 1838 in London, Ontario, Canada, to Henry and Mary (Dixon) Dalton, Wesleyan Methodists from northern England who had migrated to Canada a few years previously. In 1834, not long before Joseph's birth, Henry Dalton started a soap and candle factory in London, Ontario, which after his death two decades later was continued, under the appellation Dalton Brothers, by Joseph and his siblings Joshua and Thomas. (No relation to the notorious "Dalton Gang" of American outlaws is presumed.) Joseph's sister Hannah wed John Carling, a politician who came from a prominent family of Canadian brewers and was later knighted for his varied public services, making him Sir John and his wife Lady Hannah. Just how Joseph left the family soap and candle business to prospect for gold is currently unclear, but sometime in the 1870s, after fabulous gold rushes at Cariboo and Cassiar, British Columbia and the Black Hills of South Dakota, among other locales, Joseph left Canada and carried his riches with him to London, England, where for a time he enjoyed life as a gentleman of leisure in one of the great metropolises of the world.

Although Joshua and Laura Dalton's first married years were spent with their daughter Katherine in Hammersmith at a villa named Kenmore Lodge, by 1891 the family had moved to 9 Orchard Place in Southampton, where young Katherine received a private education from Jeanne Delport, a governess from Paris. Two decades later, Katherine, now 30 years old, resided with her parents at Perth Villa in the village of Merriott, Somerset, today about an eighty miles' drive west of Southampton. By this time Katherine had published, under the masculine-sounding pseudonym of Moray Dalton (probably a gender-bending play on "Mary Dalton") a well-received first novel, *Olive in Italy* (1909), a study of a winsome orphaned Englishwoman attempting to make her own living as an artist's model in Italy that possibly had been influenced by E.M. Forster's novels *Where Angels Fear to Tread* (1905) and *A Room with a View* (1908), both of which are partly set in an idealized Italy of pure gold sunlight and passionate love. Yet despite her accomplishment, Katherine's name had no occupation listed next it in the census two years later.

During the Great War the Daltons, parents and child, resided at 14 East Ham Road in Littlehampton, a seaside resort town located 19 miles west of Brighton. Like many other bookish and patriotic British women of her day, Katherine produced an effusion of memorial war poetry, including "To Some Who Have Fallen," "Edith Cavell," "Rupert Brooke," "To Italy" and "Mort Homme." These short works appeared in the *Spectator* and were reprinted during and after the war in George Herbert Clarke's *Treasury of War Poetry* anthologies. "To Italy," which Katherine had composed as a tribute to the beleaguered British ally after its calamitous defeat, at the hands of the forces of Germany and Austria-Hungary, at the Battle of Caporetto in 1917, even popped up in the United States in the "poet's corner" of the *United Mine Workers Journal*, perhaps on account of the poem's pro-Italy sentiment, doubtlessly agreeable to Italian miner immigrants in America.

Katherine also published short stories in various periodicals, including *The Cornhill Magazine*, which was then edited by Leonard Huxley, son of the eminent zoologist Thomas Henry Huxley and father of famed writer Aldous Huxley. Leonard Huxley obligingly read over--and in his words "plied my scalpel upon"--Katherine's second novel, *The Sword of Love*, a romantic adventure saga set in the Florentine Republic at the time of Lorenzo the Magnificent and the infamous Pazzi Conspiracy, which was published in 1920. Katherine writes with obvious affection for *il bel paese* in her first two novels and her poem "To Italy," which concludes with the ringing lines

> Greece was enslaved, and Carthage is but dust,
> But thou art living, maugre [i.e., in spite of] all thy scars,
> To bear fresh wounds of rapine and of lust,
> Immortal victim of unnumbered wars.
> Nor shalt thou cease until we cease to be
> Whose hearts are thine, beloved Italy.

The author maintained her affection for "beloved Italy" in her later Moray Dalton mysteries, which include sympathetically-rendered Italian settings and characters.

Around this time Katherine in her own life evidently discovered romance, however short-lived. At Brighton in the spring of 1921, the author, now nearly 40 years old, wed a presumed Frenchman, Louis Jean Renoir, by whom the next year she bore her only child, a son, Louis Anthony Laurence Dalton Renoir. (Katherine's father seems to have missed these important developments in his daughter's life, apparently having died in 1918, possibly in the flu pandemic.) Sparse evidence as to the actual existence of this man, Louis Jean Renoir, in Katherine's life suggests that the marriage may not have been a successful one. In the 1939 census Katherine was listed as living with her mother Laura at 71 Wallace Avenue in Worthing, Sussex, another coastal town not far from Brighton, where she had married Louis Jean eighteen years earlier; yet he is not in evidence, even though he is stated to be Katherine's husband in her mother's will, which was probated in Worthing in 1945. Perhaps not unrelatedly, empathy with what people in her day considered unorthodox sexual unions characterizes the crime fiction which Katherine would write.

Whatever happened to Louis Jean Renoir, marriage and motherhood did not slow down "Moray Dalton." Indeed, much to the contrary, in 1924, only a couple of years after the birth of her son, Katherine published, at the age of 42 (the same age at which P.D. James published her debut mystery novel, *Cover Her Face*), *The Kingsclere Mystery*, the first of her 29 crime novels. (Possibly the title was derived from the village of Kingsclere, located some 30 miles north of Southampton.) The heady scent of Renaissance romance which perfumes *The Sword of Love* is found as well in the first four Moray Dalton mysteries (aside from *The Kingsclere Mystery*, these are *The Shadow on the Wall*, *The Black Wings* and *The Stretton Darknesse Mystery*), which although set in the present-day world have, like much of the mystery fiction of John Dickson Carr, the elevated emotional temperature of the highly-colored age of the cavaliers. However in 1929 and 1930, with the publication of, respectively, *One by One They Disappeared*, the first of the Inspector Hugh Collier mysteries and *The Body in the Road*, the debut Hermann Glide tale, the Moray Dalton novels begin to become more typical of British crime fiction at that time, ultimately bearing considerable similarity to the work of Agatha Christie and Dorothy L. Sayers, as well as other prolific women mystery authors who would achieve popularity in the 1930s, such as Margery Allingham, Lucy Beatrice Malleson (best known as "Anthony Gilbert") and Edith Caroline Rivett, who wrote under the pen names E.C.R. Lorac and Carol Carnac.

For much of the decade of the 1930s Katherine shared the same publisher, Sampson Low, with Edith Rivett, who published her first detective novel in 1931, although Rivett moved on, with both of her pseudonyms, to that rather more prominent purveyor of mysteries, the Collins Crime Club. Consequently the Lorac and Carnac novels are better known today than those of Moray Dalton. Additionally, only three early Moray Dalton titles (*One by One They Disappeared*, *The Body in the Road* and *The Night of Fear*) were picked up in the United States, another factor which mitigated against the Dalton mysteries achieving long-term renown. It is also possible that the independently wealthy author, who left an estate valued, in modern estimation, at nearly a million American dollars at her death at the age of 81 in 1963, felt less of an imperative to "push" her writing than the typical "starving author."

Whatever forces compelled Katherine Dalton Renoir to write fiction, between 1929 and 1951 the author as Moray Dalton published fifteen Inspector Hugh Collier mysteries and ten other crime novels (several of these with Hermann Glide). Some of the non-series novels daringly straddle genres. *The Black Death*, for example, somewhat bizarrely yet altogether compellingly merges the murder mystery with post-apocalyptic science fiction, whereas *Death at the Villa*, set in Italy during the Second World War, is a gripping wartime adventure thriller with crime and death. Taken together, the imaginative and ingenious Moray Dalton crime fiction, wherein death is not so much a game as a dark and compelling human drama, is one of the more significant bodies of work by a Golden Age mystery writer—though the author has, until now, been most regrettably overlooked by publishers, for decades remaining accessible almost solely to connoisseurs with deep pockets.

Even noted mystery genre authorities Jacques Barzun and Wendell Hertig Taylor managed to read only five books by Moray Dalton, all of which the pair thereupon listed in their massive critical compendium, *A Catalogue of Crime* (1972; revised and expanded 1989). Yet Barzun and Taylor were warm admirers of the author's writing, avowing for example, of the twelfth Hugh Collier mystery, *The Condamine Case* (under the impression that the author was a man): "[T]his is the author's 17th book, and [it is] remarkably fresh and unstereotyped [actually it was Dalton's 25th book, making it even more remarkable—C.E.]. . . . [H]ere is a neglected man, for his earlier work shows him to be a conscientious workman, with a flair for the unusual, and capable of clever touches."

Today in 2019, nine decades since the debut of the conscientious and clever Moray Dalton's Inspector Hugh Collier detective series, it is a great personal pleasure to announce that this criminally neglected woman is neglected no longer and to welcome her books back into light. Vintage crime fiction fans have a golden treat in store with the classic mysteries of Moray Dalton.

The Case of Alan Copeland

THERE are no literal witches in Moray Dalton's *The Case of Alan Copeland* (1937), but the novel teems with figurative ones. In the village of Teene, where most of the events of the novel take place, we find:

Alan Copeland's awful older wife, Mabel. Years ago Mabel ensnared in holy wedded but exceedingly disharmonious matrimony Alan, once a promising young artist, and now she most decidedly leads him a dog's life, having both a cruelly cutting tongue and firm control over the purse strings.

Mabel's sponging best friend, Emily Gort. A pink-nosed, icily genteel and censorious spinster of the parish who dotes equally upon the austerely scholarly vicar and her great ginger tomcat, Bobo, Emily is a mistress of the prim and pious putdown, but she also knows on which side her bread is buttered.

Massive malevolent Mrs. Simmons. Like an enormous venomous spider, from her parlor she presides over the Teene's crossroads shop and garage, where she employs her "flapper" daughter Irene and her taciturn nephew, Ern.

Strange local schoolteacher Gertrude Platt. The unorthodox and acerbic pedagogue despises her young charges almost as much as she adores her unsettling art and books, including Theophile Gautier's gender-bending nineteenth-century novel *Mademoiselle de Maupin* and queer contemporary works by André Gide.

To be fair, the Vicar, Reverend Henry Perry, is not any better than this monstrous regiment of women, resembling as he does the coldly pedantic Reverend Casaubon in George Eliot's *Middlemarch*. Anyone, you would think, would murder to get out of this village. And murder someone does! But why?

Meek and fragile Lydia Hale, who works in the dreadful bargain basement of a London department store, becomes the unwitting catalyst to murder when she visits her uncle, the vicar. She and Alan fall in love, even rather unexpectedly doing the deed, Thomas Hardy fashion, at one of those scenic stone circle formations one finds in Britain. Primitive!

This is the sort of thing which fascinates me about the crime fiction of Moray Dalton. In how many mystery novels of the period does the author allow her heroine not only to have out-of-wedlock sex but to get pregnant, all without recriminations against her character? (The only people who criticize her are not people we like.) Of course from the evidence we have, the author herself, Katherine Mary Dalton Renoir, does not seem to have led the usual sort of life for a woman of her day.

Unfortunately Lydia's fling with Alan ultimately lands him in the soup when his wife dies and her body is exhumed months later, revealing that she is fuller of arsenic than one of those infamous Victorian flypapers! After Alan is arrested, can his mild, mother-dominated lawyer, John Reid--a character who seems to have stepped out of Josephine Tey's *The Franchise Affair* --and the private detective George Hayter, a former Canadian mountie, save him from the not so tender graces of the hangman?

The Case of Alan Copeland is Moray Dalton's seventeenth detective novel and the first one published after the Hugh Collier series mystery *The Strange Case of Harriet Hall* (1936), earlier reissued by Dean Street Press. (Why Harriet Hall's case and not Alan Copeland's is strange, I shall leave readers to decide.) A dozen more Dalton novels would follow over the next thirteen years. Dalton definitely had her style down now by now and her seasoned readers will be able to pick up on certain common features in her books: the poisonous older wife, the sympathetic young woman, the suffocating village, the unorthodox sexuality, the purposefully drab private investigator, the trial. Yet Dalton's characters and settings are so vividly presented it all seems fresh. *The Case of Alan Copeland* would make a fine British television mystery film, with all the darkness already in the text, making it unnecessary for any screenwriter to invent it.

As in *Harriet Hall*, the focus in *Alan Copeland* is on the characters that are impacted by a murder, but there is genuine detection, particularly in the investigation into the origin of some poison pen letters, which is highly pertinent to the solution. When readers learn the identity of the murderer, I think they will see that indications were laid throughout the book. But aside from the puzzle aspect, readers should enjoy what is an emotionally gripping and credible tale of murder.

We get some clue here of what the author was trying to do when Miss Platt tells George Hayter, "You're not true to type. . . . In novels private detectives are always either foreigners or a mass of affectations. You're more like an ordinary policeman in mufti." So while readers will not be getting Hercule Poirot or Albert Campion here, they should still feel like they are visiting the same literary world as that which was so ably fashioned by Agatha Christie, Margery Allingham and other British Crime Queens. Moray Dalton was a mystery writer who could both plot an interesting story and compose an intriguing sentence, making her mysteries superbly readable examples of the fine art of English murder fiction.

Curtis Evans

Chapter I
THE HOUSE OF DISCORD

I

EMILY Gort was having tea with Mrs. Copeland, tea and a cosy chat. It was very pleasant, after trudging across the fields in the teeth of a March gale, to sit in a well-cushioned chair before a blazing fire and eat buttered scones and a large slice of Mabel's golden sponge cake, and the fact that Mabel was a woman of uncertain temper who needed very careful handling rather added to Emily's satisfaction.

Emily enjoyed managing people, and the tiny hamlet of Teene did not give her much scope. There was the vicar, of course, who had come to rely more and more on her services, but he was almost too easy. Miss Gort had been in the dressmaking department of a large draper's shop in the Midlands before she came to live with her aunt shortly after her uncle's death. Old Gort, who was a retired builder, had put up the dreary little house of yellowish grey brick in which his niece now lived and another exactly like it a mile away at the crossroads for Mrs. Simmons, who ran a wayside garage and petrol station with a little shop for the sale of sweets and tobacco. His widow had been a tiresome old woman, but her niece had borne her incessant grumbling with admirable patience, and had been rewarded when the old lady died two years after her coming, for she had inherited the house and a tiny income which she supplemented by doing a little dressmaking. After Mabel Leach married Alan Copeland the two women had become very friendly. Emily made all Mabel's dresses and was useful to her in various ways. Mabel disliked any physical exertion, and was inclined to fuss over her health. She went out very seldom, but she liked to hear all the village gossip, and for this she relied on Emily.

As she often said, Alan was no companion. He was working very hard trying to make a success of poultry farming on a small scale. He was almost invariably polite to his wife and very rarely contradicted her, but he was only a simulacrum of the real Alan, who had withdrawn long since into some fastness of the spirit beyond her reach.

She was dimly and resentfully aware of this, and tried to get at him sometimes very much as, years ago, when they were on their honeymoon at Seaton, she had prodded the sea anemones left exposed by the tide in the crannies of the rocks. He had wanted to stop her from doing that. He had always been queer, she thought, getting so worked up and excited over his paintings that nobody would buy, forgetting to come in to meals, wasting money on brushes and what not. "Why can't you use a cheaper blue, Alan, if cobalt is so dear?" They had quarrelled over that. He was much quieter since he had given up messing about with canvases.

He was twelve years her junior, a fact which had become more obvious since, through her own slackness and the almost childish greed that was one of her more attractive failings, she had grown very stout and unwieldy. She loved good food, and much of her time was spent in her kitchen making pastry and cakes and concocting highly-flavoured stews.

"Try one of those little buns," she said now hospitably, "they're rather special."

"It's sure to be delicious," said Miss Gort, helping herself. "And what lovely daffodils you've got in that vase. Your daffodils are always finer and come on earlier than anyone's. I hope you can spare a few for the Easter decorations."

"For the altar. I won't have them messed about on the window sills."

"No. No, of course not."

The conversational duet was taking its usual course, with a note of patronage on one side, and on the other a slight effect of flurry indicating the eager deference of a social inferior.

"Mr. Copeland isn't coming in to tea?"

"No. He had to send some poultry off by rail, and something has gone wrong with the car again. He said he would leave it at the garage on the way home and walk the rest of the way."

"He won't have to do that," said Miss Gort with her tight-lipped smile. "Irene Simmons will be only too pleased to give him a lift."

Mrs. Copeland cut herself a thick slab of cake. "It's a bit heavy," she murmured, "but I do like a good fruit mixture. Irene is one of these modern girls. All that paint. And that terrible old mother of hers. They're very pushing. She's always coming here, making some excuse, but I never ask her in. They are very common. Are they making the garage pay?"

"I believe so since Irene's cousin, Ernest, has been in charge. They say he's quite good at repairs, and it's the only petrol station for miles. I called there the other day to get a pint of petrol to clean that blue silk jumper of mine, and he served me. Quite the working man, very black and oily, but civil enough. I don't envy him if Irene falls back on him. She's the sort that get what they want by hook or by crook."

"I daresay." Mrs. Copeland sounded indifferent. She was not really a jealous wife. She was far too self-satisfied for that. She might be irritated by Irene Simmons' frantic efforts to attract Alan's notice, but her natural reaction was one of amused contempt for the younger woman. She was, if anything, rather pleased to be reminded of Irene's ill-concealed infatuation. "Alan can't stand her," she said complacently.

"Did he tell you so?"

"He's not one to say things. But I know. I rather wish I hadn't taken that second piece of cake. I've got that pain again. Pass over my tablets, Emily."

Miss Gort complied. "You poor dear," she said softly, and hesitated over the selection of a fresh topic. The call for tablets was a danger signal. Mabel was always very cross when she was suffering from the effects of over-eating.

"Oh, did I tell you the vicar was expecting a visitor? A niece of his late wife's. I said to him, 'Oh, won't it be too much for you?' and I think the poor old gentleman is rather overwhelmed by the prospect, but it seems she practically invited herself, and he didn't like to say no. He said it was only for a week or two, and I must confess I was relieved to hear it. Newcomers can be very upsetting."

Mrs. Copeland looked at her friend reflectively, at her narrow shoulders, her pale light-lashed eyes, her long nose which was inclined to be pink at the tip. It was a pity, she thought, that dear Emily's sterling worth, her energy, her industry, her patience and good humour were not set off by better window dressing.

"If the vicar had any sense," she said with unusual warmth, "he'd marry you."

"Oh no!" A dull flush mounted to the roots of Emily Gort's thick, fair hair. "I never thought of such a thing. Never. I have the greatest respect for Mr. Perry, but we could never be anything more than friends."

"Dear me!" Mrs. Copeland was amused and a little surprised by her vehemence. She did not believe her. "You can't be wanting something more romantic at your age?"

Emily Gort winced. That was so like Mabel, her claws out again so soon after a moment of real kindness.

"Of course not. I don't want anything of that sort." She made an effort. She could not afford to quarrel with Mabel. "It's difficult for a woman like you, darling, with lots of sex appeal as they call it nowadays, and whom men admire, to realise that a born old maid like me can have other interests."

Would that do, she wondered. Yes. The bait had been swallowed, hook and all. Mabel preened herself. After all, she must have sex appeal or Alan would not have married her. Was that what she was thinking? Miss Gort smiled to herself as she brushed the crumbs off her lap and prepared to rise.

"You must take a pot of my lemon jelly along with you and a few tartlets left over from my last batch. You'll find them packed ready in a basket in the hall as you go out. You can bring the basket back when you come along with those patterns. You won't mind me not seeing you off. I don't care about moving while I've got this pain."

"You keep still—and thank you for everything," said Miss Gort, thinking, "How flabby she is!" as she bent to kiss her friend's cheek. "You're an angel, and much too good to me. Take care of yourself."

She picked up the basket in the hall on her way out. Mabel could be generous, she thought, if you took her the right way. She lingered for a moment at the gate, half expecting to see the tall figure of Alan Copeland coming up the road. She had a message for him from the vicar about getting a new spade for old Martin, the sexton, but that would keep. The way from the farm to her house was open to the wind, a little used path through untilled fields that had lain fallow since the end of the agricultural boom that had followed the Great War. Miss Gort's four-roomed brick villa with its grey slate roof, wore an air of bleak gentility that might have reminded a passerby, knowing Frances Cornford's poem, of the lady who walked through the fields in gloves. Emily kept her little garden neat, but there was nothing in it but a few hardy shrubs in front. At the back she grew potatoes and cabbages and catmint to please Bobo, the great ginger tom cat who came down the path to meet her, purring and arching his back as the gate clicked behind her. The house struck cold as she entered it, but it was hardly worth while to light the sitting-room fire so late in the day. It was very clean and very bare. The floors in all the rooms were covered with linoleum. There was a pervading smell of furniture polish and moth balls.

Emily Gort went out to her meat safe to put away the tart-lets and the lemon jelly and brought back Bobo's supper of boiled fish. Then she uncovered her sewing machine. She had promised to finish old Mrs. Simmons' new dress before the end of the week.

II

The vicar was on the down platform when Alan came out of the luggage office.

"Hallo, Copeland, where are you off to?"

"Nowhere. I was getting a crate of poultry labelled through to Westbury," explained Alan, with the careful patience of one who has learned to say what is necessary and to refrain from anything more. He looked anxious and pre-occupied, but that was not unusual.

"Well, there was something I wanted to say to you. I can't remember at the moment, but it will come back to me. Ah, here comes the train."

He bustled forward as the train came to a standstill. Only one passenger got out, a girl carrying a cheap imitation leather suitcase.

Alan, waiting by the ticket office, uncertain what to do, noticed that she was short and slightly built. She was not made up, and she could hardly be called pretty, but her face lit up when she smiled.

"Lydia?"

"Yes. And you must be Uncle Henry."

She offered her hand and Mr. Perry shook it limply. Secretly he resented her coming as an interruption of his well-established routine. She would expect to be talked to at meals, and he was used to eating with a book propped against the cruet. He knew that he would find it easier to be cordial when he was seeing her off a week or possibly a fortnight hence. But she seemed, on the whole, a harmless young woman. The timbre of her voice did not jar on his sensitive ear and there were no smears of violent crimson on her mouth to offend the eye. And, after all, she was poor Caroline's sister's child.

"I hope the change will do you good," he said formally. "I'm afraid you will find it very quiet."

"I shall be glad of a rest," she said. She walked along the platform with him, still carrying her suitcase. It had not occurred to the vicar, who was used to being waited on, that he might relieve her of it, and it was Alan who took it from her. She glanced up quickly at the dark, care-worn face, and he heard her catch her breath.

"Oh, thank you."

"Ah, Copeland. This is Mr. Copeland, Lydia, my church-warden. My niece, Miss Hale."

"Can I run you and Miss Hale back to the vicarage, sir?"

"No, thanks. I have hired Simmons' car from the garage. It is waiting outside. About that matter—I still don't recall—but I'll be seeing you later."

Alan had to collect some empties, and when he went out to his battered Ford the other car had gone. Just as well, he reflected as he started the engine. She was still knocking pretty badly, and he would have to leave her with Simmons to see if anything could be done to patch up the poor old crock. If he had only been able to make Mabel realise that it was better to pay a little more for an engine that was not practically worn out. He sighed. No use. She could not discuss money matters with him for five minutes without being insulting, and somehow he had never got hardened to that.

Irene Simmons came out of the little shop in which she sold sweets and cigarettes to passing motorists as he drove on to the patch of asphalt behind the row of gaudily painted petrol pumps. She was adjusting a slave bangle on a plump arm.

"Want some juice?" she asked casually. She was like one of her own sweets, one of the pink and brown sticky ones, the cheap kind. She came close up to Alan as he climbed out of the car, so close that his sleeve brushed against the rather greasy mass of dark curls at the nape of her neck. Old Mrs. Simmons, watching them through the grimy mesh of the Nottingham lace window curtains, was shaken throughout her vast bulk by her noiseless chuckle. Young Irene up to her tricks. Well—Mrs. Simmons' small black eyes, sunk in fat, like currants in a boiled dumpling, lingered on the unconscious Alan's well set dark head, his broad shoulders, narrow hips and graceful length of limb. Copeland was a fine looking chap. She couldn't blame the girl. Pity young Ern was such a little squit. But—for a moment she considered Alan apart from her daughter. What did his wife mean by letting him go about so shabby? Well, no one could say he was leading Irene on. She chuckled again, observing her daughter's ill-concealed disappointment as their brief colloquy ended.

"Will you tell Ern to do the best he can with her?"

"I will. I'd have run you back to the farm in our car, Mr. Copeland, but she's out this afternoon. Station work."

"I know."

"You were there? Then you saw the vicar's niece? How thrilling! What is she like?"

"She seemed quiet," he said vaguely. "I should think she might be delicate."

"Won't you stop for a cup of tea? Ern may be back with the car any minute, and save you the bore of trudging all that way back."

"Thanks. But I think I'll be getting on."

"Good-bye-ee," said Irene gaily, but as she walked slowly back to her little shop her eyes filled with angry tears.

She blinked them away as her mother called to her from the back room.

"Irene!"

"Yes. What is it?"

"Come here."

Irene went in reluctantly. Modern she might be, but she was afraid of her mother. Mrs. Simmons could be formidable. Not that she was a strict parent or unduly concerned with her child's morals, but she made her plans and she meant them to be carried out.

"I saw you just now with Copeland."

"What about it?"

"He's a married man, and he's not the kind to leave his wife for another woman. He hasn't the guts. Anyway, he couldn't. He hasn't a bean. It's all hers. I'm warning you, see. I'm not going to sit here and watch you making a fool of yourself."

"You wouldn't like it if I wasn't civil to customers," said Irene sulkily.

"Civil." The mountain of flesh shook with mirth. "Oh well—put the kettle on. Ern won't be long now. And we'll have those bloaters for tea."

After her friend had left Mabel Copeland rose in her lymphatic fashion and cleared away the tea and prepared the supper tray before she went back to the sitting-room. She was dozing on the sofa when her husband came in. She woke with a start.

"Alan—"

His voice answered her from the shadows. "Here I am."

"What are you doing?" Her voice was sharp with annoyance.

"Nothing at the moment. I thought of lighting the lamp but I was afraid of disturbing you."

"How very thoughtful we are all of a sudden. It doesn't occur to you that I might get dull shut up in the house all day, and be glad of a bit of company?"

Mabel always made a grievance of having been indoors, though there was nothing but her own inertia to prevent her from going out.

"I thought Emily Gort was coming to tea with you. You generally hear anything that's going on from her."

"That's just like you, Alan, making a fuss because the only friend I've got comes to see me sometimes and tries to cheer me up."

"I'm not making a fuss."

"Yes, you are."

He was silent.

She shifted her ground. "What about the car?"

"I've left it at the garage for repairs. Ern Simmons will do what he can. He told me last time it was only fit for the scrap heap."

"And you agreed with him, I suppose. A nice way to talk about a present, I must say. Talk about looking a gift horse in the mouth. I shan't give you another, Alan."

"I have to have some sort of conveyance if I'm to go on with poultry farming," he said with an effort.

"So far it's been nothing but a waste of your time and my money," she said.

He set his teeth. He knew that for some time now she had been determined to make him give up his work, just as, years ago, she had succeeded, by the combined methods of aloof discouragement and direct bullying, in stopping him from trying to paint. He had to ask her for money to buy paints and canvases. His pictures must be framed before they could be sent to a show. He had given up at last. There was some of his stuff on the walls in the sitting-room and a few dusty canvases, nibbled by mice, in an attic. He was not going to be beaten twice. He knew what her arguments were. They could live very comfortably on her income. There was really no need for him to spend his days cleaning out chicken coops, packing eggs, and plucking poultry for the market. But—he had paid her back every penny of the sum she had advanced him when he started. The enterprise was paying its way. One of these days he could buy himself a new suit, a winter overcoat, without asking her for the money to pay the bill. And he knew her well enough to be certain that while he would receive every encouragement to sell his birds and his coops and the wire netting to the first bidder, she would begin almost directly to point out that he was living on her, and idling his time away. He sought desperately for a diversion.

"I saw the vicar at the station. He was meeting his niece."

Mabel, really interested at last, brightened up and adopted her more friendly tone. "Then you saw her? What is she like?"

"A little thing with a pale face."

"Insignificant. I thought she might be. But Mr. Perry's niece must be a lady, and that's something in a place like this, where there's really no one. I shall go to church on Sunday and I shall see her then. We'll ask the vicar and her to spend an evening, supper and cards."

Alan allowed himself to relax in his chair. She would go on quite happily now, and he need not even listen.

"Chicken and mayonnaise salad and one of my cherry trifles. Mr. Perry shall have something really fit to eat for once. That old woman who keeps house for him hardly knows how to boil a potato. He needs a good wife to look after him. Emily Gort would have him I'm sure, and he couldn't do better. I suppose he's too much in the clouds to realise it, but you might give him a hint, Alan."

Alan roused himself to reply. "That hardly comes within the province of a vicar's churchwarden. Besides"—again he was being indiscreet—"I hardly think Miss Gort would suit him."

"You're always so down on Emily, and I can't think why. She always stands up for you."

"That's very nice of her. Against whom?"

"Oh, you know what I mean. I've been wondering if it would occur to you to light the lamp. It seems funny that you can't do a little thing like that without being asked. I've heard that some men are really useful about the house."

"If I do things off my own bat they're generally wrong."

"Oh, of course you say so."

He lit the oil lamp and went over to the window to draw the curtains. In the valley below a few lights glimmered in cottage windows where thatched roofs clustered about the ancient church, but those of the vicarage were hidden by a belt of trees. Beyond there were fields and more fields, most of them lying fallow, where the coarser weeds grew more thickly every year. But the marshy ground by the brook was gay with kingcups. He had seen a heron fishing in the pool by Lobb's brake that afternoon, and a bit he would have liked to paint, the silver birches by the old stone bridge. It was this countryside, saved by the merciful absence of any famous beauty spots from so-called development, that had charmed him when he first came to Strays to stay as a paying guest with Mabel and her mother. He had been commissioned to do the illustrations for a book called *On Foot in Wessex*. He had been roughing it, stopping a night here and there at wayside cottages. Within a few days of his coming to Strays he was looking so ill that Mrs. Leach sent for the doctor. He had typhoid fever. When he struggled back to consciousness after a long period of misery and confusion it was to realise that he was hopelessly in the debt of Mrs. Leach and her daughter, who had nursed him devotedly. They were unfailingly kind to him throughout the long weeks of his convalescence, and he tried to forget that when he arrived he found them pretentious and boringly persistent in asserting their gentility. He was grateful to Mabel, but she did not attract him, and he was secretly appalled when he discovered that she had fallen in love with him. She seemed to take it for granted that they would be married. Even now, looking back, he did not see how he could have escaped. How could he, after all she had done for him, subject her to the greatest of all humiliations? And materially, their marriage however lacking in romance from his point of view, seemed to have compensations. He had been making a bare livelihood with his brush. Private means

meant possibilities for further study and for travel. He had had
no conception then of the gradual process of enslavement that
had changed the tolerant affection he had once held for his wife
into a feeling he did not care to define even to himself. The death
of his mother-in-law had not eased the situation.

The sofa creaked as Mabel changed her position.

"What are you staring at?"

"Nothing."

He drew the blinds lingeringly, as if reluctant to shut out a
night that was more friendly to him than the lighted room.

CHAPTER II
DECORATIONS

I

THE vicarage at Teene had been rebuilt in the 'seventies of
the last century by a parson with sporting proclivities and
large private means. To his successors it had been an incu-
bus. No other incumbent had been able to afford the tons of
coal required to keep those spacious, high-pitched rooms and
long, draughty passages even tolerably warm, or the number of
servants needed for its maintenance. It had killed their wives
by inches, and sapped the youth and strength of their daughters. The Perrys, a childless couple, had only brought enough
furniture with them for four rooms. Mr. Perry had ignored a
suggestion from his bishop that with so much accommodation
he might take pupils, and settled down happily enough to what
he regarded as his life-work, a study of the Byzantine Church in
the fourth century. At the time the living was offered him he was
collecting material for the sixth chapter. Now, fifteen years later,
he had reached the nineteenth. His wife had died after so short
an illness that it had hardly affected the settled routine to which
his cold but tenacious spirit clung as the limpet clings to its rock.

Before she had even crossed the threshold, during the drive
from the station, Lydia realised that she was there on suffer-

ance. Her spirits sank. She had perhaps counted more than she should have done on his being really glad to see her. Mrs. Binns, who showed her up to a bare and icy bedroom, looked her up and down with unconcealed hostility and scarcely troubled to answer her.

"I haven't brought you no hot water. There's plenty of cold in the jug. Supper's at seven. The dining-room's on the right at the foot of the stairs. The vicar's study's the room on the left. Going to meet you will have put him behind with his work and he won't want to be disturbed."

"Yes, you old devil," thought Lydia. "You scamp your job. The house is inches thick in dust and you know I shall notice it. Well, it's only for a week. I shan't stay the fortnight."

She unlocked her suitcase and took out her few possessions. She worked as a cashier in a large draper's shop in north London. It was a firm that catered chiefly for the lower middle class, buying in the bankrupt stock of their less fortunate rivals, and the staff worked at high pressure. Lydia, flagging visibly after a sharp attack of 'flu, had been called to the manager's room and told that she might take her two week's holiday, not actually due until September, now.

"And I hope you'll be a bit brisker when you come back, Miss Hale. We treat our employees well, but we expect them to jump to it."

"Yes, sir."

She had not wanted to take her holiday so early. She had not begun to save up for it, and the planning for those precious fourteen days of freedom would have helped her to endure the airlessness of her glass-fronted prison, raised like a pillory above the sweltering crowds of customers in the bargain basement, throughout the summer. And so she had written to Uncle Henry, fishing for an invitation. The answer, written in the small, cramped writing of a scholar, had been stiffly worded, but Lydia, with the bright, unfounded optimism of youth, had spent the two days that intervened between his invitation and her arrival in picturing the forming of an idyllic relationship.

"My dear child, you have filled my darkening years with sunshine." "If you will stay with a lonely old man—"

It was already evident that these touching phrases would never be uttered. The Reverend Henry Perry was obviously quite satisfied with his present way of living. At supper he carved the cold mutton absently, and chewed the slice he had given himself, and the stewed prunes and rice mould that followed with the air of one whose thoughts are elsewhere. Lydia, trying to think of something to say, asked if the church would be decorated for Easter.

He roused himself to answer. "Easter? Oh, yes. I believe they gather flowers. Yes. You must ask Miss Gort. She is in charge. My right hand in the parish. You'll excuse me now. I have some writing to do."

Lydia did not see him again before she went up to bed at ten, having spent the evening finishing a novel she had bought to read in the train.

But when she opened her window the air seemed exquisitely fresh and the silence of the night was soothing to jaded nerves. She slept well and woke refreshed, to hear birds twittering under the eaves and the chattering of innumerable starlings that nested in the intricate stone corbels and jutting gargoyles of the church tower. What did it matter that her uncle and his housekeeper were dry old sticks? She found it easy to be cheerful at breakfast, and the vicar listened with more indulgence than she had expected, and even smiled once, and capped something she had said with some unintelligible quotation from the classics. On the other hand Mrs. Binns, coming to clear away, was sourer than ever.

The vicar had gone to his study, but Lydia was still in the dining-room trying to choose a book to read from among the faded collection that had once belonged to her aunt, when the door opened and a thin, middle-aged lady in grey came in laden with a pile of tattered paper-bound hymnals which she deposited on the table before she extended a hand in a grey fabric glove.

"You are Miss Hale. It's such a pleasure—I am Miss Gort. These wretched books have been on my mind, but I've been so rushed. And then I thought perhaps the dear Vicar's niece—quite simple really, just a little furnishing up with brown paper and scissors and paste. This evening perhaps and then they would be all fresh and nice for the use of the choir on Sunday. You will? Thank you so much."

"Do you want to see my uncle?"

"Oh, I wouldn't disturb him now. I'm just going to visit a bedridden old woman in the village and then back for the three hours' service. I'm afraid it will only be a tiny congregation. You'll be there, of course."

"I don't think so. My holiday is so short. I want to be out in the fresh air as much as possible."

"I see."

Miss Gort's disapproval was obvious. Darn it, thought Lydia, hasn't she just landed me with the job of re-binding her horrible little books? She smiled at the older woman. "My uncle was telling me how much you help him in the parish."

Miss Gort looked pleased. "I do what I can. There's nobody here you know—I mean, no squire's wife, or anyone. Just farmers and the quarry manager's sister, and people of that sort. No one in authority, so to speak."

"About the decorations. I thought I might go primrosing."

"A good idea. The school children bring some, but always with such short stalks. We shall be busy at the church to-morrow. Let me see—" she rubbed her nose reflectively. "We must be careful not to poach on anyone's preserves. Mrs. Copeland always sends the flowers for the altar. They've a small greenhouse at Strays and grow arums on purpose. Irene Simmons does the font, and I am responsible for the pulpit. Perhaps you could help Miss Platt, our schoolmistress, with the windows, just moss and leaves and any flowers that are left over. You can't go far wrong. Well, I must fly. Poor old Mrs. Tarrant does so look forward to my visits and I don't like to disappoint her."

II

Alan got off his bicycle on the bridge. He would have to walk up the long hill in any case and he meant to have another look at those silver birches. It was just the sort of composition and colour scheme he had always loved to paint. Greenish greys and opalescent gleams. Why shouldn't he begin again? What would Mabel say? The materials were expensive, and there was no market for his work. You couldn't make her understand what it meant to him. He sighed, fumbling for the packet of Players in his coat pocket and striking a match on the old stone coping of the bridge. The constant repairs to the car were a serious item. He did not want to get into debt at the garage. Ern and Irene were all right, but he distrusted the old woman. It wasn't only that she was horrible to look at, she couldn't help being gross and unwieldy, it was the malicious gleam in those beady eyes and the fits of silent laughter. He shrugged his shoulders. If it wasn't for Tom Bragge, the quarry manager, and his sister, he would not have a friend in the place, and his friendship with them was hampered by the fact that his wife disliked them both. They were his customers for eggs and an occasional roasting fowl for the Sunday dinner. But for that he would never have seen them, since they were not church-goers.

His eye was caught by something moving among the osiers and alders on the left bank of the stream where a patch of king-cups glittered like a gold clasp on a dark cloak. He saw a slight figure poised and clinging precariously to a branch of willow. It must be Perry's niece. Only a stranger would attempt to go down that side of the stream. The ground there was swampy and treacherous. He shouted, and there was a rather faint response. Little idiot, he thought irritably, why can't she look where she's going. But he could not leave her there floundering in the mud. He swung himself over the wall and made his way towards her, picking the driest patches, and jumping from one tussock of coarse grass to another.

"Here, this way," he addressed her brusquely, without cere-mony. "Take my hand. Now—"

She followed him meekly. The black water oozed up quickly, filling the deep imprints left by their feet as they struggled back to the bridge through a clogging mass of undergrowth.

"There—" He dropped her hand as they reached the road.

She was intimidated by the anger in his voice, not knowing it to be the result of over-strained nerves.

"I—I'm sorry to give you all that trouble. I wanted to get those kingcups."

"The village children would have got them long ago if they had been get-at-able. You'd better go straight home. The water went right over your shoes."

"And yours. I'm so sorry," she repeated anxiously.

Why had he thought her insignificant yesterday on the station platform? Her small features were exquisitely modelled, her pale skin smooth as the petal of a flower. Was it that he had grown used to the standard set by Irene Simmons whose appeal was that of a poster in violent primary colours? He did not see many young women. Just as well, perhaps. Looking at her he had forgotten to listen.

"Sorry? Oh, that's all right. I don't catch cold. Got to be going though. Good-bye."

He had turned away, pushing his bicycle up the hill. No manners, thought Lydia, and what an unhappy face.

She said nothing of her misadventure to her uncle when they sat down to high tea in the dining-room, but she asked him the name of his churchwarden—"the one who was at the station."

"Oh—Copeland. A poultry farmer. He married a woman older than himself for her money. It's turned out well enough, I believe. Mrs. Copeland is inclined to be invalidish, but they live very comfortably. Strays is a fine old house, dates back to the sixteenth century. I had a note from her this morning asking us to spend the evening there on Monday. Supper and a game of whist. I accepted, of course. Very kind of her."

During the evening parties of school children arrived, scuffling and giggling as they made their way round to the back door, with baskets full of primroses, white dog violets, trailing branches of ivy and small, tight bunches of daffodils. Lydia carried them over to the church after breakfast the following morning and found the three ladies responsible for the decorations already at work. Miss Gort came down the chancel to shake hands with her and introduce her in a hissing whisper to Miss Platt, the schoolmistress, a stockily-built woman who was dealing with a sack full of very muddy moss with the fierce efficiency of one resolved to get through an unpleasant job as quickly as possible. She acknowledged Lydia's arrival with a curt nod. Irene Simmons was busy at the font. She was wearing a bright blue coat, and a red beret that matched her lipstick was pulled down over one eye. She stared hard at Lydia as she came in, but was generally watching the door, and the reason became apparent when Alan Copeland arrived with a big bunch of arum lilies.

She slipped round the font and waylaid him in the aisle.

"Bags I some." She was smiling up at him confidently. Lydia could not see if the smile was returned, but she heard him say,

"Nothing doing. These are all for the altar."

"Who says so? Mrs. Copeland?"

Was there a tiny pause before the answer? "I say so. Don't hold me up, Irene. Miss Gort's waiting for these."

"And watching. Someday her eyes'll drop out of her head. I shan't be sorry, will you—"

She drew back to let him pass and he went on to the chancel steps where Miss Gort took the lilies from him. "Oh, how lovely. Thank dear Mabel. Really magnificent. How is she?" She went with him to the church door and they stood together for a few minutes in the porch talking confidentially in undertones before Miss Gort returned alone. She paused on her way to praise Miss Platt.

"Taking the leaves and briars out of the moss? What a good idea."

Her long nose, faintly pink at the tip, was twitching slightly.

"We shall have done before three if we all work hard. I am going to tea at Strays. Mrs. Copeland sent a message. She relies on me to cheer her up."

"Cheering up indeed," said the schoolmistress, poking a very small bunch of primroses into a nest of moss when Miss Gort had passed out of hearing. "Some women don't know when they're well off. A good husband, a good home, no money troubles."

"You mean Mrs. Copeland?"

"Yes. It makes me sick to hear of her complaining of this and that. I wish she had my job, with nothing to look forward to but a pension when I'm too old for anything else, or Emily Gort's for that matter, living on twopence half-penny a year and cadging bits of dressmaking. Mrs. Copeland's only trouble is that she eats too much and doesn't take enough exercise. And, between you and me, she makes that poor man's life a hell. Irene—" She raised her voice. "Irene, can you spare us some of your primroses?"

Irene Simmons, who had been standing back to admire the general effect of her operations at the font, came over to where they were at work.

"I've finished," she announced. "You can have my leavings. This is a hell of a job. My nails are full of earth. Wasn't it a scream to see old Emily sucking up to Alan Copeland? I wanted to die."

"This is Miss Hale, the vicar's niece," said Miss Platt.

Irene nodded, and, producing a pocket mirror and a lipstick, repaired her lips and set her red beret at a more rakish angle.

"You'll think country people have very bad manners, Miss Hale," she remarked. "I mean—Alan met you the day you came, didn't he? Ern told me he was at the station when your train came in. He never even looked at you just now. I was noticing. Rather rude, I thought. He can be rude. You mustn't mind."

Lydia smiled. "I don't."

"Okay. Don't let that bird pinch any of the daffs off my font."

"She goes to too many films," said Miss Platt when she had left them.

"I didn't know you had a cinema here."

"We haven't. She goes in to Wainbridge or Carchester with her cousin, Ern, or any other young man she can get hold of. She's supposed to be engaged to Ern, but I wouldn't give much for his chances if anyone more attractive turns up. Very bad style, of course, but she's pretty, don't you think?" said Miss Platt, making an evident effort to be fair.

Lydia would have liked to disagree with her. She detested Irene's type of good looks, but she could not deny their existence.

"Very pretty," she said with emphasis, and then, being only human, added, "in that way."

CHAPTER III
LYDIA'S FIRST WEEK

I

ALAN found his dress clothes laid out on the bed for him when he came in from the field on Monday evening. He had been setting a trap for a rat that had burrowed under the wire netting and killed three of the chicks the night before. He was tired and would have liked to get into old clothes after a hot bath and spend the evening over a book, and he cursed the vicar and his niece and his wife's social ambitions as he struggled into his boiled shirt and fumbled over his tie. Old clothes. His dress suit was old enough, since it dated from the year before his marriage, when he had shared diggings with another painter in Chelsea and had sometimes been asked out to dinner or to a dance. It was well cut. He had sold one of the small landscapes that had been hung that year at the R.A., and he had blued the cheque and gone to a good tailor—but it smelt damnably of moth balls. He heard Mabel's fretful voice calling to him from the foot of the stairs.

"Alan, do hurry. They will be here any minute."

"All right!"

The lamp was lit in the hall and Mabel hovered between the dining-room and the drawing-room, giving final touches to the long table laden with a cold supper and lighted by pink-shaded candles in the candelabra of Sheffield plate that had belonged to her grandmother, and to the card table set out with two packs and markers. Alan was startled by the extent of her preparations, by the roast chicken and duck, the ham, the galantine, the trifle and the jellies and creams.

"Good Lord! What a bust for two people," he said tactlessly.

"One must do things properly," said Mabel. "How does my dress look?"

She was wearing a claret-coloured brocaded velvet which had been made for her by Miss Gort.

"Very nice," said Alan dutifully.

Secretly he thought that the choice of colour was unfortunate. It made her look very sallow.

"Here they are," she said as the door bell rang. "No, don't go, Alan. Mrs. Tulke is in the kitchen."

The vicar and Lydia had walked up from the village, and they were obviously unprepared for so much ceremony. Lydia, who had taken off her coat in the hall, was wearing a white silk blouse with a tweed skirt.

"I hope you won't mind my coming like this," she said as she shook hands. "I only brought down what I could stuff into a small suitcase."

"It doesn't matter in the least," said Mabel graciously. "We never dress up. I just like to slip into some old thing in the evening." She turned to speak to the vicar, leaving Lydia to Alan.

"Oh dear," thought the girl, "he's terribly good looking."

But his silence was daunting. She tried to think of something to say, and remembered that she had not thanked him for helping her out of the swamp. She began impulsively. "You must have—"

He slightly shook his head with a glance at his wife's broad back bulging in her velvet frock.

Lydia understood that he had not told Mrs. Copeland of the incident, and that if it was referred to now his previous silence might be misunderstood. His dark face had the strained look of one who has to be constantly on guard.

"I hope you are feeling better for the change," he said carefully.

"Oh yes. I like the peace and the quiet after London, and I think this country is perfectly lovely."

"Yes. It's partly the colour of the earth. If you look at a field being ploughed you'll get the most glorious umbers. A plough-ing team of Shire horses and gulls following the furrow. I've always wanted to paint that."

"Do you paint?"

"I used to long ago. I—I had to give it up."

She looked about her, seeing some pictures in narrow gilt frames on the walls. "Are any of those yours?"

"Yes."

She moved across the room to look more closely at a study of a wheatfield just harvested, with the sheaves dark against a sunset sky.

"I love this," she said eagerly.

"That's just over by Tarrant's. Ten years ago most of the land about here was being farmed by small-holders, ex-officers, many of them, who invested their gratuities, God help them. It's all derelict now."

"They couldn't make it pay?"

"Apparently not," he said bitterly. "They worked hard enough, poor devils. But tithes and rates took any profits they made."

"What are you two talking about?" Mabel called to them impatiently. "We are going into the other room for supper now."

"I was admiring Mr. Copeland's pictures," explained Lydia, only to wish that she had said nothing, for it was immediately clear that this was a sore subject.

"Yes, they're quite nice," said Mabel, "but I do hope you won't encourage him to take up painting again, Miss Hale. We have no room for more, and it's a very expensive hobby. You've no idea what the materials cost, and the frames. And of course they don't look anything without frames. And nowadays one can get such charming reproductions of really good pictures that the game doesn't seem worth the candle."

Her husband said nothing. All the light and life had died out of his face at the first word she uttered. The change was, to Lydia, shocking. Was it possible that Mrs. Copeland did not realise how wounding her careless comments would be to her husband's pride? Was she being deliberately cruel, or was she merely insensitive? As the evening wore on Lydia inclined to the latter alternative. Mabel was hospitable according to her lights. She pressed her guests to eat and drink, but allowed it to be seen that she knew her pastry and her jellies were better than anything they had been accustomed to. She monopolised the conversation, and talked incessantly of herself. When they sat down to the whist table the vicar was her partner. Alan, who had uttered several civil sentences and gone through all the motions proper to a host, had not really spoken since his wife, with a stinging flick of her lash, had put him in his place.

He was playing very badly. Lydia, who, despite herself, was intensely and painfully aware of him, so that the other two people in the room seemed little more than shadows, knew that he was trying to lose, and, observing Mabel's childish exultation as she picked up the tricks, she knew why.

As she sat facing him she could not prevent her eyes from returning to his face, clear cut, fine drawn, over-sensitive, rigid with repressions. She could allow herself to watch him since he carefully avoided her gaze. He only met her eyes once, and that was in the hall, when the evening was over and they were putting on their coats. She felt an almost overwhelming desire to speak, but he forestalled her. "You see," he said very gently, "the unburied dead."

Again Mabel intervened. "What's that?" she asked, but this time, fortunately, she did not require an answer. "See them to the gate, Alan. I'm always afraid somebody will tumble over that step."

Her husband obeyed. They walked down the stone-paved path bordered with clipped box hedges to the iron gate set between pillars of stone.

"How lovely it is," said Lydia, turning back to look at the front of the house in the moonlight.

"A charming old place," her uncle agreed.

Alan Copeland unlatched the gate for them. "Yes. I remember thinking the first time I saw it that one could be happy here. Good night."

A minute later as they walked down the road they heard the house door closed.

"Quite a pleasant evening," said the vicar cheerfully. "People say that Mrs. Copeland is difficult and that they don't get on, but I can't see anything wrong myself."

II

Lydia had already discovered that her uncle's interest in his parishioners was superficial, and was due to the occasional promptings of his conscience. His heart—and she was beginning to suspect it to be a rather unsatisfactory organ, atrophied by disuse—such as it was, had long been centred in his self-appointed literary labours. She wondered if he had even noticed that Aunt Mary was dying before she died.

"I'm quite glad I came," he was saying, "but you must not expect me to go with you to tea with Miss Platt or the others. They've all invited you. Very well meant, I'm sure, and you must go. Those sort of people take offence so easily."

"I suppose so," she said vaguely. She was looking up through a network of branches at the moon. She felt happy, and was careful not to ask herself why.

The vicar cleared his throat. She was really much less trouble than he had feared before she came. He hardly saw her except at meals. "Are you leaving at the end of the week, or shall you stay a fortnight? You can if you like," he said clumsily.

"Thanks," she said, in the same far away voice. "I should like to stay on."

III

The school house had pseudo-Gothic lancet windows, and that of Miss Platt's living-room, overlooking the asphalted playground was covered with wire netting.

"The little beasts are always throwing stones, quite large ones," she explained, "at birds and at each other. Have you had much to do with children, Miss Hale?"

"Nary a thing," said Lydia cheerfully. "I suppose some are nice and some are nasty, like grown up people."

She was not yet sure how she was going to classify Miss Platt herself. Physically she was unattractive, thick-set, blunt features, with a swarthy, greasy skin; but she was vital and intelligent. The shelves and the dresser in her little sitting-room were stacked with books. Lydia looked at some of the titles while her hostess went into the tiny kitchen to make the tea. André Gide, Paul Marguerite, Mademoiselle de Maupin, *Death in the Afternoon*, *Tom Jones*, *Gulliver's Travels* and several works on criminology and famous trials. The pictures on the walls, too, showed a very definite taste for the macabre. Most of them were engravings from Hogarth, but there was one of a dying horse lying on a sun-drenched arena from which Lydia was turning away, feeling rather sick, as Miss Platt came in with the teapot and the toasted scones.

"Are you admiring my Spanish picture? I brought it back from Seville two years ago. I always try to go abroad for my summer holidays. It's a reproduction, of course, a colour print of a painting by a man who's tremendously popular over there. You see it in all the shops. I adore it, don't you?"

"I can see it is clever," said Lydia. "But—"

Miss Platt grinned. "But you hate it. I thought perhaps you might. So did Alan Copeland when I brought him in here to show it to him. Rather disappointing in his case. One does not expect that sort of sentimental reaction from a painter—and he was a painter once, and might have made his name if he hadn't been a damned fool. I'm not talking through my hat. I spent two years at the Slade before I realised it was no use in my case and became an instructress of youth. I'm the only person in Teene who can talk Alan Copeland's language, who knows why he stands for half an hour looking over a gate at a wild cherry tree in bloom. Do you take milk and sugar?"

"Yes," said Lydia. "Well, that must be nice for both of you."

"Oh, we're not specially friendly," said Miss Platt. "As a matter of fact I can't help despising him, and he probably knows it."

"Oh—why?"

"For letting himself be trapped by that awful old Mrs. Leach and her daughter. They were well named. They took lodgers, and he came. Little more than a boy, and a very handsome one. I went out sketching with him several times. He was so gay and charming in those days. And then he fell ill and they nursed him, and he never got out of their clutches. But he might if it hadn't been for that soft streak in him."

She was speaking more to herself than to Lydia, and her little deep-set eyes were bright with the anger that had burned in her for ten years. It was an old story and had ceased to have any local interest. No doubt it was a relief to find a listener who had not heard it all before.

"You have been here for some time then?" said Lydia.

"Longer than I care to think about," said Miss Platt curtly. "I knew your aunt. She was missed in the village. She used to visit the old people and listen to their long-winded complaints. They like that. There's been a great falling off in the attendance at church since she died. Why didn't you ever come to stay in her time?"

"My own mother was alive then, and we lived abroad. She couldn't stand the English winters."

"You've got a job?"

"Yes. I'm a cashier at Levine and Turnmore's."

"I know. I've had some of their sale catalogues. Astounding opportunities in the bargain basement."

Lydia smiled. "That's where I work."

"My God! No wonder you looked washed out. Why don't you make up? Or have you cut out lipstick while you're here to please the vicar?"

Lydia, being only human, was not unwilling to talk about herself. She had found the vicar's bland indifference a trifle chilling. She had been quick to realise that his detachment was deliberate, and that he meant to underline the fact that she had no real claim upon him.

"I don't think he would notice how I looked," she said. "I left off to please myself. We all have to make up at the shop. You can't have any natural colour in your face spending eight hours or more in that fug, and it might happen that one customer in a thousand really noticed us and went off saying that Levine and Turnmore's girls looked overworked and underfed, and the firm wouldn't like that."

The older woman knocked the ash off her cigarette. "Quite."

Through the faint blue veil of smoke her broad, swarthy face reminded Lydia of that of a sallow and slightly sinister figure of Buddha that she had seen every morning in the window of an antique shop on her way to business.

"You'll marry—or—" she leaned forward a little, staring. "I didn't realise it the other day, but you're definitely attractive."

Lydia laughed, but she felt uncomfortable. There was something about Miss Platt that she did not understand. She got up to go, and realised that by her haste she had betrayed her feelings. Miss Platt's eyes had narrowed. Her lips twitched as though she had found amusement in some rather bitter private jest as she rose to her feet as Lydia, made voluble by nervousness, explained that she must rush, and that it was later than she thought; and she did not press her to stay.

IV

Lydia's next engagement was with Mrs. Simmons and her daughter. Their house at the cross roads had been put up by Miss Gort's uncle, the retired jobbing builder from Plymouth, soon after he had built his own. It was an ugly brick box, with a slate roof, and the yard at the side with a shed for cars and a row of gaudily painted petrol pumps, was an added eyesore. They must have been watching for her for Irene, looking like an overblown rose in a bright pink silk jumper, opened the door before she had time to knock, and took her down the tiny passage into a stuffy sitting-room crowded with furniture, where the vast bulk of Mrs. Simmons, in her best black silk, partly blocked the light from the window.

"Ma, this is Miss Hale."

"You'll excuse me getting up," wheezed Mrs. Simmons, as she extended a puffy hand. "We ought to feel flattered, I'm sure. I said to Irene, we'll ask her, but she won't come."

"Oh—why not?"

Lydia sat down on the nearest chair. The carpet was grey with dust. She thought of Miss Platt's well-filled bookshelves and sage green distempered walls. There was no attempt at culture here. A pile of tattered fashion papers was stacked on one chair and a pack of greasy cards lay on a side table among a litter of odds and ends dimly reflected in the glass front of a case with stuffed birds in it. Tea was laid on the round table in the middle of the room, with brown and white bread and butter, two kinds of jam and a large dark plumcake. Irene had gone to the kitchen to make the tea. Mrs. Simmons eyed her embarrassed visitor maliciously.

"The vicar never comes if he can help it. He sends his she curate. That's Emily Gort. Did you have a pleasant evening at Strays? Irene gets our eggs and poultry from them. We like to do our neighbours a good turn, but we don't visit. We're not good enough for the Copelands nowadays, though the Leaches weren't anything to write home about. Guests they call it, but it was nothing but letting lodgings."

Lydia said nothing. Mrs. Simmons did not seem to require an answer. Irene came in with the teapot. "Go on, Ma. Grouse, grouse, grouse. Who the hell cares? You come from London, don't you, Miss Hale? Have you seen Marlene's latest picture?"

"No."

Irene monopolised the conversation during tea with some encouragement from Lydia, who preferred discussing movie stars to the more dangerous type of conversation initiated by Mrs. Simmons. The old woman listened indulgently, only intervening when the meal was nearly at an end to remind her daughter that Ern would be expecting her to take a cup out to him.

"And give him three lumps and a good slice of cake. I suppose he's too mucky to come in and say how-d'ye-do to Miss Hale?"

Irene giggled. "He was flat on his back under that bit of junk Mrs. Copeland calls a car when I last saw him."

Mrs. Simmons' body was immovable, but she turned her head in Lydia's direction. "She gave it to her husband as a birthday present, and he's supposed to use it for his business and to take her for a drive when she feels like it. If it had been second-hand no one would have said anything, but it's more like eighth-hand. Breaking down all over the place. Making him feel like a fool. Mean. There's not a meaner woman than Mabel Leach, that was."

Irene went out to the yard with a brimming cup of strong tea and a lump of cake. She did not return to the sitting-room, but they heard her running up the stairs and opening and shutting drawers in the room above.

"I suppose Ern's taking her off somewhere. He leaves a boy to attend to customers in the evening. If you don't have a bit of fun when you're young when do you? But don't you be going yet, Miss Hale."

Irene put her head in at the door. She was wearing her red beret.

"He's patched the old thing up and he's taking it up to Strays, and I'm going along with him. I'll get some eggs while I'm about it," she said breathlessly, and shut the door again before her mother could speak.

Mrs. Simmons moved uneasily so that the sofa creaked under her vast weight, but she said nothing at all. Lydia was silent too. From where she sat she could see herself reflected in the glass case of birds. Neat and ladylike, she thought bitterly. Irene, so young and so vital, had taken all the colour out of the room with her when she went. What did her vulgarity matter?

"I must be going," she said.

Mrs. Simmons roused herself. "Not yet, dearie," she said. "I get very dull sitting here by myself. Stay a bit and you'll be doing a kindness."

Lydia hated the oily voice, but she couldn't refuse. After all, her time was her own, and nobody wanted her at the vicarage.

"Bring over that pack of cards and I'll tell you your fortune."

She's just like an old witch, thought Lydia. If only she does not want to hold my hand.

"I'd love it," she said.

"Will you clear this end of the table then? Just like that Irene to go traipsing off leaving a mess of dirty cups to be washed up anywhere. Now, draw up a chair, cut twice, and think of a card."

She took the pack from Lydia and dealt out the cards in five heaps face downwards, wheezing and muttering to herself.

"The nine, the queen. I see a door opening for you, dearie, and a choice to be made. And this—it's either an illness or a journey."

"I've just had 'flu," said Lydia. She was growing more interested. It was becoming apparent that Mrs. Simmons took her fortune-telling seriously. She leaned forward, breathing heavily, her little eyes sunk like currants in the huge pudding that was her face, intent on each card that she picked up and laid down again. She was silent now, and for so long that Lydia felt compelled to speak. "Can't you tell me any more?"

Mrs. Simmons said nothing.

Lydia told herself that it was all nonsense, but her heart sank. "Is it—very bad?"

"I haven't said so. Too many spades. Did you think of a card?"

"Yes."

"What was it? You can tell me now. It may help."

"The king."

"What suit?"

"Spades."

"Ah." The old woman raked all the cards together into one untidy heap and pushed them aside. "Well, thank you for coming to see us. You've been invited out all round, I suppose. Have you been to Emily Gort's yet?"

"I'm going to Miss Gort's to-morrow."

Mrs. Simmons shook with silent laughter. "Poor Emily. She means to marry the vicar one of these days. What do you think, Miss Hale? Is there a chance for her?"

"I don't know," said Lydia cautiously. "Goodbye, and thank you so much for my tea, and my fortune, even if it wasn't a very good one."

She could not avoid shaking hands, much as she disliked the clinging grasp of those hot clammy fingers.

"I can't see you to the door, dearie. Can you find your way out?"

"Yes, of course. Good-bye!"

She was glad to get out of the stuffy over-heated room, with its smell of stale cooking. It had all been rather horrid, she thought.

The old woman, left alone, reached out slowly for the cards and fumbled them over. They would be returned presently to the sideboard drawer where they were kept with various boxes of pills and bunches of dried herbs.

It was getting dark when Irene came in, flushed and bright-eyed.

"We came home across the fields," she said as she lit the lamp. "I got a dozen eggs. Has she been gone long? I see you told her fortune. Had she a good hand?"

"There was death in it."

"Oh, rats!" said Irene.

CHAPTER IV
GEY ROUNDS

I

LYDIA had been facing the biting east wind all the way from the village and she had rather looked forward to sitting by a fire, but the grate in Miss Gort's sitting-room was filled with green paper shavings. The room itself looked very bare and spotlessly clean. The floor was covered with a worn linoleum, highly polished. The window curtains of Nottingham lace were dazzlingly white and stiff with starch. There was an overpowering smell of fish.

"I hope you don't mind," said Miss Gort. "The fishmonger calls Thursdays and I always get some for my cat. He's such a dear."

She lifted the huge ginger Tom that had followed them into the room on to her lap where he stood for a moment, waving his tail in front of her face, before jumping down again.

"You had tea with the Simmonses yesterday, didn't you, and Miss Platt on Tuesday? Well, you've met everybody now."

"What about the people at that big farm? I believe we get our milk from there."

"Oh, the Dawsons, at Monk's Barn. They're Plymouth Brethren and hold some kind of service of their own in their dairy on Sundays. Too bad, I think. They've got some of the men who work for them to attend instead of coming to church. And Bragge, the manager at the quarry and his sister don't go anywhere. They're not the sort of people your dear uncle would care for you to meet. That's the worst of villages, Miss Hale. The society is so restricted, especially where there is no great house to bring a little life into the place. I should feel it very much if it were not for dear Mrs. Copeland. I am always welcome at Strays, you know. She is so sensitive and highly strung. No one else about here understands her as I do. She depends on me."

"I thought Strays a lovely old house," said Lydia.

"You are interested in architecture? My uncle was a builder. He came here when he retired and built this house and the house the Simmons family live in. They are exactly alike, but you wouldn't think it, would you? I sometimes smile to myself when I go to fit poor dear old Mrs. Simmons for a new dress. Did you ever see such a clutter of old rubbish? And the dust! It's Irene's fault, but I suppose the poor girl has her work cut out cooking the meals. You'd be surprised at the amount of food they get through, though, of course," Miss Gort tittered, "you've only got to look at Mrs. Simmons to see she doesn't live on air. Just a minute. I think I hear the kettle boiling."

Miss Gort's tea was in strong contrast to the hearty meal to which Lydia had sat down the day before.

She was given a cup of weak tea and offered a plate of biscuits which had grown flabby from being left out of the tin. She ate one and was not pressed to take another.

Lydia, looking at Emily's bony, red, work-worn hands flut-tering over the sugar basin, at her sandy hair and the faintly pink tip of her long nose, wondered, with a touch of pity for a woman for whom she had hitherto felt nothing but the care-less contempt of youth for tedious middle age, if that pinched and frosted aspect was the mark of poverty. She had found Miss Gort's self-sufficiency and self-satisfaction, her evident convic-tion that the vicar and the parish depended on her, irritating, when perhaps, if she had looked deeper, she might have seen them to be heroic.

One ought not to judge without knowing a lot more, she thought. Miss Gort, meanwhile, unaware of these reflections, was explaining that ever since Mrs. Binns had scorched one of the surplices she had undertaken all the washing and the iron-ing of the church linen herself.

"I charge for the soap and the oil of my stove —that's only fair. Nothing for the labour. That I give very willingly, Miss Hale, and with a grateful heart. I'm thankful for many mercies. Let me see. It's a week to-day since you arrived. How much longer will you be staying?"

"Until next Thursday."

"Really? You've fitted in at the vicarage more easily than I expected."

"I try not to get into Uncle Henry's way."

"Yes. Of course at his age a man gets set. Well—I'm so glad you were able to have a cup of tea with me. Bobo, say good-bye to the lady. I have taught him to shake hands."

But the ginger cat slipped by his mistress as she opened the door into the passage and vanished into the kitchen with the aloofness of his race.

Lydia had imagined that it might be necessary to make some return for the hospitality shown to her, but she soon found that the vicar had no such intention. No one had been asked to a meal at the vicarage since his wife's death. Lydia, seeing that the suggestion had alarmed him, dropped the subject. In any case she had foreseen difficulties. The Simmons family could not have been invited with the others, and would have resented being entertained on another day. Miss Platt evidently did not get on with Mrs. Copeland. Lydia told herself that it did not matter. She was going back to London and was not likely to be seeing any of the inhabitants of Teene again. She could forget them all—and the sooner the better. Meanwhile she took long walks through winding lanes between hedgebanks starred with primroses, tired herself out, and went to bed early. On Sunday, at the morning and the evening services, she sat in the vicarage pew, close to the pulpit and with the main part of the small congregation behind her, joined in singing the hymns, and tried to follow the drift of her uncle's argument in a sermon that dealt with some obscure point made by a recent commentator on the Epistle to the Hebrews. His rustic hearers meanwhile shuffled in their seats, and the choirboys sucked peppermints. And then, while the last hymn was being sung Alan Copeland and his fellow churchwarden, the landlord of the Bull, went round with the offertory bags. Lydia avoided looking at him as she dropped in her coin, but as he went up the aisle to where the vicar waited at the altar steps she allowed herself one quick glance. His back was turned. It couldn't matter. I'm a fool, she thought bitterly afterwards as she hurried back to the vicarage. She might have lingered in the porch, waiting for her uncle. It would have given her a chance to speak to Alan as he came out of the vestry. "Goodbye, in case I don't see you again." She met the housekeeper in the hall and told her she had a headache and was going straight to bed. In her room she paced to and fro, twisting her hands together. Oh, why had she come to Teene? Was this love, this sick craving for a man who had no use for her? Why had she stayed on the second week? To get him away from Irene, that painted doll? After a while there was a knock at the door.

"The vicar asked me to say do you mind not walking about so much. It disturbs him. Is anything the matter, miss? Have you got the toothache?"

"Yes, a little. All right. I'll take some aspirin and get into bed."

She slept, thanks to the aspirin, and came down to breakfast looking not much paler than usual.

Monday and Tuesday passed uneventfully. She had found an ordnance map of the district in the bookcase and it enabled her to keep well away from Strays. On Wednesday, her last day at the vicarage, she had planned to walk as far as Gey Rounds. She had heard of it from her uncle. It was a hill top crowned with the remains of a prehistoric stone circle. The country people sometimes went there blackberrying, but never at any other time. It was at least twelve miles there and back, but she thought she could manage it if she allowed herself plenty of time. She asked the housekeeper for sandwiches and started directly after breakfast.

It was a fine day and Lydia was fond of walking. She followed the route she had marked on the map and found the footpath across fields that saved her a couple of miles, and brought her back to the road at the foot of the cone-shaped hill she had to climb. She had seen a couple of cars on the road and a postman on his bicycle, but that was some time ago. There was no house in sight, and she seemed to have the landscape to herself. Some young women would have been nervous of so much solitude, but Lydia was sick of crowds, and just then she felt a special need to be alone. It was good to walk on the turf, cropped close by innumerable generations of rabbits, after the hard metal of the road.

The sun was shining, and the larks were singing overhead, and the air was still even on the hill top. There were bees at work among the almond-scented flowers of the gorse. It was one of those days that early April sometimes borrows from June. Lydia smiled as the white scut of a rabbit flashed out of sight. Why can't I be happy with the earth, she wondered. I won't think of anything but what I see before me.

The sarsen stones were smaller and less impressive than she had expected. They had sunk with the passing of time into the loose friable soil and several were entirely hidden in thickets of wild sloes and blackberry bushes. She found one with thyme growing about it and sat down there, leaning her back against the sun warmed stone, to eat her sandwiches. Below, at the foot of the hill, the road wound like a shining black thread, and beyond it half a county lay, unrolled like a map, pasture and plough lands, milky jade, and pale browns, to the misty blue of the horizon.

She had taken off her hat and pushed back her hair from her forehead. She was a little tired, but not much. In any case she meant to stay here for hours and steep herself in the peaceful silence of the place. Time would slip by here like sand through one's fingers. She bent to watch a ladybird slowly climbing a blade of grass.

A shadow passed between her and the sun. She looked up and saw Alan Copeland standing before her. The shock of joy affected her as fear might have done. She was white to the lips and trembling. He was speaking, but she scarcely heard what he said. Something was happening to her that was to have a tremendous effect on her life and on his.

The personality that had been built up, not without pain and effort, during her twenty-two years, the Lydia Hale who had learned through contact with others, through the teachings of her elders, by reading books, to be reasonably unselfish, to exercise common prudence, to keep the rules of civilized society for her own sake and that of others, was quietly but firmly thrust aside by another self, far stronger and more vital but incapable of coherent thought.

"I'm afraid I startled you. I'm so sorry, but I was passing in my car and I saw you climbing the hill. I had to follow to warn you to be careful. Strangers don't know, but there are a good many adders up here. Gey Rounds has a bad name on that account. It'll be all right if you don't try to go through the undergrowth. They come out of their holes on a day like this to sun themselves." He hesitated. "I was surprised to see you here. It's a long way on foot—" He stopped again rather helplessly, as if he had lost the thread of what he was saying. "Good-bye," he muttered and was turning away when she spoke.

"Don't go."

He swung round again to face her. "I didn't expect to see you again."

"I know," she said. "I didn't mean to, but it's happened. Now you are here won't you stay and talk to me just for a little while?"

He answered heavily. "I haven't anything to say. It might be better if I went."

They looked at one another now steadily. She touched the folded coat she had spread on the grass. "Sit here by me. Please. I want you to stay."

"Are you sure? You're so young. Perhaps you don't understand. I—I'm in love with you."

She answered with a directness that matched his own. "I'm glad."

His dark face, schooled to a mask-like immobility, came to life. He tried to speak, but could not get his words out.

"Then you—you—"

The minutes passed. Larks sang overhead, dropped to their nests, and presently sprang up to sing again. A snake with the orange and black diamond markings that spell death on its packed coils basked in the afternoon sunshine and then, with an uncanny swiftness, slid away and vanished in a hole in the ground. The postman going home from his rounds on his red painted bicycle, noticed the same shabby car standing by a field gate that he had passed earlier in the day.

II

"You must write to me, Lydia. Not to Strays, of course. The Post Office, Wainbridge. I have some customers in that direction. I can call for letters. You've got to leave to-morrow?"

"Yes. In any case this mustn't happen again, Alan. It's too dangerous."

"Yes, but—I don't want you to run any risks, my sweet. Oh, God, why can't I take you right away? That would be the simple, natural thing. If I could get any kind of job. What a hope! We've got to face facts. I'm dependent on—on Mabel." He could feel her flinch at the name, but she only said, "Don't worry about all that now. Darling, we've been happy. Don't let us think of to-morrow. Why is it so difficult to live like animals in the present?"

"Because we aren't like animals—altogether," he said sombrely. "We've got the extra something that makes for misery."

"Hush, Alan. Don't talk, don't think—"

He hid his face against her breast. They were silent for a while before he stirred again.

"We shall have to go, Lydia. I can drive you back to the vicarage. I can give you a lift. No one can make harm of that. If you tried to walk back now you wouldn't be there before dark. Don't forget, if you're asked, I picked you up here at the foot of the hill. We've got to be careful. The village is full of chattering women."

"I know. We'd better not go down the hill together. We might be seen from the road."

"Hardly anyone comes this way—but I suppose you are right."

He helped her to her feet and held her close for a moment.

"God forgive me if I've harmed you, Lydia."

"You haven't. I shall never regret this. Never. I can promise you that. Go now, my dearest. I'll follow in five minutes."

They were silent during the drive back to the village. Alan stopped the car at the vicarage gate. Lydia got out and turned to offer her hand.

"Thanks for the lift, Mr. Copeland."

He answered in the same formal tone. "Not at all." Their eyes met for an instant. "Good-bye."

He heard the vicarage gate clang behind her as he let in the clutch and drove on.

Mabel came out of the sitting-room as he entered the hall.

"How late you are. Where have you been? I was beginning to feel quite worried. I really can't be left for hours and hours like this. That dreadful girl from the garage has been here. I happened to go into the back spare bedroom and look out of the window and saw someone hanging about by the yard gate. I thought I'd better go out. She said they wanted a boiling fowl. I asked her to kindly come right up to the back door and knock in future. I don't care to have people lurking about like that. It's an odd way to behave. And her manner was very surly."

"Yes," said Alan carefully, "she has too much time on her hands. She does hang about, as you say, but I have to be civil. I can't afford to offend my customers."

"Customers. That's your excuse for keeping in with that Bragge and his sister. I wonder if the quarry owners would keep him on as a manager if they knew he drank. Such a bad example to the men."

"He's a darn good fellow, and he does his job. They'll sack him quick enough if he gives them cause. And, meanwhile, please don't go spreading that about."

"I shall say what I choose. It's true. Emily heard it from the wife of one of the men. But we won't discuss it. I've had my tea. You must get your own if you want any. But I suppose you had it with the Bragges. I might have known you would be there."

He realised how dangerous it might be to let that pass.

"No. Something went wrong with the car as I came back from Wainbridge. I managed to put it right myself, but it took a long time, and then I came up with the vicar's niece and gave her a lift home."

"Miss Hale? On the road from Wainbridge?"

"She told me she's been exploring the countryside, taking long walks every day."

"Fancy. Rather unwise, I should have thought. Overtiring herself. I thought she looked delicate. Where are you going now?"

It was one of her most irritating habits to be always asking such questions. He tried to be patient. "Down the field to feed the poultry and collect the eggs. It's my usual job about this time of day, you know."

"I know the wretched birds have to be attended to whenever I happen to need you. I always say they're more trouble than they're worth. I see the bill for all that wire netting came in again to-day. Aren't you going to pay it?"

He bit his lip. "They'll have to wait. Was it addressed to you?"

"Of course not, but it was in an open envelope with a half-penny stamp. And now I suppose you are going to complain that I look at your correspondence?"

He suppressed his rising fury. "Not at all. I don't mind in the least. Why should I? It isn't as if I had any friends who wrote to me."

He left her staring after him. What an odd thing to say, she thought. Really, Alan was very queer at times. She would have to ask him presently what he had meant. It didn't do to let such things pass. She was not at all sure that she had been right to let him take up poultry farming even in a small way. He seemed to imagine that it would make him independent of her, and that, of course, was nonsense. He must not get notions, she thought. She would not have believed a psycho-analyst if he had told her how much intimate satisfaction she derived from Alan's struggles to escape. From long practice she had grown very expert at plucking at those shrinking nerves of his, but she played her little devilish tunes on those worn strings without ever being really aware of what she was doing. She did not know that her former infatuation for him had changed to a cold dislike, and that he hated her. Certain forms had always been observed between them. Though it was years since they had shared a room he always came in to kiss her good night. Though she nagged him incessantly she trusted him entirely. It had certainly never occurred to her that he could be unfaithful. On the other hand, she had no confidence in his business acumen. He would always be a fool, she considered, in worldly matters.

If she was not careful he would be wasting money again on paints and brushes. She would have to be quite definite about that, she thought, as she sat by the fire which she had lit because though the day had been so unseasonably warm it got chilly after the sun set.

CHAPTER V
PAYMENT DEFERRED

I

DURING April there was a Birthday Sale at Levine and Mentmore's. The bargain basement was more crowded than ever and the wooden balls that held the customers' bills and their money clanged incessantly across the overhead lines between the harassed assistants serving at the counters and the pale-faced girl in the cashier's desk. No daylight ever penetrated there, and very little air. Day after day the same crowds, or so it seemed, asking the same questions. "Are these reduced?" "Is this cotton mixture?" "How do I get to the hat department?" The same bored voices of the girls in charge of the lifts, "Going up. Going up. No, moddam, this is the basement." And Lydia, in her glass case, smoothing out the crumpled bills, counting out copper and silver, pressing the switch that sent the wooden ball off on its aerial journey. Doves leaving the Ark. No, not a bit like that. Don't dither, or you'll make a mistake.

One Saturday morning at the end of May she fainted, and had to be carried through the mob of women snatching at a new consignment of blouses at 2s 11d. to the staff toilet room. She soon recovered and insisted on going back to her desk though the older woman from the glove department who had been told off to attend to her tried to dissuade her.

"You look ghastly, dear, you do really. I'd go straight home if I was you. They can't stop you. In fact it's only fair to the rest of us if you're sickening for something."

"I'm not. To-morrow's Sunday. I'll have a good rest."

"I would do. Do you live at home with your people?"

"No. I've got a bed-sitter—but the landlady's quite decent."

She went on with her work doggedly and made no mistakes, but she knew that the shop walker looked at her thoughtfully each time he passed, and she was afraid.

On Monday the blow fell. She was sent to the manager's office and there she was told that she was obviously not physically equal to her work, and that she must leave at the end of the week.

"But—"

"We won't argue about it, Miss Hale. You will remember that you were ill before Easter and were allowed a fortnight's holiday. We expect our employees to be fit. That will do."

At the end of the week she left Levine and Mentmore and began to look for work. She answered advertisements without result, and put down her name at the Labour Exchange. She was, of course, drawing unemployment benefit. At the end of another fortnight the Exchange put her in communication with a manufacturer of a patent pad guaranteed to remove ink-stains from any surface. He was looking for lady-like young women with pleasant manners.

"You'll do," he said. He was good-natured. "But you've got to be pushing too, see? Polite but pushing, pushing but polite. You go from door to door, see, and, if possible you demonstrate. You take three dozen in this case. They weigh very light. And when you have sold them all you come back to me for more. I have fifteen young ladies on the job now. One pound a week and commission. If you work hard you do well." He produced a map and showed her the district she was to cover.

She was to start the next morning, and she was allowed to take the case full of pads with her when she had left a deposit of ten shillings with her new employer.

"Just a form," he said gaily as he slipped the note into a greasy pocket-book which seemed to be well filled. "I can see you are honest, a good girl, but there are some who would run away with my pads and never come back. I am sure you will be one of my smartest saleswomen with a little practice. Put on your best clothes and don't forget your lipstick. You must appear prosperous. You are not asking see. You let them have these so marvellous pads as a favour. That is sales psychology."

It was rather a long bus ride from Lydia's lodgings to the district that had been allotted to her. She started on an apparently interminable street of dreary little semi-detached villa residences and went up one side and came back the other without selling a single pad. Some housewives listened to what she had to say before they shook their heads regretfully and closed the door; some only opened the door a few inches and banged it to again as soon as they saw she carried a case, and several did not come to the door at all. She left that street, dragging her feet a little, and went to the next. Here, after several failures, her spirits were raised by one woman who let her recite the little piece she had learned describing the virtues of the pad to the end.

"It sounds all right, but how am I to know it does all you say? You come in and I'll pour some ink on a bit of rag, and if your pad gets it off I'll buy one. Can't say fairer than that, can I?"

Lydia followed her hopefully into a clean little sitting-room. Her employer had not actually demonstrated one of the pads to her, but the test proposed sounded fair enough. Her prospective customer bustled about and produced a strip of old linen and a penny bottle of ink.

"There. That's a good sized blot. Now you get to work."

Lydia rubbed it with the pad and only succeeded in smearing the ink over a larger surface. "Perhaps I'm using the wrong side," she faltered. She turned the pad over with no better success. She stared down helplessly at the mess.

"Looks as if I'd have been nicely had if I'd bought this," said the other woman grimly. "How much are you asking for these?"

"Two—two shillings."

"I've half a mind to fetch a policeman," the voice altered. "Here—sit down here."

Everything had gone black. When the light returned Lydia found that she was lying on the floor with a cushion under her head and that her face and hair were wet. She tried to sit up.

"No hurry," said the voice. "You did a proper faint that time. Don't be frightened. I can see this isn't your fault. You wouldn't have been so ready to demonstrate if you'd been in the secret. It looks like a dirty swizzle, but I'm not blaming you. Have you sold many of these precious pads?"

"No, none."

"Just as well. I've been looking at them. They're nothing but bits of carpet felt cut into squares and sprinkled with a drop of some chemical. Where did you get them from?"

"A Mr. Isaacson. He has an office in the City. I was to go back for more when I'd sold all these."

"What a hope! Is that what he said?"

The woman was brusque but not unkind. Lydia told her all she knew about the job.

"And he stung you for ten shillings? I'll bet that's how he makes his profits. That case you're carrying isn't worth more than half a crown. If he gets a deposit from every one he engages he doesn't do so badly. I'm willing to lay any money that if you went back to his office now you'd find it to let . . ."

"I shall have to go back, of course, to make sure," said Lydia. "That pad I tried might just happen to be a dud."

She scrambled rather shakily to her feet. "It was idiotic of me to flop like that."

"Not at all. You've been overtiring yourself. You'd no business to take on a job like this in your condition."

Lydia's heart seemed to miss a beat. "In my—"

The other woman looked at her quickly. "You're going to have a baby. Didn't you know?"

Lydia swallowed hard. "Are you—sure?"

"Of course. I'm not likely to make a mistake. Didn't you notice the brass plate on my door? I'm a midwife."

"Oh—I hadn't noticed. I—I think I'll be going. Thank you for—for being kind," said Lydia faintly.

The nurse laid a large capable hand on her arm. "All right," she said, "I'm not nosey. I'm not asking any questions. But you sit down—you're all of a tremble—you shall have a cup of warm milk and some biscuits before you go."

While she was heating the milk over a gas ring in the kitchen she was thinking, "She's a complete stranger. She may be a thief. And I left my gold brooch and my watch on the mantelpiece."

But when she went back to the sitting-room the girl had not moved from the chair in which she had left her.

The nurse sighed. She had seen fear on so many women's faces.

"You just sip that. Don't gulp it down," she advised. "And don't think you need hurry away. I'm alone in the house as it happens. The friend I live with is away on a case. My time's my own until to-morrow. You won't mind me asking—you're not married, are you?"

"No."

"Will he marry you, d'you think?"

"He can't."

"I see. Men are beasts."

"No. It was my fault as much as his. More, perhaps. I was mad, I suppose—"

"It's nature," said the nurse. "If we were sensible all the time the human race would die out, and I suppose there's some use in living or we wouldn't be sent here."

"I don't know what I shall do."

"I can't help you. I don't hold with that sort of thing. Women have gone down on their knees to me here, in this very room. God knows I was sorry for them, but if you once let yourself be persuaded you're done for. Why, a nurse who trained at Queen Charlotte's the same time as I did is serving a five years' sentence at this very moment."

Lydia shuddered. "I don't want that."

"That's all right, for you won't get it from me. And, what's more I think you're wise. My advice to you is not to worry too much. Try to get a rather easier job than this house to house canvassing. You've got another five or six months before anybody need notice. And don't be too proud to take all the help your friend can give you."

She glanced at the clock on the mantelpiece. She was a kind-hearted woman, but she had planned to treat herself to the first performance at the nearest picture palace, and the time was getting on.

Lydia took the hint. "I must be going," she said. With hands that still shook a little she took the mirror from her bag and adjusted her hat and repaired her complexion.

"What are you going to do about these pads?"

"I shall take a bus at the end of the road and go straight back to his office. If he's there I shall ask for my ten shillings."

"Shall you go to the police if he's flitted?"

"No. I don't want to be mixed up in things and perhaps have to be called as a witness or something. I've never been in a police court. I should be terrified."

She picked up the case and achieved a rather watery smile.

"Thank you." She was moving towards the door when the nurse called to her.

"Wait a bit. I believe I know a job that might suit you for a bit. They'd take you if I recommended you, but I should be taking a risk because it's a position of trust, and I don't know anything about you."

"I was a cashier at Levine and Mentmore's for two years. They sacked me because I wasn't strong enough, but I'm sure they would give me a reference for honesty and all that."

"Well, a patient of mine told me the other day that they want to find a companion for her grandmother, who lives with them. The old lady's sight is failing and she likes to be read to. You'd have to change her books and listen to her grumbling and write letters at her dictation and so on. It sounds easy and you'd get a pound a week and your lunch and your tea. They don't want anyone living in. It's a flat and there isn't room. The snag is that the old lady is a holy terror. On the other hand, you could rely on the rest of the family being decent to you. It wouldn't be a permanent post. My patient's husband is an American and they may be going back to the States next autumn. What about it? I was going to the pictures, but if you like I'll take you round there now."

Lydia hesitated. The post had its obvious drawbacks, but she could not afford to miss a chance of employment, especially now that she knew what lay before her.

"It's very kind of you," she said. "Perhaps we could go to the pictures together afterwards."

II

Lydia had written to Alan every week since she left Teene. She posted her letter on Tuesday morning and received his reply by the first post on Friday. They were not long letters as a rule for neither of them had the gift of expressing themselves on paper. Lydia, who was chiefly anxious not to add to her lover's worries, always said that she was all right and that his letter was enough to make her happy for the rest of the week. She had not told him that she had left Levine and Mentmore's. What was the use? He had troubles enough of his own. His letters to her were always written out of doors, scrawled in pencil as he sat in his car. There was no local news and no reference to his domestic affairs. Often there was only one sentence. Darling, I love you always. Once he wrote that if they did not meet again soon he should go mad.

Lydia had been engaged as reader and companion to old Mrs. Smith, and now travelled daily from her bed-sitting-room to the flat in Russell Square. She had not got back her ten shillings. She had taken her new friend's advice and not gone back to the office in the City. She was glad that she had not when she saw an account of his arrest a few days later, headed Heartless Fraud on Unemployed Women. Apparently no less than a hundred and sixteen applicants had paid their ten shillings for a case worth half a crown at the most and some bits of carpet felt. The names and addresses of those who were chosen out of the crowd to give evidence were published. Alan might have read all about it and worked himself into a fever.

The fact of her condition was of far greater importance. After much anxious consideration she had resolved to keep that from him for the present.

The nurse had advised her not to be too proud to take all the help her friend could give her. That was usual she knew, in such cases. There had been girls at Levine and Mentmore's. She was not too proud—but what could poor Alan do? They had already faced the fact that he was dependent on Mabel. He would suffer horribly and quite uselessly. What was her love worth if she could not spare him that?

And so the following week she wrote him one of her usual letters

"MY DARLING ALAN,

"I hope you are keeping well. We're having what they call a heat wave here. It's stuffy in the Tube and the tea shops, but how glorious it would be on Gey Rounds. I'm all right. I think of you and love you. Take care of yourself. Your own

"LYDIA."

She found her new employer less exacting than she had been led to expect. When she had paid her rent she had only eight shillings left to pay for her breakfast—she found she could do without supper—and for shoe repairs and other incidental expenses, including bus and train fares. At the end of the first week she had three halfpence left in her purse. Obviously she would not be able to save. On the other hand, she felt much stronger even after a few days' rest from the strain of her work at Levine and Mentmore's. It was a blow when at the end of the first fortnight she was told that the Smiths were giving up the flat in a few days and sailing for New York. She lay awake for a long time that night, thinking with dread of the future. There was time, there was still time before anyone would know, but meanwhile the sense of having been trapped by life that is common to all women in her unhappy position was always there, and a cold crawling fear of the inevitable shame and pain to come lurked in the shadowy background of her troubled mind.

"You're looking peaky again, Miss Hale," said her landlady.

Soon, she thought, she would be trying to avoid meeting her on the stairs. And there were moments when her courage almost failed her even now, when she longed to tell Alan, to beg him to come to her, to save her somehow, anyhow, from the inevitable consequences of her own reckless passion.

She even wrote, sitting up in bed scribbling feverishly, with her pad on her knees. Alan, come, come. If they could not live together they could die. The gas, a locked door, or the river. But when the morning came she always tore up what she had written.

Some weeks later, on a wet afternoon about the middle of June, Lydia's landlady answered the door to a young man who asked for Miss Hale.

Young or youngish, with a thin, dark face, and an air of suppressed eagerness. The landlady, who was used to dealing with attractive members of the opposite sex trying to dispose of vacuum cleaners, writing compendiums and tooth brushes, eyed him doubtfully.

"Is it to sell her something?"

"Oh, no. I'm a friend of hers. My name is Copeland. I'm sure she'll see me."

"She's out at present. Well—I've got a sitting-room vacant on the ground floor. You can wait in there for her if you like."

She showed him into the room and lingered in the doorway. "She doesn't get many visitors, and that's a fact. The way some young girls are fussed over while others are left to sink or swim—that's life, I suppose. It's heart-breaking work looking for a job, and Miss Hale isn't over strong. I've seen her when she's come in holding on to the banisters as if she hardly knew how to drag herself up the stairs. And if I call up to her if she's had any luck I can tell by her voice when she answers that tears aren't far off."

"She is out of work?"

"Yes. Didn't you know? Perhaps I've said more than I should. I'm apt to run on. But Miss Hale has been with me two years, and never no trouble. Always so quiet and considerate like, and nursed me once through the flu, which I haven't forgotten. So I take an interest. I must go back to my ironing."

Left to his own devices Alan stood at the window looking through the coarse mesh of the Nottingham lace curtains into the dreary street. Grey, all grey, but for the reflection of the pillar box at the corner like a splash of blood on the wet pavement. The pillar box in which she had posted her letters to him. Looking for a job. His little Lydia in a thrusting, pushing world.

And here she was coming up the steps, fitting her latch-key in the lock. He crossed the room in two strides and intercepted her at the foot of the stairs.

"Lydia—" his hand was on her arm.

She gasped. "Oh, Alan!"

He drew her into the room. "My sweet!" They clung together silently while he rained kisses on her hair, her eyes, her lips, and tasted the salt of her tears.

"Darling, don't cry."

"I can't help it. I've wanted you so."

"And I you. It's been hell all these weeks. Weeks—it seemed like years."

"Oh, Alan, how did you manage it? I thought you could never get away. And I didn't get your letter last week. I've been so worried."

"I'm sorry about that. I couldn't get over to Wainbridge, and I was afraid to post a letter to you in Teene. Something has happened. Look at this!" He touched the mourning band on his sleeve.

"Oh!" They were sitting on the sofa now, hand in hand, and she could see him more clearly. He looked very worn, she thought, and hollow-eyed.

"Darling," she murmured, "what is it?"

"Mabel died last week. It was very sudden. She was only ill a few hours. Of course she had been ailing for a long time. It was her digestion. She liked rich food. She wasn't well when I came in, and she went up to bed early. In the middle of the night I woke up and heard her calling me. It—it was pretty ghastly. I did what I could for her, but she got worse, and I was alone in the house with her. No one within a mile, no telephone. I had to get the doctor somehow, and the damned car had broken down again. I had to go off on my bicycle at four in the morning. I knocked up Emily Gort on my way, and she shoved on some clothes and hurried off to be with Mabel. She's really been a brick all through. When I got back with the doctor she was unconscious, and she died a few minutes later, but he said there was nothing he could have done to save her. It was a duodenal ulcer. He wasn't surprised. He had expected something of the kind. She never would take his advice, and diet. That was last Thursday, and the funeral was yesterday."

"Poor Alan," she said gently. "It must have been a shock."

"Yes. And—during that awful night she said, 'I might have been nicer to you, Alan. I know I've been irritable. You must try to forgive.' Poor woman. We parted friends."

"I'm glad of that."

"Yes. But the fact remains that—well, you know what my life was like. I don't want to put it into words. And I love you. It's been pretty damned awful all these weeks. How soon can we be married, Lydia? What do you think about it? I suppose there'd be a lot of talk in the village if we don't wait a year."

She was leaning against him, in the crook of his arm, and resting her head against his shoulder. She had made one or two little snuggling movements, but now she was quite still.

"Alan—I can't wait."

"You don't mean—"

"Yes."

"Good God! Why didn't you tell me before?"

"I didn't want to upset you."

"Lydia—I'll never forgive myself."

"It was as much my fault as yours. And it doesn't matter now."

"We'll be married as soon as possible, in a few days, at the nearest registrar's."

"But—I can't go back to Teene, Alan. Being married wouldn't stop the scandal. It would be awful for you, too. We should be pariahs."

"We can keep away for a bit," he said. "I meant to do that in any case. You'd hardly believe it, Lydia, but Irene Simmons has been up to Strays every day since Mabel died. I simply can't get rid of her. She says her mother sent her up to see if there's anything she can do. I don't know if that's true, but I'm scared of that old woman. And it's hard on Ern. I don't know if he's really fond of her and if he minds the way she goes on—he's one of those quiet, reserved sort of chaps—but they're supposed to be engaged."

"You never—encouraged her, Alan?"

"Never," he said emphatically. "She's been a bit of a nuisance for some time now, trailing around. I went over to see Mabel's lawyer at Wainbridge yesterday. He'd asked me to call round. Of course the will has got to be proved and all that, but he was prepared to advance me as much as I wanted to go on with."

"She has left you everything?"

"Yes. Except five pounds and some bits of jewellery to Emily Gort."

"You could sell Strays?" said Lydia tentatively.

He was silent for a moment. Then he said, "I'd hate to do that. I always loved the house. It could be made perfect. There's panelling under those terrible Victorian wallpapers. One of the derelict barns would make an ideal studio. There ought to be a lawn at the back where Mabel would have vegetables. All these years I've seen things that could be done. Now I can. And that isn't all. Mabel, that last night, asked me to go on living there. Don't leave Strays, she said. And I promised."

"I see," said Lydia. She understood his feeling. That long thwarted creative instinct of his was at work. Strays had made its appeal to her, too.

"She—she wouldn't mind you altering it?" she said.

"Mabel? Look here, Lydia, we mustn't be morbid. What can it matter to her now if I spend her money in ways she wouldn't have cared about? She left it to me, and she knew darned well that we didn't agree about anything. She had her own way while she lived. Isn't that enough?"

"Yes. I think it is."

"Well, then. Let's leave it at that. I'll write to the lawyer chap and tell him I'm going to travel about for a year, and I'll tell your uncle the same thing. I'll have to go down and make some arrangement about the poultry, but I shan't leave anyone in the house. Caretakers only mess up a place."

He broke off as the landlady, after rattling the handle, burst into the room with a laden tea tray.

"I thought you and your friend might like a cup," she explained. "Or is it a relative, Miss Hale?"

"Not yet," he said gaily. "We're going to be married in a few days."

The landlady beamed. "I'm glad, though it means me losing one of my lodgers. I hope you'll both be happy, I'm sure. Fancy that. This is the anniversary of my wedding day. Quite a coincidence. In the air, as you might say. I got the top of my wedding cake still under glass. You've seen it, Miss Hale, in my basement sitting-room. Lovely it is, all cherubs and horseshoes. You won't be having none of that, I suppose? Just quietly in your travelling dress? You'll have to take good care of her, sir. She's not one of the tough sort."

"I'll take care of her," he said.

CHAPTER VI
THE SECOND MRS. COPELAND

I

THE Copelands spent the rest of the summer in North Wales. After a week at an hotel in the pass of Llanberis they moved into lodgings in the village. There was a long spell of dry weather and they spent most of their days out of doors. Alan made a large number of sketches and notes for larger pictures which he hoped to paint later on. Lydia read novels and knitted a jumper. They were both as happy as human beings can be. Alan looked ten years younger. He had no longer that air of a man who is always on his guard. He talked easily and freely. He was a great favourite with their landlady, who was charmed by his devotion to his wife. She liked to linger, talking to them when she came into the sitting-room to clear away their meals. Lydia did not mind, but Alan found her conversation boring.

"I must say I'm looking forward to having a place to ourselves," he told Lydia.

"Yes, but—"

"I'll have to send for some more cadmium." They were sitting on a rock on the southern shore of Lake Padarn. Alan was working quickly, trying to get an effect of light before it changed.

Lydia was watching his dark face, satisfied, absorbed in the effort he was making to transfer the colour of the sky and the water reflecting it to his canvas.

"We're half way through September," she said. "We shall have to leave before long."

"I know. You haven't been bored here, darling?"

"Of course not. I've loved it."

He painted in silence for a few minutes. Then he said, "How about Leamington for the next stop? There's some good country round, and it would be all right for you. I mean, doctors and nurses and all that. But I'll go anywhere else you like."

"Leamington will do," she said. "But, Alan, I don't want to be a worry, but how can we go back to Strays next Spring with a baby three months old. I—I suppose it's cowardly of me, but I simply can't face it."

"I've been thinking that over," he said. "Luckily you don't correspond and never have with your uncle. He really knows nothing about you. I suggest that we give out that you were secretly married when you came to Teene last year to a man who was killed in a motor smash soon afterwards. I shall have met you round about next February, a young widow with a baby, and married you. What about it? I don't see why they shouldn't swallow that."

She hesitated. "It's very ingenious, but it means telling a lot of lies."

"I'm afraid it does, but can you suggest any alternative?"

"No. But I wish it wasn't necessary."

The light had changed. He closed his paint box and began to wipe his brushes. "It won't hurt anyone," he argued. "It will be for the child's sake as much as our own. That ought to make it easier for you. We shall have to work out all the details. There is an art of lying. I seem to remember something of Kipling's. Not a little place at Tooting but a country house with shooting sort of lie. I'm looking forward to overhearing people saying how touching it is the way Copeland adores his stepson. Come along, take my arm, old lady, over this rough bit of ground."

She said no more. After all, he was right. There seemed to be no alternative but a brazening out of the situation of which she knew herself incapable. But she did not feel so sure as Alan that they would convince their neighbours at Teene. It was about this time that she began to have recurring dreams about them. In her dream she was trying, vainly, to put on her clothes while a crowd of people stood round her, pointing and staring, and Irene and her mother were there, and Gertrude Platt, and Miss

Gort with her ginger cat in her arms. And sometimes it seemed that the crowd was not looking at her at all but at a dead horse lying on a patch of blood-stained sand. At this point she usually woke up crying and clutching at Alan. They had found comfortable rooms at Leamington. Alan still went out sketching when the weather permitted, but Lydia no longer went with him. In the evenings he read aloud to her while she lay on a sofa drawn up to the fire. On Christmas Eve she went into a nursing home farther down the street. Their child was born on the 28th of December. It only lived three days.

"Poor little beggar," said Alan sadly, "perhaps he realised he wasn't really wanted."

"But he was!" cried Lydia. "I wanted him. Oh, Alan—didn't you!"

"As a matter of fact," he admitted, "I did. But I should have hated him to suffer for no fault of his own."

They both looked forward now with growing eagerness to going back to Strays.

II

Emily Gort glanced about her with the eye of a general reviewing the disposition of his forces. The jam jars filled with daffodils were effectively concealed by banks of moss and trails of ivy, and the pots of ferns had been so arranged that the vicar could not possibly fall over them when he entered the pulpit. She looked at her watch. They had just finished in time. Mrs. Dilke would be coming at three to wash down the chancel and the nave. She joined the schoolmistress, who had just finished decorating the window ledges with the primroses that had been brought during the morning by the village children.

"Very nice," she said graciously.

Gertrude Platt said nothing. She resented Miss Gort's attempts to patronise her. Miss Gort moved on to the font where Irene Simmons was pushing some kingcups into one of the jars standing round the base.

"Have you finished?"

"Just about." Irene stepped back to survey her handiwork. She had coarsened a little in a year, but she was still very pretty. She was never very regular in her attendance at church, but she was fond of flowers and really enjoyed helping with the decorations.

"It does you credit, Irene," said Miss Gort.

Miss Platt strolled up to them. She had lately taken to wearing a beret, a dark blue cloth beret like a man's. It became her broad, ugly, clever face better than a hat. Her lips twitched with suppressed amusement as she watched Irene, who had just produced a pocket mirror and a powder puff.

"My dear—" Miss Gort's long nose grew a shade pinker at the tip. "Think a moment. Not in a sacred edifice. I know you mean no harm, but—"

"Oh, gosh!" grumbled Irene.

"The chancel doesn't look so well as usual," said Miss Platt judicially. "Can't be helped, I suppose. We're bound to miss poor Mabel Copeland's arums. Well, may as well be getting home."

The three women left the church together and walked down the path towards the lych gate. Miss Gort was enquiring after Mrs. Simmons, who, according to her daughter, was much about the same.

"And how much longer are you going to keep your cousin Ernest waiting?" enquired Miss Gort playfully. "You're a naughty girl, you know. It's no wonder the poor fellow looks glum. I called at the garage the other day to get a little petrol to clean my grey silk jumper and I could hardly get a word out of him."

Irene reddened. "If Ern told you I was engaged to him he's a liar—" She broke off as the vicar came up the path and, instead of following his usual custom and hurrying by with a mumbled good afternoon, stopped to speak to them.

"Ah, the decorations. To be sure. How quickly the time comes round. Dear me. Was it last year or the year before that my wife's niece came down for a few days?"

"Last year, vicar. She helped you, Miss Platt, with the windows. Is she coming down again?" enquired Miss Gort.

"Well, that's just the point. I've had some very surprising news," said Mr. Perry. "It's really—I hardly know what to say.

It has taken me so completely by surprise. It's disturbing. And yet, of course—" His voice died away. He stood looking helpless and bewildered.

Miss Gort's light lashes flickered. "Oh dear," she said, "have you been offered another living?"

"No. Oh no!"

She bit her lip. Gertrude Platt observed her with malicious interest. It was generally assumed in the village that Miss Gort was trying to catch the vicar. The pursuit had lasted a considerable number of years, and Emily's backers had begun to lose hope.

"It isn't anything to do with me," said the vicar. "My sanction has not been asked. I am faced with the *fait accompli*. Obviously I could hardly have approved. Less than a year. To be candid I regard such haste as unseemly."

Gertrude Platt's deep voice intervened. "We don't know what you're talking about, Vicar." Irene, standing between the two older women, was trying, not very successfully, to suppress a giggle.

"I was about to explain," said the vicar. "I have had a letter from Alan Copeland after never hearing from him all these months. Not that I expected him to write, and I'm sure he needed a change. I'm not blaming him for that."

"Is he—coming back?" asked Irene, trying, and failing, to sound indifferent.

"Yes. He's returning to Strays. Apparently he is planning to make alterations in the house and the garden. He says he is engaging Tom Welland, who used to help him with his poultry, and Tom's wife as servants. I suppose that the late Mrs. Copeland lived well within her income. I seem to remember that she only had a daily woman."

"But—" Gertrude Platt's heavy brows were drawn together. "Why should you be upset by his return, Mr. Perry? Surely it was expected?"

"Oh, of course. It isn't that. The point is that he's married again. I don't blame him for that either. He's comparatively young. But he should have waited the full year. She should have known better. It's really an extraordinary coincidence. He has married my wife's niece, Lydia Hale. It seems that they met in London a few weeks ago. He scarcely saw her when she was staying at the vicarage last Easter. Oh, we spent an evening at Strays, I remember, but poor Mrs. Copeland always took the lead. Rather a dull sort of man I should have said. Quite a good fellow, but so very silent. I can't get over it."

There was an odd little pause. Emily Gort was the first to speak.

"I must say"—her voice was higher pitched than usual and not quite steady—"he has shown a lack of respect to poor Mabel's memory. I was her best friend, and I feel that. I'm sorry to have to say it, Mr. Perry, as the—second Mrs. Copeland is your niece."

"My wife's niece," the vicar corrected her. "I feel that as much as you do."

"But isn't that rather hypocritical?" enquired the schoolmistress, with her twisted smile. "After all, we all know they led a cat and dog life."

Irene Simmons turned away abruptly and went over to her bicycle which she had left leaning against the churchyard wall. Miss Platt glanced after her as she rode down the lane.

"Well, Mr. Perry, we don't often hear anything exciting in this place. You've given us quite a thrill, hasn't he, Miss Gort? Married within a few weeks of meeting again. It sounds romantic."

Mrs. Simmons, fingering the greasy cards of her old pack, cocked a knowing eye at the dingy sitting-room ceiling. She had heard the banging of the bedroom door followed by the creaking of much tried springs as Irene threw herself on her bed. Another row with Ern, whose temper had got very short of late? But Ern had been busy all day in the garage decarbonising a car. She waited a while and then struggled to her feet and lumbered into the passage.

"Irene!"

A muffled voice replied. "Coming!"

Mrs. Simmons waddled deliberately back to her sofa and waited until her daughter came down and began to get the tea, slamming cupboard doors and clattering the crockery.

"Aren't you going to light the lamp? It's nearly dark. You'll break something."

"Oh, all right."

Mrs. Simmons watched the girl's face as she bent over the table to turn up the wick. Powder and rouge hastily and recklessly applied, did not hide the ravages of recent tears.

"What's the matter?"

"Nothing."

Her mother was silent for a moment, shuffling her cards. Then she said quite quietly, "Don't be a fool. I'm on your side, whatever you've done. I might be able to help you."

Irene filled her mother's cup and cut her a thick slice of the heavy plum cake before she answered.

"I haven't done anything." She swallowed hard before she went on. "Down at the church just now the vicar told us Alan Copeland's coming back. He's married again. He's married Mr. Perry's niece, the one who was here a year ago."

"Fancy that!" said Mrs. Simmons with relish. "The dirty dog. One in the eye for Gertrude Platt."

Irene stared at her blankly. "Miss Platt? You don't think she—"

"She knew him before Mabel Leach married him."

"But she's quite old. That old trout," said Irene contemptuously.

"Did Mr. Perry seemed pleased about it?" enquired Mrs. Simmons.

"No. He said it was too soon, and so did Miss Gort. She said it showed a want of respect to her dear Mabel's memory."

"Ah, she misses her pickings. Up at Strays most days, wasn't she, and never without a basket of apples or the remains of a rabbit pie, or what not. I've heard all about that from the women who worked there. So he's married that little Miss Hale. You never can tell with men what they're going to fancy. I remember her coming to tea with us."

Irene sniffed resentfully. "A white-faced thing, nothing to look at, not a bit smart."

Mrs. Simmons finished her cake and pushed aside her empty cup to take up her cards. "I told her fortune. It was in the cards, Rene—and something else too. I've often wondered about it since. Don't you fret, dearie. You're well out of it. With your looks you can do better than that. Come August you shall go to stay with your auntie in Plymouth and help her in the bar. It's time you saw a bit of life. This was her card."

She rubbed a broad splay thumb over the smug face of the queen of hearts. Irene reached for the card and tore it in half.

"I'd like to do that to her."

"I lay you would, I lay you would," said her mother, and was shaken with silent laughter.

III

Gertrude Platt left the vicar and Miss Gort by the vicarage gate and walked briskly back to the school-house. Her sitting-room fire was laid ready and she put a match to it before she put her kettle on the oil stove. It was burning well when she sat down half an hour later to enjoy her tea. There were toasted muffins with plenty of butter, and there was a parcel of books of the kind booksellers describe as curious, which she had brought down with her the last time she had spent a day in London. She dipped into one of them and read with gusto until the light began to fail. Then she lit a cigarette and lay back in her chair, thinking over what she had heard that day. Once she smiled to herself, but it was not a very pleasant smile. The firelight flickered over the green walls, the green curtains, the rows of books and the dead horse lying in a pool of blood on the sunlit arena.

IV

The vicar was upset and Emily Gort had to spend some time proffering the comfort and reassurance that he needed.

"He's not your churchwarden now. He resigned, and you've got old Twitten in his place. You needn't see more of them than you want to."

"I can't have Lydia always running in and out of the vicar-age," he said. "Mrs. Binns was very troublesome when she was here last year, and burnt the bacon at breakfast for a week after she'd gone. I can't get on with my work if I'm worried."

"I'll give her a hint if you like, but it may not be necessary. She knows how important it is that you should have time to get on with your book," said Miss Gort soothingly. "I must go home now. My cat will be wondering what has become of me. I'll be along in the morning in time to ring the bell for the eight o'clock."

"Oh dear, of course. Easter morning. This news has driven everything else out of my head," he said in his flustered voice. "Very inconsiderate at a time like this when I have so much to do. I must say I'm surprised at Copeland. He should have waited. Such haste is hardly decent."

"I must confess I am surprised," said Miss Gort regretfully. "But we must not judge, must we. We don't know the circum-stances. I always try to be charitable."

"I know you do, Emily," said the vicar with unusual warmth. "I rely on you, and you never fail me. But I mustn't keep you any longer standing in the cold."

"All very well," thought Emily Gort as she trudged the long mile and a half back to her gaunt little brick villa on the hill side. "I do your dirty work, and you're too afraid of your housekeeper to ask me into the vicarage for a cup of tea."

The big ginger cat was waiting on the doorstep and came mewing down the path to meet her, arching his back to meet the flattering palm of her hand. "Well, Booboo, have you missed your missis, and how many birds have you caught?"

It was very cold in the bare little sitting-room, but Emily did not light the fire. In her opinion fires were not necessary at the end of March. She put a kettle on the oil stove in her scullery. There was nothing much on the larder shelves. A piece of boiled fish for the cat's supper, a bit of mouldy cheese for her own. A year ago there would have been a cake of Mabel's making, jam tarts, a thick slice of veal and ham pie, all sorts of savoury titbits from the well stocked larder at Strays. The very dress she was wearing had been one of Mrs. Copeland's which had grown too tight for her, and had been passed on to Emily to be altered and taken in for her. Mabel, in spite of her knack of saying sharp things that hurt and her bullying ways, had been generous. Emily Gort thought of the mound in the churchyard on which she had laid her home-made wreath of primroses and ivy that morning, and her pale blue eyes filled with slow tears.

CHAPTER VII
COVENTRY

I

THE morning after the Easter Bank Holiday three vans drove up to Strays and the lane was blocked for several hours while men in sacking aprons carried out Mabel Copeland's heavy mahogany sideboards and marble top wash-stands and shuffled down the path with rolls of carpet and dark tapestry curtains with trailing crimson tassels and cords. The furniture was to be sold by auction in Wainbridge. Emily Gort saw a notice of the sale in the local paper and walked three miles in the rain to catch a bus to attend it. She had not much money to spend, but the bidding was far from brisk, and she secured Lot 51, which included a set of draughts, a tea caddy and a firescreen for two shillings.

Tom Welland and his wife had spent the day after the vans had left scrubbing the floors. Subsequently one van arrived from London with furniture for four rooms. The Wellands moved in and waited expectantly for their employers.

"Can't make head nor tail of it," Tom Welland told the landlord of the King's Head. "Mr. Copeland wrote we to put the furniture in the upstairs rooms and leave the dining-room and the sitting-room be. What's the sense of having me and the missus to wait on 'em if they be going to live all hugger mugger?"

On Saturday afternoon, Irene Simmons, riding pillion on a boy friend's motorcycle, passed a small dark blue saloon car just beyond the cross-roads. Alan was driving and his wife sat by him, and there was luggage at the back. She went to church the next morning, out of curiosity, but was disappointed. There was nobody in the Strays pew.

On Monday Alan and Lydia called on the vicar. His housekeeper admitted them reluctantly and left them to wait in the dusty dining-room. They were both nervous. Alan had only come to please Lydia. He had never been really interested in parochial affairs. It had been Mabel's idea that he should become the Vicar's churchwarden. He meant to keep out of the village in future. Strays, after all, was on the extreme border of the parish. Still, the fact remained that old Perry was Lydia's uncle by marriage and that they had to be civil. The vicar came to them presently and shook hands limply.

"This is a surprise," he said. "I can hardly take it in even now."

They conversed jerkily and with increasing difficulty on general subjects and then Lydia got up to go.

"I hear you've sold the furniture?" said the vicar as he accompanied them to the door.

Alan answered. "Yes. It was all pretty ghastly. We're going to strip the paper from the walls. I'm certain we shall find some fine old oak panelling. We shall furnish by degrees with period stuff and replace those fearful sash windows with leaded panes. We mean to do it all ourselves, room by room. We're re-making the garden too. When we've finished you'll see Strays looking as it looked in its prime."

"I see," said the vicar frigidly, and Alan, realising that Mr. Perry was incapable of understanding what the old house, so lovely and so neglected, had meant to him during his long years of serfdom, reddened and relapsed into silence. The vicar's parting handshake was as flabby as ever, and he did not ask them to come again.

They were both rather silent during the drive home. Lydia was wishing, not for the first time, that they could have made a fresh start somewhere, but she did not say so to Alan. It had been a relief that the vicar had been too preoccupied and indifferent to ask them any questions about their marriage. They had agreed to say that it had been three weeks previously at a London registrar's office.

"I do hate telling lies," sighed Lydia at last. "We didn't have to. That was one comfort."

"Wait till the women get at you," said Alan grimly as he turned the car into the yard. "You'll have to be polite, Lydia, but for God's sake don't be too cordial. I shan't be able to stick Emily Gort running in and out as she used to. Gertrude never came because Mabel was rude to her, and the Simmons child only hung about the chicken run and the back door, but they'll be all over you if you aren't careful."

But when Lydia met the schoolmistress in the lane a few days later and was about to stop and speak, Gertrude Platt passed on with a cool little nod, and the morning she stopped at the garage for petrol Irene, who had been in the yard talking to Ern, met her rather uncertain smile with a blank stare and then turned her back and walked into the house.

Ern, on the other hand, who was usually grumpy and mono-syllabic, spoke to her with unaccustomed gentleness, helping her to reverse the car. She had not long learned to drive, and easily forgot what she had to do. Her face was burning, and it was not easy to start, knowing as she did that Irene and her awful old mother were jeering at her efforts as they watched her from behind the dirty lace curtains.

She said nothing of either encounter to Alan. After all, she thought, it would be easy so to arrange her life that she never saw anything of her neighbours. There was so much to be done at Strays, and they had the car if they needed a change. They were going to make their own electricity, and a firm from Wain-bridge was doing the wiring. Another firm was carrying out Alan's long-cherished plan of turning one of the barns into a studio. Bessie Welland had been in good service before her marriage and was quite a satisfactory cook, and with her to help him Tom was learning to be an indoor servant. Alan was spending several hours a day scraping the numerous layers of wallpaper from the dining-room walls. Lydia often helped him. He had explained to her that it must be done carefully to avoid damaging whatever they might find underneath. To his intense satisfaction the foundation proved to be oak panelling with a linenfold pattern, though it had been obscured before the first paper by a coat of green paint.

They were both at work on this with sand paper one afternoon when Bessie came to announce a caller.

"Please, ma'am, Miss Gort."

"Oh hell!" grumbled Alan. "I hoped we'd finish this corner before dark. Get rid of her as soon as you can."

"Be quiet," whispered Lydia, "she'll hear you. The door's open." She shook back her loosened hair, wiped her hands on a rag, and crossed the passage to the living-room where Miss Gort, in the slate grey costume she wore on Sundays, stood clutching her handbag and her umbrella. The pale pink tip of her long nose was twitching. Like a rabbit trying to get at a cabbage leaf, thought Lydia, suppressing an hysterical desire to laugh. Had she overheard? Lydia thought not, but, in case she had, she was more friendly than she might have been.

"How kind of you to come and see us. I hoped you would. Do sit down."

Miss Gort looked about her. "You won't mind me saying it looks bare? It's the new fashion, I suppose, but in poor Mabel's time this was such a cosy room."

"We shall have some more furniture, and carpets and curtains later on. We want to get the walls stripped first."

"Oh!"

"Alan says Strays has been like a beautiful woman in the wrong clothes. It will be lovely when he has carried out all his ideas. We're doing all we can ourselves. That's why I'm such a mess in this old overall. I hope you'll excuse that. I've told Bessie to bring the tea."

"It's nice for your husband to have all poor Mabel's money to spend on his notions," said Emily, "but I don't know that she'd have approved. She was very proud of that mahogany suite. Most of her furniture was good old stuff came to her from her mother. Ducks and Drakes. That's what it looks like. But it's no business of mine."

"He is staying on here to please her, because she asked him to," said Lydia quickly. She felt uncomfortable and unhappy, as she always did when she was reminded that they were living on Mabel's money. She might have enjoyed it when she was living, but she had preferred to hoard it. What they were doing now could not hurt her.

Bessie came in again, wheeling the tea wagon. Miss Gort addressed her affably. "Bessie was in my Bible class, you know, Mrs. Copeland. I daresay she thought she was leaving service for good when she married, and yet here you are back again in cap and apron, Bessie."

Bessie reddened and muttered below her breath as she left the room. Miss Gort eyed the tea service with mild surprise. "You don't mean to say Mr. Copeland got rid of the old Worcester? But I suppose you put it away. Too good to use. I'm glad you have. Poor Mabel took such care of it." She helped herself to bread and butter.

"We've all been wondering how you met again. It really was extraordinary, wasn't it, in a city like London. I forget how many million inhabitants. How did it happen exactly?"

This was the inquisition Lydia had been dreading. She braced herself to meet it.

"It was on the steps of the National Gallery. We went in together. I'm interested in pictures, but I don't know much about them. He was kind in explaining things. We had tea together. We were both lonely."

"And when was this?"

"Oh—about the beginning of February."

"Dear me. Scarcely eight weeks ago. Were you married in church? You won't mind my asking'"

"Not a bit. We were married at a registrar's office. We didn't want any fuss."

"I quite understand that," said Miss Gort sweetly. "Very natural, under the circumstances. After all one can't get over the fact that poor Mabel passed away last June. It is usual to wait a year, I believe, unless there is some special reason—but of course in your case there couldn't be. Fuss. It's a funny way of describing the church's blessing. Quite amusing really."

Lydia looked at her silently.

"You must not be offended at anything I say," added Miss Gort with her tight-lipped smile. "It is best you should know. It is only what other people think. I'm sorry for Alan, and for you, too, because I'm afraid you've made a bad start here. We're old-fashioned in the country. I can't help fancying that Alan realises that already. I saw him the other day driving past my house in his new car, and I must say he didn't look as if he was as happy as a newly-married man is supposed to be. Not at all the blissful bridegroom."

"Really. He has had toothache. Probably he was driving in to Wainbridge to the dentist. Will you have a second cup?"

"Thank you. And another lump of sugar this time, please. I hope my being here isn't preventing your husband from coming in to tea?"

"No, of course not. He gets so absorbed in his work. He probably doesn't know it's ready. I'll fetch him."

Lydia jumped up and left the room quickly, shutting the door after her before she crossed the passage to the dismantled room where Alan was still busy sandpapering the panelling.

"Darling, you've got to come and be nice to her. She doesn't like me, and I can't cope with it."

He looked at her and his face changed. "What has she been saying to you?"

"Never mind that. It doesn't matter. Just come and smooth her down."

"Oh—all right."

He followed her back to the room where Miss Gort sat sipping her tea and darting quick glances about her. She rose as he came in. "Oh, Mr. Copeland—I didn't want you to be disturbed on my account—and I really must be going. You're looking thin, I must say. Not so much rested as I should have expected—" She seemed at a loss for words.

He held her hand in the grey fabric glove in his firm clasp and his dark eyes were smiling as they looked down into hers.

"I'm all right. How are you? Still doing most of Perry's work for him? He's lucky to have you to rely on. Mabel always said so. She was fond of you, Miss Gort."

Her light lashes flickered as she withdrew her hand. "She had to have someone to turn to," she said. "Well, I must be going. Good-bye, Mrs. Copeland."

Alan went with her to the gate. When he came back he found Lydia sitting on the rug before the fire. He drew up a chair and felt in his pockets for his pipe.

"What did she say to you, Lydia?"

"Oh—she was just rather catty. We must expect that, I suppose. I'm afraid she overheard what you said about getting rid of her."

"Was that it? I'm sorry. She's a good sort really, and she was really kind and helpful last summer, you know, when it happened. But she was Mabel's friend, not mine. It's no use pretending I'm craving for her society. She does work hard in the parish, but I don't know that she's exactly popular with the villagers. She's a bit of a busybody."

"She asked where we met. I told her the National Gallery."

"That's as good a place as any."

"She's a prying sort of woman. I can see that," said Lydia anxiously.

"Don't worry about her. You needn't see much of her. I'll take you over to call on the Bragges' to-morrow. You'll like them. We'll ask them over here. They never could come in Mabel's time. She took a dislike to them. Let's forget it."

She sighed, leaning back to rest her head against his knees. It was warm and pleasant in the firelit room, with the curtains drawn to shut out the pallid moon peering like a prisoner through bars of cloud, and the cold, alien life of the valley, the furtive glances, the whispering voices.

She told herself that she ought to be a happy woman. Alan, she knew, was content. He had her, and he had Strays. When all the changes he had planned had been made he would still have work to do. When the studio was ready for him he was going to paint. He had a portfolio full of the sketches he had made in North Wales. But one of the barbs planted by Miss Gort still rankled.

"Alan, when you drove in to Wainbridge last Monday to have that tooth out did you go by the upper road?"

"No. That's the longest way."

"Then it was another day you passed Miss Gort's house?"

"Must have been. I went that way yesterday as a matter of fact. Why?"

"She saw you."

He laughed. "I don't suppose she misses much." He was stroking her sleek brown curls.

"Go on," she murmured, "I like it. Oh, Alan, I love you so."

"My sweet."

Yes. She still felt safe, quite safe, in his arms.

II

There were workmen at Strays on and off all through the summer, replacing the sash windows with lattices more in keeping with the stone mullions, converting a part of the disused cattle sheds into a power house and wiring all the rooms for electric light, laying crazy pavement and putting down turf for a lawn where there had been a cabbage patch. Alan and Lydia went twice to London to choose rugs and stuff for curtains and loose covers that would tone with the silvery grey of the old oak panelling.

"It has cost more than I expected, but it's been worth it," said Alan contentedly. They had worked hard themselves. Lydia had bought a sewing machine and had made all the curtains. She seldom went beyond the gate except in the car. She had not seen Mr. Perry again since the first call they had paid on him together. They never went down to the village or to the church. Bragge, the quarry manager, and his sister came to dine with them on Saturday evenings, and they played bridge afterwards. They were a gaunt, grey couple, rather silent and reserved, with the watchful, defensive manners of people who have been snubbed often enough to have developed a technique. Lydia was drawn to them because of their evident affection for Alan.

They neither had nor needed any other friends.

They were fond of going out in their car, taking their midday meal with them. Alan studied his A.A. map, but Lydia seldom knew where they were going. One warm, still day in early September they left the car in a lane and climbed a hill, following a winding sheep track to the top. There was a magnificent view, and Lydia gazed at it for a while in silence. The descent on this side was more gradual, the smooth turf, close cropped by generations of conies, broken with outcrops of grey rock and patches of furze and briars, with a few of the gnarled old yews that are supposed to mark the ancient pilgrim tracks from shrine to shrine in the days when much of the low-lying land was under water half the year, and the remains of a stone circle.

Lydia caught her breath. "Alan! This is Gey Rounds."

He laughed indulgently. "I was beginning to wonder when you'd spot that. We've come to it from the other side."

"You knew?"

"Of course."

There was no answering smile on her face. She half turned.

"Let's go back to the car."

"Lydia!" His voice sounded hurt. "I don't understand you. Ever since we came back to Strays I've been wanting to come here. Don't you feel the same about it? We can't go back yet. You ought to rest after that climb. Let's sit down here on the grass." She yielded and sat down, clasping her knees with slender, sunburned hands, her eyes fixed on the misty blue horizon.

Alan watched her anxiously.

"Have you got a complex or something about this place, darling?"

"Perhaps I have. Hadn't we better leave it at that? I don't want to upset you. I daresay I'm silly."

"No. We've got to have it out. Is it that you blame yourself for what happened here? Lydia, you mustn't. The fault, if it was a fault, the blame, if there must be blame, is all mine. Lydia, I'm a different man now. Then I was a poor devil in a hell of my own making. You were divine in your sweetness, your generosity. I was pretty near the end of my tether, nearer than I've ever told you. I'd got as far as planning the way out, an accident with a shot gun—you saved me from that."

She turned her head slowly towards him. "Really, Alan?"

"Yes, really. Does that help?"

She nodded. "I've a mixed up feeling about it. Glad and sorry. At the time I gloried in being able to make you happy, but when the baby was coming I realised the terrific responsibility. Sometimes I wonder if he would have lived if I hadn't worried so much the first few weeks. I was wasting the strength that should have been going into him in being frightened and—and ashamed."

Alan groaned. "Lydia, don't. You make me feel such a criminal."

"It was you who insisted on dragging this out of me. I can't help what I feel. Darling; my heart has never been sorry for that day, but in my mind I know it was wrong."

"Well, you've paid anyhow. You're quits with that jealous God of yours," he said bitterly. "But it's you who are wrong, Lydia. You were sinned against, not sinning. Try to get that into your head. I never dreamed you had these morbid fancies."

"I know," she said. "And there may be thoughts in your mind that I have never guessed at. I wake in the night sometimes and think of that. However much we love we are still two people. We can never be sure that we understand—"

"You are much too good for me," he said humbly. She sighed. "I'm not good. I don't deserve my happiness."

"Are you happy?"

"Of course."

They sat for a while silent, while larks sang overhead. They could hear in the distance the voices of children blackberrying on the lower slopes of the hill and the barking of a dog in a farm down the valley. It seemed to them both then that the shadow of the old unhappy far off things lifted and passed away and that the future lay before them serene as that autumn landscape.

Presently he helped her to her feet and they went down the hill again to their car.

CHAPTER VIII
THE BRIGHT DAY IS DONE

I

"A GENTLEMAN to see you, ma'am."

Lydia had been half asleep on the sofa. The novel she had been reading had dropped from her hand. She roused herself.

"Who is it? Did he give his name?"

"No, ma'am. He asked for Mr. Copeland first and I told him he was out."

"He's probably trying to sell something."

"He said he hoped to see some of Mr. Copeland's pictures."

"Oh!" Lydia was quite awake now. A possible patron. Alan had said very little about it, but she knew he was eager to prove that his work had some commercial value. His faith in his talent was apt to waver. It had not yet recovered from the prolonged cold douche of Mabel's determination that he should not waste her money on paints and canvas. "Show him in, Bessie."

She felt in the pocket of her jumper for her powder compact, and patted the bunch of curls on the nape of her neck before she walked round the room rearranging the cushions. Bessie showed the stranger in. He was a tall, heavily-built man with a hard, red clean-shaven face and sandy hair. Lydia decided not to offer her hand, but she smiled at him.

"I'm so sorry my husband isn't here. He's out painting. It's the sort of day he likes. So much depends on the light. Won't you sit down."

He remained standing. "Does he sell his pictures, Mrs. Copeland?"

"Oh, yes."

"I hoped I might see some of them."

"You can, of course. Come into the studio."

He followed her through the house and across the yard, pausing only to admire the lead Cupid on the pedestal.

"Very pretty. This was just a farm originally, wasn't it?"

"Yes. But my husband always saw its possibilities."

The northern slope of the barn roof had been filled with glass and a clear light poured into the converted studio. A half length portrait of Lydia occupied the easel and faced them as they entered. It was unfinished, the figure roughed in with charcoal but the painting of the head was nearly completed. The small, pale face with its characteristic upward tilt was luminous against a dark background. Portraiture was not Alan Copeland's forte, but this was the woman he loved. He was never likely to do anything better. The stranger eyed it gravely.

"Very nice," he said, "but what I wanted was just some little thing. A birthday present for the wife, as a matter of fact."

Lydia brought forward a portfolio of sketches, and stood by while he looked them over, holding each one up to the light. Not quite a gentleman, she thought. A gentleman says my wife. And he did not really know much about painting.

"How much would one of these cost?"

Fortunately she knew that. Alan had sold several sketches to visitors at Llanberis.

"Three pounds."

"I see. This one with the water is pretty. Would that figure sitting under the tree be you?"

She laughed. "Yes. But it's too small to be recognisable."

"I'll take your word for it. Is it one of those lakes in Cumberland?"

"No. It's Lake Padarn. That's Snowdon in the background."

"I'll take this one." He laid it on the table while he took three pound notes from his case. Lydia found some paper and wrapped it up for him. She had changed her mind about asking him to stay for a cup of tea. There was something heavy and unattractive about him.

"Are you just passing through?" she asked as she walked with him to the gate.

"In a manner of speaking. On business. Tomorrow I may be the other side of England." He laughed abruptly as if he had made a joke, and checked himself as if he felt that his amusement was out of place. "Well, I'm obliged to you, Mrs. Copeland. It's a pretty picture, and I'm sure the wife will be pleased with it when she sees it. Good afternoon."

He raised his black bowler hat and got into the Ford saloon car he had left waiting in the lane.

Lydia went back to the studio to replace the sketches that had been left strewn over the table in the portfolio. She was glad he had chosen that one; there were others she would have been sorrier to part with. Dolbadarn Castle black against the sunset, for instance. In July, was it, or August? They were all dated in the left hand corner under Alan's signature.

"Oh!" she said aloud, and stood very still for a moment. She had been off her guard when she admitted that she was with Alan in North Wales. The sketch would show that it was last summer. It just proved how easy it was to make a slip. Not that it really mattered in this case. The buyer of the sketch was a stranger in the neighbourhood who would neither know nor care about their affairs. And yet—how had he found his way to Strays? Who had told him that Alan was a painter.

"I'm getting worked up over nothing at all," she told herself, and she was careful not to refer to her gaffe when Alan came in to tea and she gave him the three pound notes.

He was satisfied with his afternoon's work, and in one of his sanguine moods, and he was boyishly elated over what he described as the first of the queue.

"What sort of chap was he? It's possible he heard of me in Wainbridge. The people at that art shop in the High Street seem quite eager to show some of my stuff in their art gallery to sell on commission. Was he a knowing sort of bird? There was some good brush work in that Padarn thing."

"He was a stodgy sort of person, and his only adjectives were nice and pretty."

"Gosh!" Alan laughed, but she could see he was disappointed. Her heart ached for him. It was natural that he should long for encouragement.

"You'll be giving a one man show in another year or two, and then all the art critics will be falling over themselves to say things, and I shall start a book of press cuttings and sleep with it under my pillow."

"I'll tell you what we'll do with this three pounds," he said, "we'll start a post office savings account book for Alan Copeland, junior. What about it?"

Alan Copeland junior had recently become a possibility.

"All right," she said, "I'd like him to be thrifty. Turn on the wireless or we shall miss the news."

II

The weather broke up early with a gale that raged in the Channel for twenty-four hours, bringing sea-spume twenty miles inland and stripping the trees of their leaves. All night the casements rattled and the wind howled in the chimneys of Strays. Lydia, unable to sleep but unwilling to disturb Alan, slipped out of bed at last and went over to the window. The shadows of the tormented trees danced wildly in the moonlight across the lawn where the sundial that only marked the sunny hours showed a blank face. Lydia, looking beyond into the valley, was surprised to see a dim light burning. She had just seen by the luminous dial of Alan's watch lying on the night table that it was a few minutes past two. "Somebody ill, I suppose," she thought. The light seemed to be near the church. Could it be shining from one of the vicarage windows? Could there be trouble there? The vicar was an old man. Ought she to call again at the vicarage, risking a repulse? No, she was not wanted there. She had taken the measure of her uncle's icy self-sufficiency during the few days she had stayed under his roof. She went back to bed and forced herself to listen to Alan's quiet breathing rather than to homeless crying of the wind until she, too, fell asleep.

The bad weather persisted, and Alan went out less with his sketching easel and spent more time in his studio. Lydia often sat for him in the morning, but after lunch she usually lay down on the big divan in the sitting-room. She was determined that this time her baby should have every chance. She was going to rest, and not worry. There was nothing to worry about. She and Alan were not only lovers, theirs was a comradeship that would outlive passion. He was invariably kind and considerate. He was easy to live with, partly perhaps because he was not a great talker. After lunch he would see her comfortably settled among her cushions with her book before he lit a cigarette and went back to the studio to work until the light began to fail.

On the Monday afternoon a week after the great gale Lydia slept longer than usual and woke to see the windows streaming with rain. Bessie always brought up her tea at four o'clock, and it was now half past four. Lydia rang the bell and waited.

Nobody came. She rang again and went into the hall.

"Bessie!"

The house seemed unusually silent. The Wellands were not a noisy couple, but when Tom was in there was generally a murmur of voices from the kitchen, and at this hour there should have been an agreeable aroma of hot cakes fresh from the oven. Bessie prided herself on her scones and her Sally Lunns. Lydia, after a moment's hesitation, pushed open the baize door that shut off the servants' quarters from the front of the house and walked into the kitchen.

It was empty.

Everything was in order. The fire was burning under a covering of slack and the table had been scrubbed. Tea had been laid ready on the wheeled waggon. But there was no sign of the Wellands, and Lydia, glancing about her in growing bewilderment, noticed that Bessie's alarm clock and the pair of blue vases Tom had won at a coconut shy had gone. As she moved round the table she saw a letter lying on the dresser. It was unstamped and was addressed to herself in a straggling, uneducated hand. She opened it and read it:

"DEAR MADAM,

"We are sorry to have to leave you sudden like this as you and Mr. Copeland have always been good to us and we are quite satisfied with the place. But it is all over the village that she has been dug up, and Tom and me don't want to get mixed up with the police so we have got a lift from the baker. Sorry to put you out, but it can't be helped.

"Yours respectfully,
"BESSIE WELLAND."

Lydia read the letter hurriedly, and gained a general impression that the Wellands had got into some kind of trouble. As servants they had been irreproachable, but of course they must have some life of their own. Still it could hardly be anything serious.

"If only they had told us," she thought, "Alan might have been able to help." She had grown fond of Bessie, and she had imagined that Bessie liked her, and Tom had seemed a good fellow in his slow, silent fashion. The kettle was beginning to boil over. She moved it to the side of the stove.

It really was too bad of them to leave their employers like this. It would not be easy to replace them. Good servants did not care to live in the depths of the country. Running away. It was extraordinary. Did the letter mean that the Wellands had been involved with the police before; that they were crooks? Absurd. Bessie was born and brought up in Teene and Tom came from a village five miles distant. Everyone would have known. Besides, their honesty was too obvious.

She was beginning to suffer now from the shock of surprise. Her knees were shaking. She sat down to re-read the letter.

This time one sentence stood out from the rest.

She has been dug up.

She threw the letter down violently as if it had stung her and sat very still. She felt as if someone had thrust before her something obscene. No use feeling sick. She must try to pull herself together and understand. The silence of the house was oppressive. She missed the friendly ticking of Bessie's clock. She was startled by a loud, authoritative knocking at the front door. Her spirit seemed to have withdrawn to a little distance, to have become an onlooker, but her body rose obediently and went to answer the summons.

There were three men outside and they pushed by her into the passage without speaking. They were all big and broad-shouldered, and seemed to fill all the available space so that, instinctively she drew back against the wall.

"Who are you? What do you want?" she said breathlessly.

"Sorry, Mrs. Copeland. We don't want to upset you. Where is your husband?"

She looked at the speaker and recognised the man to whom she had sold the sketch of Lake Padarn two weeks earlier.

"He—he's in the studio."

"That's all right. I know the way. You go into the sitting-room, Mrs. Copeland."

"What right have you to order me about?"

He turned to one of his companions. "On second thoughts you'd better stay with her, Bell. We shan't be long."

"Who are you?" she asked again faintly.

"My name is Ramsden, madam. Detective-Sergeant Ramsden. Please don't try to detain me now. You will hear all about it soon enough."

He passed on down the passage with the other man.

The sitting-room door was open. Lydia walked over to the divan and sat down. The man called Bell stood near her awkwardly. He was younger than Ramsden and she could feel that for some reason he was sorry for her. There was a grand-father clock in this room. She had been with Alan when he bought it in an antique shop in Wainbridge. It had ticked away ten minutes when Ramsden and his companion came back with Alan. She tried to stand up and sank back again.

"Alan—"

He stood before her, meeting her eyes. He was white to the lips but his voice when he spoke was strong and confident.

"Don't be frightened, Lydia. I have to go with these men, but I shall soon be back. There's been some ghastly mistake. Tell Tom and his wife I rely on them to take good care of you, and don't worry."

"But, Alan, I must know. What is it? What has happened?"

"I've been taken into custody. They've got a warrant for my arrest."

"How—how ridiculous. What for?"

For the first time he seemed to have some difficulty in answering. He moistened his lips. "Mabel. She's been—exhumed. They seem to think I murdered her. I don't have to tell you I'm innocent, Lydia."

"Oh! Alan, of course not."

Detective-Sergeant Ramsden intervened. "Perhaps you would pack a suitcase for Mr. Copeland, madam. Just a change of linen and so forth. Not a razor. Bell, you go up with her and see that there's nothing contrary to the regulations. And as quick as you can, please, Mrs. Copeland."

Lydia's body, still mechanically compliant, went upstairs and dragged a suitcase out of the cupboard on the landing. The North Wales and Leamington labels were still on it. She moved about, opening and shutting drawers, catching occasional glimpses of her white, set face in the glass. Bell carried the case down the stairs for her. The others were in the passage, and the third man was helping the prisoner on with his raincoat.

"Now, sir, if you don't mind." There was something that clinked in his hand.

"Just a minute," said Alan huskily.

He took his wife in his arms. She clung to him desperately. "Don't go. Don't go."

"Darling, I must. Don't make it more difficult. Listen. Go to Reid, at Wainbridge, to-morrow. He'll look after things for you."

Ramsden, anxious not to prolong a painful scene, touched him on the arm. He stepped back and a ring of steel struck cold on his wrist. The front door was opened and the four men stepped out into the driving rain and gathering darkness. The headlights of their car were shining in through the gate. Bell closed the door after them.

Lydia was left alone. She woke from a kind of coma, to find herself kneeling on the hearthrug in the sitting-room and striking a match to light the fire. A fire was company, and besides, she was chilled to the marrow, as cold as if she had been lying in churchyard clay. The grandfather clock ticked on steadily. It was difficult to believe that less than an hour had passed since she woke up wondering why Bessie had not brought the tea.

Tick, Tick, Tick, Tick. The clock was saying something.

Lydia turned her head to listen.

She has been dug up.

The round brass face of the clock, placidly expressionless, unconscious of its cruelty, looked down on the shrinking figure huddled on the bear skin in the flickering firelight and covering her ears with her hands.

Tick, Tick, Tick, Tick.

CHAPTER IX
THE DAMAGING TRUTH

I

REID, Reid & Pearmain were an old-established firm of solicitors in Wainbridge. Their offices were on the ground floor of the Reids' old house of mellowed brick, facing the Town Hall in the Market Square, and John Reid, once a very junior partner and now the only surviving representative of the firm, had only to lift his eyes from his desk to see the sardonic countenance and curled periwig of His Majesty King Charles the Second in his niche over the entrance to the Court room where the magistrates were to meet that morning.

John Reid had been a delicate precocious child. At school he had never been able to play games, and he had spent two years in his late teens lying on a spinal couch. He had recovered in time to pass his examinations and enter the firm with his father and his uncle—his mother had been a Miss Pearmain—and old clients who had begun by referring to him as a poor little fellow had learned in time to value his painstaking loyalty to their interests and to say to one another, "If John Reid says he'll do a thing he'll do it. He doesn't laugh so heartily as old Pearmain, but he's steady."

He was getting on for forty now and thinking of taking his managing clerk, Mr. Carver, into partnership. He was unmarried, and his mother kept house for him.

He was standing at the window when Carver came in and he spoke without turning his head. "Look at the carrion crows."

Carver glanced out at the long row of wet umbrellas, like black toadstools, of the waiting queue across the square.

"There's bound to be public interest in a case like this," he said tolerantly, "and there's very little room inside. I doubt if half that lot will squeeze in. I suppose between ourselves there isn't any doubt about who did the woman in?"

In private Carver was sometimes regrettably colloquial. Reid frowned. "That's a very improper suggestion. We are undertaking Mr. Copeland's defence."

"Yes, sir. And that's what I really came about. Mrs. Copeland is here asking to see you."

Reid's thin face flushed. "Did you tell her he was being brought before the bench at eleven?"

"Yes. She said she wouldn't keep you long."

"Oh well—show her in."

He moved forward to meet his unwelcome visitor. Lydia, as they shook hands, realised that he was as nervous as she was. "Can I be present in Court, Mr. Reid?"

"If you wish it. But it will be an ordeal for you."

She ignored that. "Shall I be able to speak to Alan?"

"That can be arranged after the Court rises."

"Is there any chance of his being released to-day?"

"None whatever, I'm afraid, Mrs. Copeland." He cleared his throat. "I know practically nothing about this case as yet. The police rang me up last night on your husband's behalf. I went over at once and had an interview with him. He had not made any statement beyond affirming his complete innocence of the charge against him. I hear that Mr. Vereker is appearing for the Crown, or rather, at this stage, for the police. He will outline their case to-day and call witnesses. We've got to face facts, Mrs. Copeland. The police wouldn't have obtained authority from the Home Office for an exhumation and proceeded to—to make an arrest if they hadn't what they regard as a strong case. Mr. Copeland will be able to meet it, we hope, but meanwhile he will almost certainly be committed for trial at the Assizes. That will give us several weeks to prepare the defence."

"I see," she said dully.

He was silent for a moment, trying to think of something encouraging to say. He found himself wishing she had been older and more obviously able to take care of herself. But of course he reflected her fragile prettiness was exactly what would appeal to Copeland after his unfortunate first marriage.

"I'm wondering," he said, "whether it might not be better for your husband if you kept away. You did not meet him, did you, until several months after the death of the first Mrs. Copeland?"

Lydia had taken off her gloves and was smoothing them over her knee. She answered without raising her eyes. "I spent a week at the vicarage the Easter before last. Mr. Perry is my uncle. We went to supper at Strays one evening and played bridge and I met Alan once or twice when I was out for walks." Reid tried not to betray the fact that this news was unwelcome. The existing doubt in his mind which he had refused to admit to Carver was strengthened.

"Well," he said, "we reserve our defence."

"I suppose this is going to cost a lot of money?" she said.

"I'm afraid so. Mrs. Copeland had lived well within her means. She left a very considerable balance at the bank. I suggested investing it to Mr. Copeland, but he was very keen on some scheme of restoration at Strays, and, as I expect you know, it has been spent. But don't you worry about that. Means will be found in one way or another. And now I fear we must be going. Are you quite sure you wish to be present?"

"Yes."

"Have you any friend with you? Your uncle, perhaps?"

"No."

He picked up his despatch case, cast a final look round the room, and held the door open for her.

He hurried her across the square and took her into the Town Hall by a side door. A breath of warm, exhausted air met them as they entered the court room. Lydia, following Reid as he forced his way through the crowd, was painfully conscious of the curious eyes, the nudging and whispering.

"Mrs. Copeland."

"That's the girl he married."

Reid found a place for her on a bench just behind his own, and left her. She looked round timidly and saw Alan standing in a sort of pen with a policeman on either side. He looked handsome but haggard, with the strained expression that had been habitual with him when she first knew him. He turned his head after a moment and saw her. She smiled and he smiled briefly in reply, and then bent to speak to his lawyer, who had come to stand by the dock. An usher shouted something and everybody stood up. The magistrates were taking their places on the dais. The acoustics of the court room were bad, and Lydia found that she had to listen intently to hear all that was being said. Mr. Vereker, who was outlining the case on behalf of the police, had been speaking for some minutes before she was able to pick up the thread.

"Facts, indisputable facts, and dates which, as I shall submit, are of the utmost significance. On the night of the tenth of June, fifteen months ago, Doctor Anderson, of Collingford Magna, was awakened by the ringing of his night bell. He went downstairs and found the husband of one of his patients, a Mrs. Copeland, of Strays. Mr. Copeland, who appeared to be agitated, explained that his wife was very ill. She had been vomiting and was in great pain. His car was out of order and he had ridden seven miles on his bicycle to fetch the doctor, only stopping on his way to ask a woman friend to go over to Strays. There was no servant living in, and he had been obliged to leave the sick woman quite alone. The doctor got out his car and they drove back to Strays.

The friend, a Miss Gort, had arrived meanwhile and had done what she could for the patient, but she was already unconscious and she passed away a few minutes later."

Mr. Vereker paused as though to mark the end of the first act in the drama he was about to unfold, and drank some water.

"Dr. Anderson had attended Mrs. Copeland for digestive trouble. The symptoms seemed to indicate the breaking of a duodenal ulcer and he had no hesitation in attributing her death to this cause. The funeral took place on the Monday. Mrs. Copeland had been an only child and had no near relatives. She had made a will leaving all she possessed to her husband. Mr. Copeland, who had been running a small and not very profitable poultry and egg business, arranged for the sale of his stock, shut up the house and left the neighbourhood for a while. Nine months later, on the twenty-eighth of March of this year, he wrote to the vicar of Teene to inform him that he was returning to Strays and announcing his recent marriage to a Miss Lydia Hale, a niece of the vicar, who has spent the previous Easter in the village. There was, one gathers, a pretty general feeling that Mr. Copeland might have waited until his year of mourning was over before he remarried, and the couple were coolly received, so much so that they ceased to take any part in the social life of the parish or even to come to church. The first Mrs. Copeland had been twelve years older than her husband. She had the money. He had no means of his own. Though she could be generous to her friends, it was rumoured that with her husband she was inclined to be close-fisted and that they had not been on the best of terms. On his return Mr. Copeland embarked on expensive schemes of demolition and of restoration at Strays, he bought a new car and engaged a staff of servants. There was no actual harm in these proceedings, but they were a piece of imprudence in so far that they emphasised the fact that he had gained considerably by his first wife's death. People, in short, had begun to talk, and the police judged it advisable to make a few enquiries with a view to disposing of certain sinister rumours."

Mr. Vereker made another effective pause. Lydia was holding herself rigidly erect on her bench, keeping her eyes fixed on the wall opposite where a blotch of damp stained the plaster. The reporters at the Press table were scribbling busily. Alan, in the dock, gripped the rail before him. His face wore the wooden expression that had been familiar to Mabel. He stood like a block. Only his eyes lived and suffered.

"The enquiries revealed certain facts—we shall call witnesses to prove them all. During the fortnight Miss Hale spent at the vicarage at the end of March and beginning of April she and her uncle had supper once at Strays and played cards afterwards. A very harmless affair. But she and Copeland were seen together some miles out of the village on the last day of her stay. The landlady of her lodgings in London will testify that after her return she received a weekly letter with the Wainbridge postmark. She lost her job and found another which only lasted a few days. She seemed poorly and in low spirits, and the good woman was getting quite anxious about her when a young man arrived, was rapturously received, and introduced as Miss Hale's fiancé. There was nothing, it appeared, to wait for, and the happy pair were married at the nearest registrar's office the following week. The contracting parties were Alan Copeland and Lydia Hale, and the date was the twenty-fourth of June, a fortnight exactly after that night on which the anxious husband had bicycled seven miles to fetch the doctor to his dying first wife. Lest you should be shocked by such haste I must add that there was good reason for it. Mr. and Mrs. Copeland spent the summer in North Wales, where he resumed the practice of his art of landscape painting. In the autumn they moved to Leamington. In a nursing home in Leamington the second Mrs. Copeland gave birth to a child, who only lived a few hours. The date of this birth, which was not premature, was the twenty-eighth of December last."

Reid groaned inwardly. Why hadn't she told him? He supposed her courage failed her. He fancied he heard her sigh in the pause that followed. The court had been paying Vereker the tribute of a very complete attention.

Vereker resumed. "I have no wish to inflict unnecessary pain on anyone, but I have to point out the significance of these dates. They furnish the motive, the very strong motive, for the crime of which the prisoner stands accused. The police, with these facts in their possession, felt justified in applying to the Home Office for permission to exhume the body of Mabel Copeland. Every effort was made to avoid publicity. The exhumation was carried out at dead of night and at the height of the great gale a fortnight ago, in the presence of Sir Ronald Beaton. Sir Ronald is here this morning. He is anxious to return to Town as soon as possible to keep an important appointment. I will therefore ask your permission to call him now."

Sir Ronald, a youngish man of athletic build, with the poker face of the successful specialist, stepped briskly into the witness-box. Inured to horror, he was cool, efficient, unimpassioned, dealing with sickening details with a calm precision that verged on the inhuman. But a few of his hearers noticed that he was careful to avoid looking at the motionless figure standing in the dock.

He had taken certain organs and samples of the hair and of the skin of the deceased for analysis. His experiments with the available material had proved the presence of a relatively large quantity of arsenic, showing beyond a doubt that a fatal dose of not less than two grains had been taken a few hours before death. There were traces of arsenic in the skin and the hair which indicated that previous small doses had been successfully assimilated.

"Does that mean that there had been previous attempts to poison this poor lady?"

"It looks like that, certainly."

"Apart from the inflammation due to an irritant poison were there any signs of disease?"

"It was hardly the body of a healthy woman, but there was nothing definite."

"You are definitely of opinion that the cause of death was arsenical poisoning?"

"I am."

"Thank you, Sir Ronald. I don't know if my friend—"

Mr. Vereker looked at John Reid.

The young solicitor rose rather stiffly to his feet.

In point of fact he was numb with dismay.

"There are people who take arsenic in small quantities for medicinal purposes?"

"Yes."

"Patients, and especially women like Mrs. Copeland, with a valetudinarian tendency, have been known to dose themselves with quack remedies without the knowledge of their doctors?"

"Yes. That is so."

"Thank you. I have no further questions to ask at the moment."

He sat down with some inward satisfaction. To cast a doubt. It was all he could do at that stage.

The Home Office expert had left the Court and the magistrates were conferring in undertones. Reid could guess what they were saying. It was ten minutes to one.

II

The attendant in the ladies' room looked up from her knitting as Lydia entered.

"Lunch interval? How's it going?" she asked.

"I don't know."

The attendant, glancing at her white face, put down her knitting.

"You sit down here under this open window. It's stuffy in there. Men don't seem to need air to breathe. Haven't you noticed it in railway carriages? A spot of brandy wouldn't do you no harm, but they're all that rushed this morning that I doubt if I could get it for you short of running across to the King's Head myself, and I'm in charge here, see?"

"It's all right," murmured Lydia.

"You're not strong enough to go standing in crowds that's what it is. And from all I hear it's one of those cases that give one the 'orrors. Tell you what, I was just going to make myself a good cup of tea. Kettle's on the ring here behind my table and just on the boil. You shall have one with me, and then, if you take my advice you'll go straight home and read all about it in the papers to-morrow." She bustled about while she talked, bringing another cup and a biscuit tin out of her cupboard.

"Why, there's a young chap does all the reporting of court cases for the *Wainbridge Herald* said to me only this morning, 'This is a fine chance for me,' he said, 'tremendous luck,' he said. 'We're all going to be in the limelight over this, Mrs. Pike.' Oh dear, she's gone right off."

Lydia had indeed slipped from her chair to the floor.

Mrs. Pike, clucking sympathetically, dipped a corner of a towel in water and wiped the ashen face.

"There, there. You'll be better soon."

Lydia sat up after a minute. "Sorry to be such a nuisance."

She drank the tea gratefully and felt really better for it.

Reid, when the court rose, had said something about seeing her later in the corridor. She must go back or she might miss him. As she went out she passed two women coming in. The elder of the two, who was enormously stout, nodded to Mrs. Pike.

"Hallo, Maggie," she said wheezily. "I heard you'd got this job. Steady work, eh, if a bit monotonous. I'll sit down for a bit if that chair'll hold me. It's four years since I've been out, and Irene didn't want me to come, but I was always one for a good murder, and I wasn't going to miss the treat of seeing Mr. Johnnie head-in-air in the dock. This is my girl, Irene. Mrs. Pike and me served in the same bar at one time, Rene."

Irene ignored this introduction. She had been waiting impatiently to stem the flow of her mother's conversation.

"Ma, did you see who that was went out as we came in?"

"I didn't notice. Who was it then?"

"It was her. The one he married."

The chair creaked ominously as Mrs. Simmons sank into it.

"Why didn't you nudge me or something? Not but what I picked her out in the court."

Mrs. Pike joined in. "Do you mean to say that was Mrs. Copeland? Well, I never. She came over faint. Well, fancy that now. A nice spoken quiet little thing, quite the lady."

Mrs. Simmons snorted. "You weren't in court, Maggie, to hear, what we heard. I declare I was quite sorry I'd brought Irene. It's hardly fit for a young girl. But I couldn't trust myself up and down steps without someone to hang on to, even with my stick. My nephew Ern brought us over, and he'll fetch us in the evening. We're going to the Pictures after this. Here's your penny, Rene. How's the world been treating you, Maggie Pike?"

"Not too bad," said Mrs. Pike. "I got this job after my husband died. That girl of yours reminds me of what you were like when I first knew you, but they lay it on thicker nowadays. I can't get over that being Mrs. Copeland. How's the case going, Bella?"

Mrs. Simmons' little black eyes twinkled malevolently in the vast expanse of her face. "Badly for him. He done it all right. He's one of those chaps have got a way with women. Mabel Leach made a fool of herself over him. There was a time when my Irene had a pash for him, but she soon got over it. She can pick and choose. Plenty after her, but I daresay she'll end by marrying her cousin Ern. He's not showy, but he's steady."

Irene had rejoined her elders and was standing before the glass applying a thick coat of scarlet lipstick to her pouting lips. She had not yet recovered from the shock of her mother's renewed activity. That Mrs. Simmons, who in the last four years had never travelled farther than from her bedroom to the family sitting-room and back again, should have wedged herself into a car for a ten mile drive and struggled in a crowd for a place in the public gallery of the Wainbridge Town Hall was in the nature of a miracle. So far she seemed none the worse for her exertions. Her best blue velvet toque and her fur coat had been resurrected for the occasion from a box that was kept under her bed. The coat, which was made of innumerable skins of some anonymous animal dyed a hot reddish brown had split several times since they started. Every time she moved she diffused a mingled odour of brandy and mothballs.

Mrs. Pike had resumed her knitting. Her lips were pressed together. Bella had not changed, she was thinking. She was always one of the bouncing sort, and turned very nasty if she was crossed, and it was easy to see that her girl took after her. There she was spilling her face powder over the clean linoleum.

"If you don't go now you won't get a good place," she reminded them.

"Wherever I go I get a front seat," said Mrs. Simmons complacently. "It's a knack. You've got to use your elbows. But I daresay you're right. I don't want to miss anything. I'm enjoying this. Give me a hoist up, Rene."

Her daughter complied sulkily. She had been hoping all day that none of the boys who took her for rides would see her in her present company. She was ashamed of her mother's blue toque and her mangy fur coat, and a little frightened by her unconcealed high spirits.

They were moving towards the door when another woman came in. It was Emily Gort, neat and trim as ever in her slate grey coat and skirt and well-darned thread gloves. She would have passed them by with a little nod and her tight-lipped smile, but Mrs. Simmons blocked the way.

"Looks as if they'd got him, doesn't it, Miss Gort," she said.

"I fear so," said Miss Gort. "It's been a great shock. Very trying. I'm being called as a witness, you know. I hope I shall be given strength for poor Mabel's sake. It's terrible for the vicar, isn't it. I do so feel for him. How wonderful to see you out and about like this, Mrs. Simmons. You must be careful and not overdo it. I must not keep you now. They tell me there isn't much time."

III

Dr. Anderson gave his evidence after the lunch interval. He was inclined to be on the defensive, but Vereker handled him carefully. He had been called in by Mrs. Copeland ten days before her death for gastric trouble. He had advised careful dieting and prescribed some medicine. She had taken the medicine.

He had seen the bottle, with only one dose remaining, on her table after her death. No, there was no arsenic in his prescription. He had never given her arsenic in any form. He had not been prepared for a fatal outcome, but it was the sort of thing that might happen. He had not heard the village gossip, and had no idea that Mrs. Copeland was not on good terms with her husband.

Emily Gort was the next witness and her evidence was listened to with close attention.

"You knew the late Mrs. Copeland well?"

"Yes. I was her dearest friend."

"You were often at Strays?"

"Yes, she was invalidish and seldom went out beyond the garden. I used to run in three or four times a week just to cheer her up a bit."

"Did she complain of her husband?"

"Not exactly complain. She was very fond of him. But she sometimes said he never told her anything."

"Anything else?"

Miss Gort had removed her grey fabric gloves before she took the oath. She was smoothing them out on the ledge before her while she was speaking very much as if she might have stroked the back of her ginger cat. The tip of her nose twitched slightly.

"Must I answer that?"

"Yes."

"On one occasion when I found her crying she said he wished she was dead. I told her that was nonsense, and that she must not give way to such fancies. I knew, of course, that they got on one another's nerves, but I didn't take it seriously."

"You were in her confidence?"

"Yes, I think so. It was a relief to her, poor dear, to pour out her troubles."

"Did he give her any occasion for jealousy? I don't want what she said to you. Did you see anything yourself of his association, if any, with other women?"

"One of the girls from the village came rather often to fetch eggs. I've seen her myself hanging about the lane, and when he

came down the field to feed the chickens they'd be standing by
the gate talking for a good while. But I didn't think there was
any harm in it, and I don't now."

"Still, it caused unpleasantness."

"Yes, Mabel was on at him. She didn't like the poultry business."

"Why was that?"

"She thought it made him too independent. You see, he hadn't
any money of his own, and she'd always kept him very close, just
doling out a few shillings for tobacco. I think she always regret-
ted that she'd advanced him twenty pounds to make a start with
poultry farming. He worked very hard, and he had paid her back
and was beginning to make a profit."

"And she resented that?"

"Well—there's no denying that poor Mabel was one of the
bossy kind. I used to try to persuade her to go a bit easier with
him, but it was no use."

"And that was the state of affairs on the fatal tenth of June.
Thank you, Miss Gort. You've thrown a good deal of light on the
unhappy relations of this man and his wife. Were you at Strays
on the tenth?"

"Yes. I had tea with Mabel. She was upset and I tried to patch
things up."

"Was it then that she said he wished her dead?"

"Must I answer that?"

"Yes, please."

"It was then. But I didn't take it seriously."

"Apart from being, as you say, upset, did she appear to be in
her usual health?"

"Yes. She'd been baking scones. She made a good tea. She
was a splendid cook."

"Scones. Was there anything else?"

"Oh yes. But they were hot. We both ate several and she gave
me those that were left over to take home with me. I finished
them the next day."

"Can you remember anything else about your last visit, Miss
Gort?"

"She persuaded me to stay longer than I had meant to. It seemed as if she didn't want to be left alone. She came with me to the gate and we said goodbye, and I promised to look in again in a day or two. She said, 'He'll be back before long. I declare I'm half afraid of him. He's been so queer lately!' Those were her last words."

"You weren't alarmed?"

"Oh, no. I just laughed. I said, 'Queer. All men are queer.' Like that."

There was some laughter in the court and the Chairman of the Bench looked round angrily.

Vereker waited for silence to be re-established before he resumed.

"Copeland came to fetch you that night?"

"Yes. He threw gravel up at my window. He told me Mabel was very bad and he was on his way to get the doctor and would I go to her. I hurried on my clothes and went at once. I found her in a terrible state. I did what I could to make her comfortable."

"Did she speak to you?"

"Only a few words and not very clear."

"Can you recall them?"

"She said 'It was the cocoa. It tasted bitter.'"

"You attached no importance to that statement?"

"Not at the time. No."

"She died a few minutes after the arrival of the doctor with her husband?"

"Yes."

"Did she usually have cocoa for her supper?"

"Yes."

"You had no suspicion at all?"

"None. He seemed dreadfully upset. He said, 'It's been awful.' I was truly sorry for him."

"Just one more question, Miss Gort. Do you recall a conversation that took place in your presence between Mr. and Mrs. Copeland the previous summer on the subject of weed killer?"

"Yes. Mabel was complaining that he spent all his time on the poultry and didn't bother about the garden, and that the paths were in a disgraceful state. He said he would see about it. When I came a few days later the weeds on the front path were all shrivelled and brown. Mabel told me he had got a tin of weed killer and they had had a row about it because she thought it an unnecessary extravagance as he could very well have got them up with a hoe, and it was dangerous stuff to have about. He came in while we were talking and he said it was all right. He had it on the top shelf in the shed he used as a garage where no unauthorised person was likely to get at it, and he didn't mean to use it much, anyway, because of the poultry. I never heard any more of it after that."

"I see. Thank you. That will be all, Miss Gort, unless my friend, Mr. Reid—"

John Reid rose and bowed. "I have no questions to ask this witness at this stage."

The next witness was Maria Povey, a short, stout woman with a broad, good-humoured face.

"You let lodgings, Mrs. Povey?"

"Flatlets. It's much the same thing."

"I see. Miss Hale was one of your tenants?"

"That's right."

"She left you on the twenty-fourth of June the summer before last."

"That's right."

"Will you tell us in your own words what led up to her departure?"

"Well, she's been a bit down over losing her job and altogether I was a bit worried about her. She hadn't been the same since she went away for Easter, and I did think there might be some trouble over a man. I'd noticed she was always on the look-out for a letter one morning in the week, and very gay for a bit after it came. I know what girls are, sort of silly like. Mind you she wasn't one of the flighty ones. I'd no fault to find in the two years she was with me. Quiet and well behaved. I don't allow gentlemen visitors, but when a young man called to see her and said he was a friend of her uncle's I made an exception and let him have a vacant sitting-room to wait in. She was out, and when she came in I left them together for a bit and then I took them up some tea, and they were sitting on the sofa holding hands, and he told me they were going to be married as soon as ever he could get the licence. And married they was on the twenty-fourth, and I was one of the witnesses."

"What was the name of the bridegroom, Mrs. Povey."

"Well, he signed the register as Alan Copeland."

"Do you see him here?"

"Yes. Standing in the dock."

"Would it have surprised you then to hear that only ten days before that he had been attending the funeral of his first wife?"

"I wouldn't have believed it—not then—he seemed such a—"

John Reid sprang to his feet. "I protest—"

"I am sorry," said Vereker blandly. "The reactions of decent people are not admissible. I apologise. I've no further questions to ask this witness."

CHAPTER X
MOTHER AND SON

MRS. Reid's drawing-room on the first floor of the tall Queen Anne house in the Market Square was very much as it had been when she came to it as a bride. It had a white wallpaper with a satin stripe and white paint, and there were rose-coloured Bokhara rugs and chintz with a pattern of roses. Photographs in silver frames stood on the piano and the occasional tables. The only modern note in the room was the telephone on Mrs. Reid's rosewood writing table and that had been put in to please John Reid. His mother secretly disliked it and used it as little as possible. She picked it up now with her usual slight tremor of distaste. She was not deaf but she was always afraid that she would not be able to hear.

"Oh . . . is that you, John? It was hopeless keeping dinner any longer. Cook will do her best for you, and I have had something on a tray. Isn't it over yet?"

His voice came faintly over the wire. "Yes. Committed for trial. I say, Mother, about Mrs. Copeland. She's very young and hasn't a soul to stand by her. I hardly like to leave her. May I bring her over?"

"Oh!" Mrs. Reid was startled and slightly shocked by the suggestion. "I don't think so, dear. I'd so much rather not be mixed up in it. In fact, definitely, no. I'm sure it would be unwise. You know I—John—"

He had rung off. "Oh, dear!" she said to herself. She replaced the receiver and went back to her chair by the fire. She did not regret her refusal, for one had to be firm sometimes, but it had made her unhappy.

When her son came in half an hour later she looked up at him deprecatingly. "John dear, I hope you understood—"

"It's all right, Mother," he said, but he avoided her eye. He looked tired and dispirited. "It's been a long day." He sank into a chair and took a cigarette from his case.

"What about your dinner, Johnnie?"

"I don't want any. I saw cook just now and told her. I had a scratch meal at the King's Head with Mrs. Copeland. She's spending the night there. She drove over from Strays this morning, but she's only just passed her test, and she was afraid to go back alone after dark. In the state she was in, shaking like a leaf, it certainly wouldn't have been safe."

"The King's Head. Is that a nice place?" murmured Mrs. Reid.

"They take commercials. It's all right. Quiet and seems clean. And she'll be on the spot tomorrow morning. She's to be allowed to see her husband then before he's moved to the county jail to await his trial."

"I suppose you think I was very hard-hearted?" said his mother.

"Not at all," he said coldly. "I daresay you were quite right from your point of view." He bent to pick up a crumpled edition of the local evening paper. "Did you send Parker out for this?"

"Yes. I heard the newsboys. There doesn't seem to be any doubt of his guilt, John."

He was silent for a moment. Then he said. "She believes in him."

"My dear boy, of course she would say so. It's the least she can do, isn't it? After all, he did it for her."

"Yes," he said slowly. "That's the general view, of course. There's no doubt of their mutual devotion. And the damnable part of that is that it's going to weigh in the scale against him."

"One can't help feeling sorry for him in a way," said Mrs. Reid. "The first wife must have been an awful woman. On the other hand one can't feel much respect for a man who marries a woman years older than himself for her money."

"He's very likable," said Reid.

"I suppose the wife's friend, that Miss Gort, is the chief witness for the prosecution?"

"Yes, and she gave her evidence well. She's an odd little prim, spinsterish person, just the type the first wife would be likely to choose as her confidante. Physically she's unattractive so there would be no fear of her catching the eye of her husband. I must say she showed a decent reluctance to come out with the most damaging bits."

"I suppose he is one of those men who turn silly women's heads."

"I don't know," said Reid reluctantly. "There's nothing fulsome about his manners. A quiet sort of chap. I suppose he'd be called good looking."

"What line will the defence take?" She had always tried to enter into his interests, but he was still on his guard with her.

She had disappointed him.

"I have not the least idea," he said.

"It is such a—" She could not hide her distaste. "A horrid case. Can't you pass it on to another firm?"

"Impossible. It would look as if I thought him guilty. He's handicapped enough by his own folly, poor wretch. That marriage, only a few days after his first wife's death, is bound to prejudice any jury."

"How strange it is that a man who did not stick at murder should be so keen on respectability," she said.

"My dear mother, must you assume his guilt?"

"I'm not assuming anything, John. It's perfectly obvious after what came out in court to-day. I'm very sorry you have to be mixed up in it, and I don't really want to discuss it."

He lay back in his chair, trying to relax and enjoy the pleasant warmth, the quiet security of that familiar room, but he could not help recalling the dingy passage redolent of stale beer that led to the only room he had been able to engage for Lydia Copeland. The girl was so friendless, so forlorn.

Mrs. Reid threaded her needle. "They say murderers are extraordinarily callous," she remarked. "He must be. Fancy going back to live in the house where the crime was committed."

"But if he did not know there had been a crime?" Reid was dangerously polite, but his mother did not notice it.

"Don't be silly, Johnnie. You need not pretend to me."

"Would it really be too much to ask you to keep an open mind about this case? Copeland came back to Strays because he wanted to restore the place. It had fallen into decay, but he's an artist and he saw its possibilities. Actually it's one of the finest sixteenth century houses of its size in the county. He's wanted to for years, but his wife wouldn't spend the money."

"Parker was telling me that her cousin, who is engaged to a policeman, told her that they found out about the second marriage through a water colour sketch of North Wales signed by Copeland and dated—"

"It is their job to pry and spy," he said with startling bitterness.

"That's not a nice way of putting it, John," she reproved him. "It would be a great mistake to get sentimental about this—this young person he married. She may be more to blame than he is. Between them they murdered that unfortunate first wife for her money. You can't alter facts."

"Well," he said, and he was surprised at the effort he had to make to keep his voice under control, "that is one point of view. I think I'll turn in now. Good-night, Mother."

He bent to kiss her, knowing how hurt she would be if he omitted to do so. "We'll leave it at that, shall we?"

He was to go over to the King's Head at nine to take Lydia across to the police station, where she was to be allowed to see her husband for a few minutes before he was taken away to the county goal. Three men came out of the coffee room as he was waiting for her in the stuffy little entrance hall.

Lydia was just coming down the stairs.

"Mrs. Copeland, we want to take a picture—"

"We'd like your exclusive story—"

"Mrs. Copeland—"

Reid forced his way past them to her side. "I am Mrs. Copeland's solicitor. You can take it from me, gentlemen, that she has nothing to say for the Press beyond the fact that she is convinced of her husband's innocence, and that we are going to put up a big fight."

The youngest of the trio, a reporter from the office of the local paper, grinned. "That'll do to go with, thank you, Mr. Reid."

More than one camera clicked as Reid hurried Lydia across the square, but she did not notice them.

"We're not late, are we?" she said anxiously. "They wouldn't take him away before we came?"

Alan was waiting for them in a bare little room adjoining the charge room. A constable was on duty by the open door. It was a brief and poignant interview.

"Alan, can't I come round this table to you, dear?"

"No. Its one of their rules. You might pass me dope, or a knife, or something. Are you all right, darling? I want you to go home now and take care of yourself. Don't worry. Reid, look after her, will you?"

Reid, standing by, was deeply touched by the misery of that worn, dark face. "I'll do my best," he promised. "I'll be seeing you again soon."

"I can have visitors?"

"You can see me at any time, because I shall be preparing your defence."

The constable at the door cleared his throat. "Time's up, sir."

Lydia allowed herself to be led away.

"What are you doing now, Mrs. Copeland?"

She roused herself from her icy stupor of despair to answer. "Get the car from the garage and drive home, I suppose."

"Will you come over to my office first? I'd like to talk things over."

"Very well," she said dully.

There was a bright fire in his private room, and he made her sit near it and produced a decanter of sherry, a vintage wine which the custom of the firm had always reserved for specially favoured clients. John Reid did not stop to ask himself if his late father Henry Reid or his uncle Eustace Pearmain would have approved of him filling a glass from one of the last bottles in that bin for the wife of a murderer.

"It'll do you good," he said. "I'm having some myself."

"Its a lovely colour," she said, "like my amber necklace Alan gave me for my birthday. You are kind, Mr. Reid. And I'm afraid I'm taking up a lot of your time."

He sat down by his writing table. "You're not wasting it, Mrs. Copeland. We shall engage counsel, of course, to represent your husband at his trial, but we've got to do the preliminary spade work. Now how about suicide?"

"You mean that she might have taken the arsenic on purpose?"

"Exactly. What's your reaction to that suggestion, Mrs. Copeland? Would it go down with a jury?"

She shook her head decidedly. "If it had been sleeping stuff it might have been intentional. And she had veronal tablets. I remember Alan saying she used to take them sometimes, though not very often. Why should she go out of her way to kill herself with something that hurts frightfully when she could just go to sleep and not wake up? It doesn't make sense."

He made a note. "Not suicide. I'm inclined to agree with you. What about accident?"

"Very unlikely. If the tin of weedkiller was kept on the shelf in the garage it couldn't get mixed up with the groceries."

"We can't be sure of that. For instance Copeland might have left a parcel of groceries in the back of the car when he reversed in to the garage. The tin of weedkiller had been overturned and some of its contents dripped on to the parcel, impregnating a few lumps of sugar. They might be discoloured, but the dead woman was a person of rather miserly habits, close in some ways, and she would not throw them away. How's that for a theory?" cried Reid.

"Quite good, I think. I wonder if that is really what happened," she said eagerly.

John tilted back his chair. "There's another alternative, you know, and that is that she was deliberately poisoned, not by your husband, but by someone else. I think we can leave out Miss Gort. She was Mrs. Copeland's best friend and had nothing to gain and a good deal to lose by her death, but there might easily be somebody who hasn't appeared at all as yet in this case. I—may speak frankly? I don't want to hurt you—"

"Of course."

"Well then—there was some reference to a girl in yesterday's evidence. Copeland was much younger than his wife and it wasn't a happy marriage. Isn't it possible that there was some entanglement in the days before he met you?"

"You must ask him about that," she said wearily. "There was nothing to my knowledge. That girl—Irene Simmons—did run after him, but I don't think there was any harm in it. She was just a nuisance. When I first stayed in the village with my uncle—before I knew Alan—people were always talking about him and his wife and how she bullied him."

John Reid was silent for a moment. He lacked the courage to say what was in his mind, which was simply that Alan Copeland's guilt was so obvious that the step he was about to suggest would be a sheer waste of money.

"I think we should hire a private detective to make some enquiries in the village. Juries are human and don't like convicting. A loophole, that's all they need. A loophole. I'll send one of my clerks round to the garage to bring your car here, Mrs. Copeland. I'll keep you in touch. It's a pity you're not on the phone at Strays."

Chapter XI
THE CUP THAT CHEERS

Miss Platt, standing in the doorway, saw the last of her scholars clatter down the path into the lane. An hour's work that evening correcting exercises, and then she need not think of them again for two blessed days and nights. Little beasts. Not that they gave her much trouble. Miss Platt was an excellent disciplinarian. She never used the cane, but there was something behind her cool self-control that the children dimly realised though they had never actually seen. It was something they could not have described. It kept the rougher specimens in wholesome awe of the short, thick-set woman who seldom raised her voice to them, and it vaguely repelled the gentler spirits.

She was, in fact, completely indifferent to them. Her real interests were elsewhere. During school hours hers was the soulless efficiency of a robot.

She stretched herself now, shrugging her strong shoulders and moving her fingers as if coming to life again after the numbing influences of the week. She was going to tea with old Mother Simmons, and that might be amusing. And then, when the exercises had been corrected, a cosy evening by her sitting-room fire with cigarettes and *Anthony Adverse* and her thoughts. She put on her hat and coat carelessly, without troubling to look at herself in the glass and went round to the shed to get her bicycle.

As she rode down the straggling village street in the gathering dusk of the late autumn evening, lights were beginning to glimmer here and there in the tiny windows deep sunk under thatched eaves, and the smell of bloaters being fried for tea mingled with that of wood smoke. At the cross roads the row of petrol pumps reminded her of Noah and his family. She glanced, as she always did, at the second- or more probably third-hand cars labelled for sale. She longed for the freedom that the possession of a car would give her, but she knew she could not afford to keep one. It would mean giving up her trips abroad, and she could not do that.

Ern, emerging from behind the chassis of a derelict marked down to eight pounds, touched his cap sulkily. The door bell rang as she entered the little shop, and Irene, who was sitting behind the counter engaged in polishing her nails, greeted her unsmilingly.

"You can go in, Miss Platt. Ma's expecting you."

"Thank you, Irene. I'll have a packet of my cigarettes. Your mother is none the worse for her exertions, I hope?"

"You'll see for yourself."

Irene jerked her customer's shilling into the till and turned away.

A fire was blazing in the sitting-room grate and a mound of buttered toast was keeping warm inside the fender while the table was spread with a lavish supply of cakes and three kinds of jam. Gertrude Platt noticed that there were four cups. Ern, she knew, never came in on these occasions, so evidently another guest was expected. Mrs. Simmons, enthroned as usual on the sofa, was wearing her best black silk and stays that creaked with every movement. Nothing could diminish her bulk, but she seemed more alive, if not actually younger, than when Miss Platt had last seen her.

Miss Platt took a seat as far as possible from the fire and from her hostess. She had remarked, when they shook hands, a smell of spirits.

"So the age of miracles is not past," she said pleasantly.

"You mean me going to Wainbridge? Ern says the springs of the car'll never be the same again, and that we'll have to knock a fiver off her selling price, but I don't care. I enjoyed meself, and that's the main thing. We went to the pictures afterwards, but give me real life. If they'd adjourned the hearing I'd have gone again, but they got it done in the one day. No defence, see. Well, I mean to say, it was as plain as the nose on your face. You've read the accounts in the papers, I suppose?"

"Yes."

"Well, there you are. Even a worm will turn, as I could have told Mabel. We got a good view of the dock, didn't we, Rene?"

Her daughter, who had come in from the shop, was taking the kettle from the hob to make the tea, and did not answer. Gertrude Platt glanced rather curiously at the pretty, sullen, mutinous face before she spoke.

"How did he look?"

Mrs. Simmons smacked her lips. "Like death. And as for her—well, she always did remind me of a mouse that got drowned in the milk jug. And to think of the carryings on there must have been that fortnight, and her staying at the vicarage and all, so prim and proper. There's the shop bell, Rene. Better go and see who it is."

As she went out Mrs. Simmons lowered her voice to a stage whisper. "I asked Emily. She thinks I'm low, but you won't catch her saying no to a square meal. Its my belief that woman lives on what that nasty ginger cat of hers leaves on his plate."

Irene came back with Miss Gort and sat down to pour out tea.

Miss Gort shook hands. "How do you do, Mrs. Simmons. How do you do, Miss Platt."

"And how's the star witness?" enquired Mrs. Simmons with elephantine playfulness.

Miss Gort looked down her nose. "Oh, please," she said plaintively. "If I hadn't felt it to be my duty I don't know I could have got through it. And fancy you coming all that way. Oh dear, I must confess my heart sinks when I remember that I've got to go through it all again at the Assizes."

Miss Platt chose quince jam, and spread it carefully on her bread and butter. "Of course, that's a nice, womanly attitude, but, to be candid, didn't you get a kick out of it?"

Miss Gort shuddered. "Certainly not. If it wasn't that wickedness must be exposed—"

"Ah!" said Mrs. Simmons with relish. "The vicar's niece. And poor Mabel asking her to supper and cards, and all. Mabel thought she'd got him on a string, didn't she. Why, Rene here could have had him, but luckily she's got too much sense to think twice of a married man."

"I'm sure she has," said Miss Platt blandly. "And it's just as well, isn't it, because the defence will probably try to suggest that there may have been other people beside Alan Copeland with some motive for getting rid of his wife. This jam is delicious. I must try to make some next year. There's a quince tree in the school playground."

"Oh dear," said Miss Gort, "do you mind if we change the subject. It distresses me. I miss Mabel very much. She was my best friend."

Irene Simmons made her first contribution to the conversation.

"There's a stranger in your tea. A large one." Her mother craned forward to look. "So there is. I'll bet it's a policeman. Don't mind me, Emily. I must have my joke."

"A robust sense of humour," murmured Miss Platt, who at the moment would willingly have turned a machine-gun on the whole party. She allowed herself a moment's relaxation, playing with the idea. The sharp metallic patter as of deadly rain, the silly, fixed surprise on the white, upturned faces, the dark spreading stains on the dusty carpet. Dust. What a little slattern Irene was. Her cousin was a fool to want to marry her. She roused herself to join again in the conversation.

"Has the vicar said anything to you, Emily?"

"About the—the case? Oh no, not a word. He made it clear when they came back that he disapproved of the marriage less than a year after poor Mabel—and all communications ceased. She's no relation really, you know. His wife's niece, not his."

"They've had a high old time all these months," observed Mrs. Simmons, rather indistinctly, with her mouth full of cake. "A good car, and a couple of servants to wait on them, and money spent like water doing up the house. But I wouldn't be in her shoes now. Ern says Tom Welland and Bessie hopped it when they heard there was going to be trouble. She's alone there at Strays. It's a biggish house to run. Alone there at night, knowing what she knows. On the other hand, maybe she's lucky not to be standing in the dock with him. Don't tell me she didn't egg him on. It was for her he did it. All right, Rene. We've finished."

Irene got up and began to pile the crockery on the tray to be carried out to the scullery. Her thick, red fingers were unsteady, and she dropped one spoon and had to fumble for it under the table. Gertrude Platt got out her cigarette case. "Do you mind?"

"Well, since you ask," said Mrs. Simmons, "I'd rather you waited until you got outside. I don't hold with it, not for ladies. I daresay I'm old-fashioned."

Gertrude laughed with real enjoyment. "Mrs. Simmons, you are priceless. Of course I won't smoke if you don't approve. I should hate to shock you. I didn't know it could be done."

Her eyes met those of the old woman. There was no sound, but each was conscious of something like the clash of steel on steel.

Irene had carried out her laden tray. Mrs. Simmons reached for her pack of cards. "Shall I tell your fortunes?"

Miss Gort looked up with her tight pale smile. "Ah, now I'm afraid it's my turn to say no. You mean kindly, dear Mrs. Simmons, but it isn't right. The witch of Endor, you know. It's explicitly forbidden. Though, of course, I know that you don't take it seriously. A pastime. Nevertheless—And the choir practice is at six. I really must be going."

"So must I," said Miss Platt. "We can walk down to the village together."

"That will be nice," said Miss Gort civilly.

Irene had not come back. They took leave of Mrs. Simmons and went out through the shop.

They had a mile to walk to the village by a road that wound through fields that lay dim and silent under the stars.

Gertrude Platt drew a long breath of the raw mist laden air.

"I couldn't have stood it any longer. That room stinks. Couldn't she see that she was putting that girl of hers on the rack? Or was it deliberate? I like Ma Simmons. A bout with her is good exercise. The witch of Endor. You're a brave woman, Miss Gort. I shouldn't have dared. A frontal attack. I only skirmish on the outposts. But I've got an even better name for her. The rump fed runnion. Don't be too horrified. It's a Shakespearian quotation."

"Shakespeare is often very coarse," said Miss Gort repressively.

She thought Miss Platt talked a great deal of nonsense, and not very nice nonsense either. It was quite impossible to follow.

"I always tell myself that Mrs. Simmons doesn't mean half the things she says," she added. "One tries to be charitable."

After her companion's deep and husky contralto her voice sounded very thin.

Meanwhile, in a patch of shadow beyond the crude flood-lighting of the cross roads garage Ern Simmons was stroking the touzled brown head that burrowed into his shoulder with a clumsy and unaccustomed gentleness.

"Don't cry, Rene. Don't cry like that."

CHAPTER XII
A TERRIBLE POSITION

THE afternoon after the day Alan Copeland was committed for trial George Hayter called at the office of Reid, Reid and Pearmain, and having sent in his card, was shown immediately into John Reid's room.

Reid, who had not had much experience of private enquiry agents, was favourably impressed. He had been expecting a furtive-looking person with a tendency to cringe. George Hayter was a big man with a wholesome, weather-beaten face and remarkably steady grey eyes. He might have been a farmer come to consult him professionally about a mortgage. "You're not my idea of a sleuth," he said as they shook hands.

Hayter smiled. "I've been a good many other things in my time. Bronco buster. Canadian mounted police, second engineer on a tramp steamer, chicle gatherer in British Guiana. And that isn't half. But I've held this job down for three years now. I was in the same battalion in 1917 with a chap who's now high up at the Yard. We're still good friends, and that's given me a pull. Now about this case, Mr. Reid. I read all the newspaper accounts in the train coming down. Can you give me the inside dope?"

Reid sighed. "I'm afraid the police have a very good case against my client," he began. "The undisputed facts are that

Copeland was not happy in his married life. His wife was years older, and he had, I fear, married her only for her money. I managed her affairs and I remember suggesting to her that she should make him a regular allowance. No. She doled out every penny. It seems that she even resented his attempt to earn a little by poultry farming. There's no doubt that she was a thoroughly disagreeable woman, and that she made the poor devil's life a burden. She died a year ago last June after a few hours' illness. Copeland fetched the doctor and he made no bones about signing the certificate. Mrs. Copeland had made a will leaving everything to her husband. He left me to settle his business affairs, probate and all the rest of it. I had to forward any papers that had to be signed through the London branch of his bank. He remained away until last April when he returned, bringing with him the second Mrs. Copeland, and set about restoring Strays. The place was a manor in the seventeenth century and has come down in the world, passing into the hands of farmers, who replaced the lattice windows with sashes and plastered cheap wall papers over the oak beams. It had always been Copeland's dream to do what he and his wife have been doing these last few months, but of course it has cost a good bit of money." Reid hesitated a moment as if he found some difficulty in proceeding. "This—this girl he married was a niece of the vicar of Teene. She stayed at the vicarage for a fortnight, two months before Mrs. Copeland's death. They do not deny that during her visit she—they became lovers, with the result that she—"

"Yes. That came out in the evidence. I'm afraid it supplies a motive," said Hayter, gravely.

Reid was drawing circles on his blotting paper one inside the other and a dot in the centre of them all. "He'd no money to help her through her trouble, and he couldn't marry her."

"But he did marry her within a fortnight of his first wife's funeral. Yes, I agree that it looks black. But you've undertaken his defence, Mr. Reid?"

"He was my client. If I'd had time to consider I might have passed him on to some other firm. I've no experience of the criminal courts. It's not our line of country at all. We're family solicitors. I confess I find it worrying, but I don't regret it. Guilty or innocent, it's a terrible position for a man. Worse, in a way, if he's guilty. I mean to do my best for him. His wife was sitting in that very chair yesterday. She's quite certain he didn't do it."

"There is this about poisoning," said Hayter slowly. "It is very hard to prove, and especially after such a lapse of time. Shoot your victim or strike her on the head with a hammer and there will be finger-prints, bloodstains. But a death that, at the time, appeared to be natural is different. You see why the police are making such a point of his secret love affair—why this unfortunate girl, who is probably quite innocent of complicity in the actual crime, either before or after, has to be dragged into the case. I have listened to trials where the prosecuting counsel has said that the motive didn't matter, it wasn't their business to prove a motive. But in that case they had plenty of material evidence. The murderer had been found practically red-handed. But here, but for the motive, the crime might have been committed by anyone who had access to the farm kitchen during that evening. Half a dozen people may have been in and out for all we know. It'll be the job of the defence, Mr. Reid, to point that out to the jury."

Reid nodded. "That's what I thought. If you could get on to that. How will you start?"

"I'd like to see Copeland himself first and ask him a few questions. Can that be arranged?"

"I think so. I was told we should be allowed every facility. I'll ring up the Governor of the prison now and ask if we can go over at once."

The permission was accorded, and within ten minutes Reid was steering through the traffic of the High Street with Hayter by his side. On the outskirts of the little town he accelerated and in less than an hour they were entering the prison gates. They were shown into a waiting room and after a brief interval Alan Copeland was brought in. He looked very haggard and hollow eyed, but he seemed pleased to see them.

"Lydia—is she all right, Reid?"

"Quite. We shall be seeing her very soon. Mr. Hayter is going to help prepare your defence."

"Thank you."

"You can help," said Hayter. "I want you to cast your mind back to the day before Mrs. Copeland's death. We know now that there was arsenic in something she ate or drank during those hours. Who came to Strays during that time, to your knowledge? Think carefully. You've read that tale of Chesterton's where the murder was committed by the postman. Nobody thought of counting him as a person."

"I see what you mean," said Alan. "Wait a minute. I was out all the afternoon delivering eggs to customers. Miss Bragge, at the Quarry House, had ordered a roasting fowl. They're friends of mine and I had a cup of tea there. When I came in about seven the postman had been, for there were a couple of circulars in the letter box. Mabel was in the sitting-room. She told me her friend, Miss Gort, had been to tea with her. She—we had one of our usual scenes. She was angry because she had seen a girl from the village hanging about, as she described it, by the yard gate. She said she had gone out and told her to clear off, and that the girl was impudent. I tried to smooth things over. I told her the girl meant no harm and that probably she'd come to get some eggs, but she went on and on about being insulted, and so on. I tried to keep my temper. The only thing was to leave her. I was tired and had meant to put off washing the car until the next day, but I went out to the shed where I kept her and gave her a rub down. Later that night when I tried to take her out to fetch the doctor her engine wouldn't start and I had to go on my bicycle. When I went back to the house Mabel had prepared her supper and was having it on a tray in the sitting-room. She said she wasn't feeling well and was going up to bed. I wasn't surprised. She upset her digestion when she got into those rages, though, in a way, I know she enjoyed making scenes."

"What did she have for supper?"

"Always the same thing. A cup of cocoa made with milk, and a few sandwiches made with potted meat, or sometimes lettuce and tomato. But that evening she ate nothing."

"What happened then?"

"She went up to bed. I sat up for an hour longer, smoking and reading. Then I went up too. I had the room across the landing from hers. I didn't get to sleep for some time. I was worried and unhappy. The reason why is public property now. I was awakened by her crying out. I went to her and found her very ill and in great pain. I did what I could for her and when she seemed a bit easier I dressed and went down and lit the fire and made her some tea. She'd asked for it, but she couldn't keep it down. I thought I'd better get the doctor. She—she clung to me, poor woman, and didn't want to be left. She said, 'Forgive me, Alan, if I've been hard on you.' I said, 'Of course,' and tried to cheer her up a bit. I'm glad to remember that now. She was unconscious when I came back with the doctor."

"You had to leave her quite alone in that state?"

"I got Emily Gort. Her house is about a mile along the road. She got up at once and rushed over. She and Mabel were great friends."

"Yes. Well, the essential time for us is some hours earlier. Did Mrs. Copeland prepare her own supper?"

"Yes. We had a daily woman from the village. We had dinner at one and she had usually washed up the plates and dishes and cleaned the kitchen by about half past two, when she left. Mabel did a lot of cooking, and she sometimes spent an afternoon making cakes. She was a very good cook. We had large meals and a lot of rich food, but she never ate much supper."

"Would she have gone out to the kitchen to make the cocoa while you were cleaning your car, after the quarrel?"

"She'd have to heat the cocoa, but the tray was ready before that. She probably prepared it after washing up the tea things after Emily Gort left. That would be between five and six o'clock."

"And the girl who was the cause of the disagreement. Who was it, Mr. Copeland?"

"Irene Simmons. She was a bit of a nuisance, always coming up to buy eggs, but there was no harm in it. You know what fools girls of her age can be. She was just a flapper. About seventeen."

"And imagined herself in love with you?"

"Well, something of the sort, I suppose," said Alan uncomfortably. "But she had nothing to do with this."

"Would the kitchen door be locked?"

"Not until I locked up for the night. That was generally between ten and eleven."

"I want to get this quite clear. From, say, six o'clock until Mrs. Copeland came to heat the cocoa the tray would be standing on the table in the empty kitchen, and the cocoa—"

"Ready mixed in a saucepan beside the tray."

"And could anyone come to the kitchen door without being seen from the sitting-room windows?"

"Oh yes, easily. Through the yard gate farther down the lane and round behind the shrubberies to the back of the house."

"Would any of the tradesmen have called that afternoon?"

"The milkman, that is, Tommy Burton, from Yeolands Farm, and possibly the man from the Wainbridge Co-operative Stores."

"I see. Thank you, Mr. Copeland."

The haunted eyes sought his wistfully. "Does that help at all?"

There was something forlorn about him at that moment, the hunted look of a lost dog, that touched them both with an almost intolerable pity. The lawyer cleared his throat uneasily. Hayter answered gently. "I think it may. I really think it may. You have no theory of your own, Mr. Copeland?"

"None. It couldn't be suicide. I can't imagine Mabel doing that—and if she did it would have been an overdose of sleeping stuff. People didn't like her much, she was too given to fault-finding, but I can't believe she had any actual enemies. My feeling is that it may have been an accident. Don't they use arsenic in making chocolate? If only the cause of her death had been discovered at the time the rest of the packet of cocoa might have been analysed. How can one hope to discover the truth after all these months? I can only go on saying that I didn't do it, and that doesn't cut much ice," he added, with an attempt at a smile, "even with Reid."

"No, no, don't say that," said Reid hurriedly.

They shook hands again and left him, and, as they went down to their car, heard the clash of iron doors echoing down the long stone-paved corridors.

"What next?" asked Reid as he let in the clutch.

"The woman in the case, I think."

"Mrs. Copeland? Right. We'll go round by Strays."

He had been over the house more than once when the furniture was being valued for probate after Mabel Copeland's death and remembered an untidy, neglected garden and a depressing atmosphere to which a dark brown wall paper spattered with monstrous blue flowers had contributed, clumsy chairs upholstered in crimson rep, and a huge mahogany sideboard suggestive of funeral baked meats. It was good furniture of its kind and it had been well cared for by Mabel, but the auction sale had been ill attended.

"They'd come now all right, for souvenirs," he thought.

It was growing dusk as they stopped at the gate and looked through the bars at the paved walk leading between hedges of clipped box, to the front door. Reid rang the bell and they waited. There was no light in any of the windows, but presently they heard steps and the door was opened on the chain.

"Oh—is it you, Mr. Reid? I shut up rather early. I suppose it's silly to be nervous, but I'm all alone here. Please come in."

Lydia opened the door wide and stood back to allow them to pass in while she sheltered the flame of the candle she held from the draught. "Come in here. I've got a fire in the sitting-room."

"This is quite different to my recollection," said Reid. "It was rather a narrow passage, with a hat rack and umbrella stand."

"Yes. Alan discovered that it had been a square hall. A partition had been put to make the little room on the right. It was quite easy to pull down and it's much nicer like this."

She led the way into a long, low-pitched room, lit only by a blazing fire of logs on an open hearth. "This is where we found the linenfold panelling. Alan and I worked hard stripping the walls of seven layers of paper, and I think the poor room was glad to be clean and simple and beautiful again after so many years of dreadful Victorian fustiness. It's always felt friendly.

Does that sound mad? But I've always felt that some rooms hate you and try to push you out." Her voice trailed away into silence and she stood for a moment looking vaguely at the candle before she set it down.

"I know what you mean," said Reid. "I've wanted to see what you've made of Strays. I didn't altogether approve of such an outlay, you know, but you've certainly effected a transformation. If we could have more light—"

"I'm sorry," she said. "Tom Welland looked after the power plant and he and Bessie left before the police came. The current gave out yesterday so I have to manage with candles."

"You ought not to be staying here under such conditions."

"I'd rather be alone just now," she said simply. "Have you seen Alan? How is he?"

"We come from—from him now. He says you are not to worry. This is Mr. George Hayter, who has come down from London to help us."

"Won't you sit down?"

"Thank you, Mrs. Copeland."

She looked from Reid to Hayter. "How can his innocence be proved after all these months? The more I think of it the more hopeless it seems."

"The prosecution," said Hayter, "have painted their picture with a large brush to get their effect. I think the same scene may make a different impression when the details have been brought out. Mrs. Copeland's cocoa was left ready mixed in the saucepan on the kitchen table for a considerable length of time. The door was on the latch and anyone could come to it by way of the yard gate without being seen from the front of the house. If we can induce the jury to harbour a few doubts about any possible visitors to Strays they won't convict."

"Yes," she said slowly. "Alan didn't—but somebody must have done it. I wonder—"

"Can you make any suggestions, Mrs. Copeland? You can say anything to us, you know."

Lydia, drooping in her chair, sighed as she held out her hands to the blaze. "Sometimes," she said, "I feel I shall never be warm again. It's so horrible. Irene Simmons was in love with him, and so was Gertrude Platt. Irene didn't care who knew it, but Gertrude is clever. I guessed, because I cared for him too, but I don't think anyone else did. I'm sure Alan didn't."

Hayter made a note. "Who is this Miss Platt? Does she live near?"

"In the village. She's the schoolmistress."

"I see. It's in your husband's favour, Mrs. Copeland, that the police have committed themselves to the theory that the poison used was the weedkiller kept in a tin on a shelf in the garage. Anyone could have got at it there while he was away with the car. I think we shall be able to pick a good many holes in their case."

"There's one thing that puzzles me," said Lydia. "Why have the police acted now, and not sooner? What made them think there was something wrong?"

Hayter looked at her with approval. "That's a very interesting point—in fact it's of major importance. It wasn't the doctor. It would have come out in his evidence. He was perfectly satisfied at the time, and the average general practitioner doesn't spend much time wondering if he made a mistake fifteen months ago. Village gossip perhaps, intensified by the fact that you didn't try to placate your neighbours. You'd be the last to hear it, naturally. But if we could trace it to its source we might be on to something."

Reid leaned forward eagerly. "You mean—"

"I mean that a perfect crime—perfect from the perpetrator's point of view—has often been spoilt by over-elaboration. This may be a case of a murderer not satisfied to let well alone. Or—there's another possible motive."

"You think the actual criminal may have been working to get Copeland arrested? Isn't that rather far-fetched, Hayter? They'd have been safer if no suspicion had been aroused."

"Exactly. They would. It was a mistake. We must hope to profit by it. And now, Mrs. Copeland, I can't do any more to-night, though I hope to be busy to-morrow, but if Mr. Reid can wait for half an hour I believe I can put your electric plant to rights. I'm a bit of a Jack of all trades."

"Will you really? That's very kind."

She took him out to the shed that was used as a power house and left him there. Reid sat with her by the fire while Hayter was at work. He asked her what she thought of the detective.

"He has made me feel more hopeful," she said.

"But I wish he had thought, as Alan does, that it was some kind of accident. It horrifies me to think that the actual murderer is at large. I wonder—"

she checked herself with a murmured, "Oh, no—"

"What?" he encouraged her. "Don't be afraid to say."

"I was thinking of Mrs. Simmons. She's rather a dreadful old woman and she's supposed to be unable to move farther than from her bed to the sofa and back again. But she was actually at the police court the other day with her daughter. I saw them. I went to tea with her when I was staying with my uncle. She's—one doesn't like to say it of anyone—but she really is repulsive."

"What motive would she have?"

"To clear the way for her daughter. It wouldn't occur to her that Alan might not want Irene." The lights had gone on unnoticed by either of them while they talked. Hayter rejoined them. "The back of the house is much as it was?" he said. "I thought so. I had a look at the kitchen and it confirmed my theory. It would be easy to slip in and out unnoticed by anyone sitting in this room. Now I shall be making a good many enquiries in the village and I've got the names of Miss Platt and Miss Simmons. I want any others who were friends either of Mrs. Copeland or her husband, not as suspects, you understand. It's just that they may be able to throw some light on the dark places. People sometimes hold clues whose importance they don't realise."

Lydia thought a moment. "There's my uncle, the vicar. Alan used to be his churchwarden, and they were on friendly terms, but my uncle didn't approve of our marriage so soon after—though we were pretending then that it was several months after—and we haven't seen anything of him since we called on him last April. Then there's Miss Gort. She was a great friend of Mabel's. She called on me once, but she was rather rude, and she hasn't been again. Mr. Bragge and his sister were always Alan's friends. Mabel didn't like them, and they never came here in her time, but through the summer they've come in usually one evening a week to play bridge. I thought they'd stick to us, but now I'm not sure. Annie has written to say she's sorry she can't come over as she's got sciatica. Then there are the Wellands. Tom used to help Alan with his poultry farm, but I don't think he had anything to do with Mabel. And there was a Mrs. Butt who did the housework."

Hayter nodded. "She's one of the witnesses for the prosecution. It's our job to find sources they haven't tapped. Well, that'll do to go on with. Good night, Mrs. Copeland."

CHAPTER XIII
ENTER JUSTICE

I

HAYTER had booked a room at the King's Head. He dined in the coffee room and strolled into the office afterwards for a chat with the landlord. It proved very easy to direct the conversation in to the desired channel. The Copeland case had been the chief topic for discussion in the bar for some days past. Hayter soon saw that while most of the frequenters of the house sympathised with Alan Copeland they had no doubt of his guilt. It was all summed up in one phrase. "A woman like that would drive any man to murder."

"I suppose you knew him and his friends and neighbours personally?" suggested Hayter, as the barman brought in the drinks he had ordered.

"Never heard of any of them before this case. Teene is one of the outlying villages, nine miles by road, and it's on the Ritswell circular bus route. The Teene people come into Wainbridge to do their shopping and go to the Pictures. There's a special late bus on Tuesdays and Fridays to take them home. But we don't go there. Why should we? I don't say they won't get a few visitors now, out of curiosity. They're a queer lot there, I fancy."

"What makes you say that?"

"Well, there was a party of them came into the bar the evening of the day Copeland was committed for trial. We were more crowded than usual and I asked them into the coffee room. There was an old woman like a moving mountain. I've never seen anything to beat her outside a show. And a girl with her, a pretty little painted piece, hot stuff by the look of her, and a young chap who looked unhappy and hardly spoke except to say it was time to be going. The two women had gin and it, and, believe it or not, the young fellow asked for lemonade and didn't seem to care how much the old woman chipped him about it. I learnt something about them one way and another before we closed. They run a petrol station and garage at the crossroads just beyond Teene, and some say the old woman hoped to get Copeland for her daughter after his wife died. She's got her knife in him now all right. She was gloating over it all. I was in and out, attending to my customers, and she didn't bother to lower her voice, and the girl and the young chap smoking their cigarettes and listening, and every now and then trying to persuade her to go home."

"Mr. Reid will get him off if anyone can," said Hayter.

"Ah, you know him, sir, don't you. I saw you pass in his car this afternoon. Yes, the Reids have always been much respected. His mother was a Miss Pearmain. She keeps house for him. Some say it's her fault he hasn't married. Nobody's good enough for her boy. Mind you, she makes him comfortable. A cousin of my wife is parlourmaid there. Everything has got to be just so, she says, but it's a good place. Well, if you'll excuse me, sir, I've got to lend a hand in the bar while the wife takes her dog for a run."

The following morning, directly after his solid British breakfast of smoked haddock and bacon and eggs, Hayter crossed the market square to the police station and asked to see the Superintendent. A constable took his card, and, after a brief interval, showed him into the office where the Superintendent, who had just arrived, was going through the reports of the men who had been on night duty. He rose and shook hands with Hayter.

"It's about the Copeland case, I suppose? I saw you in Mr. Reid's car yesterday."

"Quite right, Superintendent. We think you've made a mistake this time, and we hope to prove it."

"I'm afraid you won't. I shouldn't be sorry if you did. We don't get a whole lot of fun out of hounding a man down. He'll have a square deal, Mr. Hayter."

"I'm sure of it," said Hayter heartily. He liked the Superintendent. He was not quite so much taken with Detective-Sergeant Ramsden when that officer was sent for and introduced to him. Ramsden was not exactly cordial, but there was nothing to complain of in his manner.

"Ramsden has been in charge of the case from the first, Mr. Hayter. He has been to London, to North Wales and on to Leamington tracing Copeland's movements during the months he was away from this neighbourhood."

"There's just one point, Mr. Ramsden," said Hayter deferentially. "What made the police think there might be something wrong? Was it information received?"

"Something like that."

"Could you be more explicit?"

Ramsden glanced at the Superintendent, who nodded.

"We'd been getting anonymous letters."

"Ah!" Hayter's eyes brightened. He did not disguise his interest.

"When did they begin?"

"They've been going on all the summer. The first—I'm not sure—it might have been in May. We didn't take much notice for a bit. But they kept on coming, and we thought we might as well look into it. As soon as I found the notice of Copeland's second marriage at a registrar's in London a couple of weeks after his first wife's death I rang up our Superintendent here and he got hold of the Chief Constable. Within twenty-four hours we had our permit to exhume the body from the Home Secretary."

"Smart work," said Hayter mechanically, seeing that it was expected of him. "Did you trace the letters to their source?"

"No."

"You mean that you tried and failed?"

"No. No doubt they were written by someone in the village who had their suspicions but didn't want to be mixed up in the case. They served their purpose. We get lots of that sort of stuff, some written by people with a screw loose, some sheer spite, and some that's really useful to us."

"I should like to see those letters," said Hayter. The Superintendent answered. "We didn't take them seriously at first so they weren't kept."

Hayter, with an effort, refrained from any comment. He was rewarded for his self-control. "As a matter of fact," the Superintendent added, "I believe I've got the last three put away in one of these pigeon holes. Wait a bit. Yes, here we are."

He laid the three sheets of writing paper down side by side. Hayter hitched his chair nearer to the table and produced a pair of spectacles. "White paper of a cheap quality. Probably all taken from the same block. Have you the envelopes? Ah, thank you. The postmarks will give us the dates. Posted at Wainbridge on the 28th of August, the 8th of September, and the 16th of October." He wrote them down in his notebook before he began to read.

"Alan Copeland poisoned his wife. Is he going to get away with it? It's up to you Mr. Policeman.

"JUSTICE."

"The wicked shall flourish like a green bay tree. That stands for the fine gentleman at Strays with his new wife and his posh car. Police are no use.

"JUSTICE."

"Are you waiting for another murder before you make a move? He did it. Alan Copeland. He looks one thing and means another. Look in the grave.

"JUSTICE."

"Very interesting," said Hayter. "It reminds me of the Zoo."

The Superintendent stared. "Why?"

"The flicker of a snake's tongue. There's enough venom spilt here to furnish a whole nest of rattlers."

"I agree. Copeland must have rubbed somebody up the wrong way. The writer is obviously bursting with spite. But he wasn't lying. The woman was murdered, and if it had not been for these letters we should never have initiated the enquiry that led to his arrest."

"Words and letters cut out of newspapers and stuck on."

"That's very common with anonymous writers," said Ramsden.

"Is it? Yes, I daresay," said Hayter absently. "Could you lend me these?"

"I'm afraid we could hardly do that."

"Well, will you allow them to be photographed? I'd like exact facsimiles."

"I see no objection," said the Superintendent rather doubtfully. "One of my men is quite good at camera work. Are you in any hurry?"

"I'd like them as soon as possible."

"Very well. He'll be pleased to do it. He's quite an artist in his way. But I don't quite see what you're driving at, Mr. Hayter."

"It's just an idea. It may not lead to anything," said Hayter vaguely. "The envelopes are addressed by hand with printed characters. I suppose Mr. Justice thought the newspaper stunt might attract too much attention in the sorting office. I'd like photographs of them too, please."

"I don't see what the defence can gain by identifying the writer of these letters," said Ramsden. "It's somebody in the village naturally. When I started making enquiries I found the place a hotbed of gossip."

"They often are," said Hayter, rising to go. "Well, thank you very much. If I call in this evening will the prints be ready?"

"Yes. I'll put Henderson on to it at once. And I think you'll find he'll turn out copies that can hardly be distinguished from the originals."

The Superintendent shook hands, and at a sign from him Ramsden accompanied their visitor to the door.

When he had seen Hayter off the premises he returned to his chief. "What is he driving at, do you think, sir?"

"I don't know. But he's welcome to any odds and ends he can pick up here, Ramsden. We can afford to be generous with the case we have. Copeland's for it all right, whatever they may do."

II

Mr. Perry was at work in his study when his housekeeper brought in Hayter's card.

"I told him you was busy, but I can't get rid of him," she said resentfully.

"Oh dear, how very tiresome." The vicar's mind came back slowly and reluctantly from the fifth century. He had been very much harassed and distressed by recent events in his parish. The chapter dealing with the Arian heresy had suffered in consequence. He had found it unusually difficult to concentrate. "I suppose I shall have to see him," he said crossly.

The housekeeper went back to the hall where she had left Hayter. "You can go in," she said, "and I must get back to my ironing."

The vicar was standing before the fire filling his pipe from a bowl on the mantelpiece when Hayter entered. He eyed him coldly and did not invite him to sit down.

"I gather that your business is urgent, Mr.—ah—Hayter—"

"It is. I have been engaged by the firm of lawyers representing your niece's husband to assist in the preparation of his defence."

"Indeed. I suppose you refer to the unhappy man who is now awaiting his trial. You have been misinformed. The present Mrs. Copeland was a niece of my late wife's, not mine. And I have nothing to add to what I have already told the police."

Hayter, who in the course of his business had had some practice in ignoring snubs from people who did not want to answer questions, merely looked sympathetic. "You've been shocked and horrified. I quite understand. The illicit love affair. Very wrong, of course. But he's not to be tried for that, Mr. Perry. If you could dissociate that from the awful crime imputed to him—"

"That is impossible," said the vicar gravely. "The two go together. If you have come here to try to persuade me that he is innocent I am sorry. You are wasting your time and mine."

"You have not visited Strays since Mrs. Copeland died?"

"No. He called on me with his second wife when he returned here last spring. I made it clear that I disapproved of his having married again before the year of mourning was up—and of course I had no idea then that the marriage had actually taken place within a fortnight of poor Mabel Copeland's death, I have not seen either of them since. They gave up coming to church, and I am told they never set foot in the village."

"You don't see your way to giving your—Mrs. Copeland—your moral support now?"

"If you mean by publicly affirming my faith in her husband, certainly not. And I hardly see what else I can do. I was obliged to be present at the exhumation, and I have only just got over the chill I got as a result. This quiet and peaceful parish has gained a very unwelcome and undesirable publicity. Once and for all, Mr. Hayter, I am determined not to be involved in this most unsavoury affair."

"Well, I accept that, Mr. Perry," said Hayter good-humouredly.

He had noticed that the old man's hands were shaking. He did not feel disposed to blame him for shrinking from any contact with such harsh realities. His eyes rested for a moment on a pile of newspapers and reviews stacked on one of the chairs.

"I see you take the *Spectator*. How do you get your papers down here?"

"Ben Cattermole is our newsagent. He delivers them. He's rather slow, but he's sure, and it's a charity to employ him."

"Can he get weekly reviews and magazines too?"

"Oh yes, everything. He's very reliable. Sings in the choir. We make a point of employing him."

Mr. Perry had warmed up with the introduction of a more congenial topic. His tone as he wished Hayter good morning was almost cordial.

Hayter, who had hired a car from a Wainbridge garage, took a stroll round the churchyard before returning to it. He found Mabel Copeland's grave. It was marked by a red granite cross with her name and the date of her death on it. Mabel, the beloved wife of Alan Copeland. He wondered if Copeland had sanctioned that formula, or if he had given a general order to the stonemasons. The lumps of trodden clay round the mound betrayed the fact that the grave had been disturbed recently. He went slowly and thoughtfully back to his car. He was going to call now on the Bragges.

The manager of the quarry and his sister lived in an ugly little house near the entrance to the quarry and one of the ground floor rooms was used as an office. Miss Bragge answered Hayter's ring at the bell. She was a little elderly woman with a nervous, deprecating manner.

He introduced himself. "I understand that you and your brother are friends of the Copelands. I am helping to prepare his defence."

"Oh—I—will you come in?"

She led the way into a shabby but comfortable living-room. He noticed well-filled book shelves and, in the place of honour over the mantelpiece, a framed sketch in oils of a group of silver birches against a bank of white clouds. Hayter was apt to look at pictures. "That's a lovely thing," he said involuntarily. "What a feeling of space. It's like the wind on a hill top."

"Yes. Alan painted that this summer and gave it to us."

Hayter was taken by surprise. He had forgotten that Copeland was a painter.

"It has meant such a lot to him," said Miss Bragge, "being able to paint again. He hadn't for years. She was always keeping on about the expense of the materials, so he gave it up. She was cruel. Sometimes he couldn't contain himself, and he told us the things she said to him. It was incredible. Mind you, she wasn't so bad at first. It came on gradually."

"Why didn't he leave her?"

"He nearly did more than once, but she was quick to see when she'd overstepped the limit of his endurance, and then she made another kind of scene and begged his pardon. He couldn't forget that she'd saved his life at the beginning. She really did nurse him devotedly through that long illness he had when he was lodging with her and her mother."

"I take it that you are convinced of his innocence, Miss Bragge?"

She was silent for a moment, then she said in a low voice,

"Don't ask me that. He was in an impossible position. He hardly knew what he was doing."

"You didn't attend the police court proceedings, Miss Bragge?"

"No. We're both terrified of being called as witnesses for the Crown. You see, poor Alan used to let himself go when he came to us, and sometimes he used violent language. We didn't take it seriously, and I don't think anything would have happened if it had not been for Lydia. We saw the change in him after that Easter, though we didn't know the reason for it. He never so much as mentioned her name to us. Please don't think I'm blaming her. They couldn't help it, either of them. It was one of those—those overpowering attractions."

"You and your brother have been frequent visitors at Strays?"

"Ever since they came home. Yes. We never went there before. Mabel Copeland didn't approve of us. You see we're Rationalists and Pacifists, what people call cranks. It's a wonder really that my brother has been able to keep his job, but the men like him and respect him in spite of his opinions somehow. The owners made him promise that he wouldn't address meetings or parade his views, so we both keep very quiet."

Hayter reflected. He saw that the Bragges would be worse than useless to the defence. He could only hope they would not be called by the other side. A clever counsel would soon extract from Miss Bragge a most damaging account of Copeland's relations with his first wife. He realised that it would be dangerous to leave her convinced of his guilt.

"Look here, Miss Bragge," he said earnestly, "hasn't it occurred to you that this murder might have been committed by someone else? It's not like one of those cases where the victim is in bed and the poison can only have been administered by one of two or three people who have access to her. Anyone could have got into the kitchen at Strays. I haven't been on this case long, but it's been long enough to convince me that there's more in it than has yet come to light."

"Oh!" she said, "do you really think so? But who would do such a thing? Oh, I do hope you are right."

"Those are the lines we are working on," he said, "and we're hoping to spring a big surprise on the prosecution when the times comes. I see you take the *New Statesman*. Do you get your papers from that old chap in the village?"

"Ben Cattermole? Yes. One of his sons works at the quarry. I ought to thank you for coming, Mr. Hayter. You have cheered me up. I feel now that it was wrong of us to take it for granted that poor Alan—"

It was just four o'clock. There was still time for one more call before he went back to Wainbridge. He drove slowly on the outskirts of the village to avoid the straggling parties of children just out of school who scattered at his approach.

A light appeared in Miss Platt's sitting-room window as he drew up at the school gate. She answered his knock at the door promptly.

"It's the sleuth, I suppose?" she said before he could speak. "Please come in. You're just in time for a cup of tea."

"That's very good of you," he said as he followed her in. "But how did you know?"

She laughed. "My dear man, it's all over the village. You called at the vicarage. Mrs. Binns, the vicar's housekeeper, doesn't miss much. She probably listened at the door while you were having your heart to heart talk with Mr. Perry. She told the baker when he called, and now everybody knows. I suppose it doesn't matter? You don't seem to have attempted any disguise."

"It doesn't matter in the least," he said, though he was rather disconcerted. "I'm simply a humble gleaner hoping to pick up a few stray ears of corn that escaped the attention of the police."

"If I'd known you were coming," she said gaily, "I'd have cut some sandwiches. We must make do with cake and biscuits. What fun this is."

"It's very nice of you," he said, "to give me such a welcome."

He watched her curiously as she moved about the room, bringing the cake from the cupboard and bending to take the kettle from the hob. He found the short, thick-set figure and broad, sallow face of the schoolmistress definitely unattractive, and he was puzzled and slightly repelled by her high spirits. Perhaps she read his thoughts, for she glanced at him with an odd smile as she sat down to the tea table. "You think I'm hardhearted because we're all more or less involved in a tragedy? If you knew how dull my life is here. So dull that death is an agreeable change—and especially, of course, the death of a woman I hadn't much use for. And as for Alan—well, he's rather asked for it. Why did he have to marry the girl at once? This passion for respectability has spoilt more than one good murder. Why did he have to come back? Still, I hope he puts up a good fight."

"I think I can promise you he will do that," said Hayter blandly.

"Good. Do you take sugar? I hope that's strong enough."

"Did you attend the police court proceedings, Miss Platt?"

"No. Couldn't give the children a holiday unfortunately. Mrs. Simmons, at the cross road garage, did, though she hasn't been out of the house for four years. Very sporting of her. But there was a very full account in the *Wainbridge Echo*, and I read that. I'd love to go to the trial. You couldn't call me as a witness for the defence, I suppose?"

"What can you do for us in the way of evidence?"

"Not a thing." As she met his eyes her defiant smile became a grimace, her febrile gaiety flickered and died. "As a matter of fact," she said huskily, "I very seldom saw him. I used to like him when we were fellow students at Slades. I admired his talent, and he was always very decent to me. They weren't all of them."

For an instant she sat frowning, brooding over remembered slights. "When he came to lodge at Strays with old Mrs. Leach and her daughter he and I used to go sketching together. Then he fell ill and they took complete possession of him and never let go. I was furious with him for being such a fool. Mabel and I never hit it off. I wasn't asked to Strays. I didn't have to go to know what it was like. I may have some queer tastes, but even I drew the line at looking on while she crucified his pride." She pushed aside her cup and lit a cigarette.

"It will go against him that they didn't get on," said Hayter stolidly. His matter of fact tone steadied her, as he had hoped it would. There was something refreshingly normal about his florid, good-humoured face, his steady grey eyes and deliberate manner.

"You're not true to type," she said, "in novels private detectives are always either foreigners or a mass of affectations. You're more like an ordinary policeman in mufti. You haven't been lying to me?"

"I've never been in the English police force," he said. "I was in the Canadian Mounted Police for some years. I've been bodyguard to a Mexican president and to a film star. I've travelled with a circus. But I'm not so young as I was. This job suits me all right."

"Oh," she sighed, "how I envy you!"

He let that pass. He had accomplished his purpose. The tension had relaxed. "They tell me Strays has been transformed in the last few months," he said casually.

"Yes. Alan's carried out his ideas. The house was only a shell with frightful accretions. He's cleared all the mess away and laid down turf where the Leaches planted cabbages. Mabel belonged to the class that likes an aspidistra on a bamboo stand."

"I thought you said you never went there."

She laughed. "You haven't really caught me out. I've not been inside. For one thing I wasn't invited. And if I had been I don't think I should have accepted."

"How's that, Miss Platt?"

She looked at him, a glint of mockery in her small dark eyes.

"Perhaps, like the vicar and Miss Gort, I was shocked by his unseemly haste. Does it matter? I know about the exterior changes to Strays because I often ride up that way and back by Little Holme and Dancing Hill. The surfaces are fairly good and one doesn't meet much traffic."

"After school, eh, on summer evenings?"

"Exactly."

"I suppose," he said, "it is too much to hope that you were up that way the evening before Mrs. Copeland's death."

She sat very still for a moment, looking fixedly at the ash on her cigarette before she flicked it off. "As a matter of fact I was."

"Did you see anybody about the place?"

"I passed Irene Simmons coming up the lane. She called to me that she was going to get some eggs. That was just an excuse, of course, for a word with Alan and a chance to make goo goo eyes. You know what some flappers are. She was always hanging about the place."

"Did he encourage her?"

"I don't think so. But you never know with men. She's pretty in her way."

"Anyone else?"

"No. Why? What's the idea?"

"You didn't see Copeland himself?"

"No. He was out. I know that because the door of the shed he used as a garage was open and the car wasn't there."

"You could see that from the road as you rode by?"

"Yes. It faced the yard gate. It's not there now. It was one of the shabby outbuildings he pulled down this summer."

"I see. Thank you very much, Miss Platt."

"You know," she said as she went with him to the door, "I think the modern legal processes are very clumsy and stupid. It's a pity we can't go back to the ordeals by fire or water. Much more amusing for the onlookers. They say three old women were drowned in the pond down the village for bewitching the parson's pigs in the days of Matthew Hopkins. I wonder if Mrs. Simmons would sink or swim."

"I have not met her yet," said Hayter.

"Look out when you do. She hates Alan."

"That's interesting. Thanks."

He glanced back after he had settled himself in the driving seat and saw her shadow cross the sitting-room blind.

"A clever woman," he thought, "wasted here, and she knows it. Thwarted, frustrated, and without many scruples. Untrustworthy. But—does she know more than she has chosen to tell me?"

He called at the police station on his way back to the King's Head. The photographs were ready for him and, after dining in the coffee room he had a fire lit in his bedroom and spent a not unfruitful hour examining them with his magnifying glass and making notes of the results of his scrutiny. It was nearly ten and he was thinking of turning in for the night when the chamber maid came up to tell him he was wanted on the telephone.

He went down to the office where the telephone was situated. He recognised John Reid's voice at once. The call, late though it was, did not surprise him. He had seen that the young solicitor had the Copeland case very much on his mind.

"What have I been doing? Oh, just spade work. I'll come round now and report if you like. I didn't know if you'd care to be bothered out of office hours."

He went upstairs again to fetch the photographs and put on his overcoat, for the night had turned cold, with a blustering north-west wind and an occasional scud of rain. The market square was deserted at that hour, and but for the street lamps looked much as it must have done in the days of the second Charles, though modernity in the shape of Picture Palaces and chain stores had invaded the High Street. An elderly parlourmaid admitted Hayter, showed him into the dining-room, and left him, murmuring that she would tell Mr. Reid. Hayter glanced about him at the gleaming silver and the well polished mahogany, at the heavy portraits of dead and gone Reids and Pearmains, solid and seemly in their nankeen breeches and bluchers, flowered waistcoats and starched cravats. Not one of them, he thought, but would take the hanging of a client composedly, as a regrettable incident. John Reid, he fancied, was made of more brittle stuff.

Reid came in at that moment. "You'll have a glass of port? My father laid it down. My father and grandfather were both good judges of wine. I'm afraid I'm not. I hope you didn't mind my ringing you up? I was so anxious to know if you'd made any progress."

Hayter sipped his port appreciatively and set down his glass.

"I've made one discovery, Mr. Reid. The police have been getting anonymous letters, signed Justice, and urging them to arrest Copeland for the murder of his wife. They ignored them for a time, and finally took action. Unfortunately they only kept the last three letters, and they don't seem to have attached much importance to them. They wouldn't part with them, but they had them photographed for me. Here they are if you'd like to see them."

He placed them side by side on the long dining-room table.

Reid studied them in silence.

"What do you make of this?" he asked at last.

"I can't say at present," said Hayter cautiously, "but it seems to me that we must make every effort to trace these to their source."

"Will that be possible? I have heard of outbreaks of anonymous letter writing. It always seems to take months to trap the writers. And this method of cutting words and letters out of newspapers makes it useless to call in handwriting experts."

"The addresses on the envelopes are written by hand."

"Yes, but in print."

"We shall see," said Hayter.

"But if you do find out who wrote them how will that help Copeland? It will only show that he was suspected by someone in the village who takes this rather unpleasant method of setting the machinery of the law in motion."

"Perhaps. But I'd like to know a little more about the writer's motives. Consider the wording of these letters. There's a cold malignity about them that chills one's blood. Don't you feel it?"

"Yes. By God, Hayter, you're right."

"The more I study this case the more strongly I feel that there is something more at the back of it than the police will admit. On the surface it's obvious enough. A man murders his tiresome, nagging wife because he wants to marry another woman. One thinks at once of Crippen, and there have been others still more recent. I'll be quite frank with you, Mr. Reid. When we discussed the matter yesterday in your office I hadn't really a doubt that your client was guilty. Even after seeing him—but now—"

Reid leaned forward, his eyes bright. "You've changed your mind? I'm glad of that. I believe in him, too, in spite of everything. We must save him somehow, Hayter. As it is I lie awake, worrying."

"We'll do our best," said Hayter. "You'll brief the best counsel available, sir?"

"Of course. I've been considering that. I thought either Ellis Churchman or Hugh Barrymore."

Hayter nodded. "Either of those. There isn't much time. He's committed for the next Assizes."

"Have you anything definite, any clue?"

"We have these," said Hayter. He was replacing the photographs in the large manila envelope in which he kept them. "I have a theory, Mr. Reid, but I'd rather not say more until I've got some evidence to support it. I'm going to carry on with my frontal attack, calling on people in the village and asking what may seem to be fool questions, but I've got assistants who will be working on other lines. Good night, sir."

CHAPTER XIV
WHAT IRENE SAW

As HAYTER drove up the lane the four petrol pumps of the cross roads filling station were silhouetted against the sky line. In the cold grey light of a cheerless November morning these gaunt robots of a mechanical age had a sinister effect, as if their round, blank faces might at any moment become threatening. There was nobody about when Hayter pulled up, but the dingy lace of the Nottingham curtains that screened the sitting-room window was parted for an inch or two as he got out of his hired car and went into the shop. A pretty, painted girl with a mob of black curls was lounging behind the counter reading a novelette. He asked for a packet of cigarettes. She pushed them towards him and resumed her reading.

"Miss Simmons, isn't it?" he asked as he counted out six coppers.

"That's right. What about it?"

"I'm collecting evidence for Mr. Copeland's defence. I thought you might be able to help us."

"Me? I don't know anything."

"There may be some detail which to you seems unimportant," he said. "Mrs. Copeland never bought anything at the door and she was rather brusque in her manner with the people who came round trying to sell brushes and letter pads and so on. We have a theory that this crime may have been committed by a hawker. Can you remember seeing anybody of that sort near Strays that evening? You'd gone up, hadn't you, to get eggs?"

He saw her moisten her lips. "I—"

They were interrupted by a raucous voice calling from the room behind the shop. "Rene, who's that you're talking to?"

For once in her life Irene welcomed her mother's interference.

"All right, Mum, I'm coming. Excuse me a minute," she said and left the shop, closing the communicating door after her. But Hayter was too quick for her. He went round behind the counter and followed her into the sitting-room before she could speak a word. She moved aside with a little gasp of dismay as he entered just behind her, and left him to face the black, mountainous figure of Mrs. Simmons on the sofa.

"Who's this, Rene?"

Hayter answered for himself. "My name is Hayter, ma'am. I'm employed by Mr. Copeland's lawyers to collect what evidence I can for the defence."

She looked him up and down with smiling insolence. "Fancy that. A big, hefty chap like you. You're more my notion of an auctioneer, or maybe a pig breeder."

He smiled back at her good-humouredly. "We can't all look like Sherlock Holmes. I'm just a plain, straightforward fellow. I don't profess to work any miracles. I just ask straight questions and hope for straight answers. I was telling Miss Simmons here we're inclined to think the murder was committed by a hawker."

"A hawker?" she said. "Rubbish. The police are mostly fools, but they're right for once. They've got the man who did it, and he'll get what's coming to him one of these days round about nine o'clock."

Hayter glanced at the girl and saw how her natural colour had faded, leaving hard, red patches of rouge on her cheekbones.

"That's still a matter of opinion," he said blandly.

"I was just asking your daughter if she had happened to notice anyone of that sort, a tramp or a pedlar, near Strays that evening. You'd gone up to the farm to get some eggs, hadn't you, Miss Simmons?"

The old woman did not move her head, but the beady eyes in the vast yellowish expanse of flesh that was her face turned towards the girl.

"Well," she said in her wheezy voice, "did you, or didn't you?"

They had to wait for Irene's answer. "I went for eggs, but Alan was out. I—I believe I did see a shabby-looking man at the farther end of the lane. He—he was sitting in the ditch. I didn't notice him particularly and I haven't thought of him since."

"Thank you, Miss Simmons. That supports our theory, you see. Would you be prepared to swear that you saw this person?"

She moistened her lips again. "I—yes."

"You little liar," said her mother contemptuously. "You won't save him that way, my girl, nor any other. I wonder you haven't more respect for yourself."

Irene had remained standing, gripping the back of a chair.

"I did see a man," she persisted.

"And if you did? You aren't going to kid me that any tramp would walk into the kitchen at Strays and poison any food that was about? Mabel Leach was poisoned right enough, and the man that did it was the one who had every chance to do it, the chap she'd married and kept on a string till he was sick to death of it all. And now, Mr. What-is-it, you may have nothing in the world to do but talk, but my girl's got to get the dinner."

Hayter was not sorry to get out of that airless, over-heated room. He had gained something, though he was inclined to agree with Mrs. Simmons that Irene had been lying. It was at any rate evident that she and her mother did not take the same view of the Copeland case. Was Mrs. Simmons the writer of the Justice letters? From the way she talked of Copeland it seemed likely. But could she have prepared and posted them without the knowledge of her daughter and her nephew? He meant to have a word with Ern before he drove on. Meanwhile Irene had followed him into the shop.

"You mustn't mind what Mum says," she said rather breathlessly. "She don't mean half of it."

"That's all right, Miss Simmons," he said easily. "I quite understand."

He had decided not to put her on her guard by letting her know that he had heard through Copeland that his wife had gone out to the gate to speak to her as she loitered in the lane. He had suggested that a hawker, driven away with hard words, had crept back and revenged himself. It could have been done. The tin of weedkiller stood on the shelf in the open garage not ten yards from the kitchen door. The tray with the cocoa ready mixed in the saucepan stood on the kitchen table by the open window. Yes, it might even have been done without entering the house. And the motive he had suggested would operate in the case of Irene. The dead woman was a nagger, accustomed to say whatever she liked to her silent husband. In her desire to wound this girl she might have gone too far. If Irene was the actual culprit her lie was accounted for. She would want to save Alan if she could do so without risking her own safety.

But how did Mrs. Simmons fit into that theory? Hayter did not make the mistake of under-rating Irene's mother. To him, as to so many others who had been drawn, always more or less reluctantly, into the stuffy little parlour behind the shop, its occupant had loomed in her terrifying immobility like a spider in her web. He had seen that her daughter was afraid of her, and he did not wonder at it. But he did not believe that Mrs. Simmons was an unnatural mother. She loved the girl in her fashion and was proud of her showy good looks. Probably her unconcealed hatred of Alan Copeland was founded on the fact that when he might have had Irene he had chosen elsewhere. Would she, knowing, or at least suspecting, what her daughter had done, feel an evil satisfaction in seeing Copeland pay the price? Would she, with that knowledge or that suspicion, despise the unhappy girl for her half-hearted attempt to invent some evidence in his favour? From what he had seen of her Hayter thought he could answer both those questions in the affirmative.

"It's just talk," said Irene anxiously. "Nobody can stop her. But about that man, I did see him really and truly, and I'll swear to it if you want me to when the time comes."

He thanked her and promised he would let her know later on if her evidence would be required. Actually he meant to advise Reid against taking her story too seriously.

"I want a fill up. Will there be anybody in the yard?"

"Yes. My cousin Ern is somewhere about. Ring the bell if you don't see him."

But Ern was in the yard when Hayter went back to his car, and he came forward at once. He was an ordinary-looking young man with small, blue eyes set rather too close together and a well greased squiff of mouse-coloured hair. The kind of ordinary person who may sometimes do extraordinary things. Hayter asked for a gallon of Shell. Ern said nothing but he glanced sharply at his customer. No doubt he had seen him go into the shop half an hour before and was wondering what had detained him so long.

"I suppose Mr. Copeland got his petrol from you," said Hayter as he counted over his change.

"He used to when he had the bone shaker the old girl got for him," said Ern. "He hasn't lately. In fact I haven't set eyes on him since he came back to Strays last Spring. Are you the police? How many times do they want to hear the same thing?"

"I'm not the police. I'm trying to get evidence for the defence."

"Then you've come to the wrong shop," said Ern bluntly.

"I gather that your aunt disliked him."

"You've said it." Ern had picked up the rag with which he had been polishing the battered chassis of a fourth or fifth rate car marked with chalk on the windscreen £8 A BARGAIN, and rubbed away a smear on the door.

"And so do you?"

"I haven't said so," said Ern with unexpected force, and Hayter discovered that though his eyes were small they were not shifty. "If you want to know I'm sorry all this has come out. Hanging him won't bring her back—and who wants her back anyway? She gave him hell. He had to take her out for drives in that old tin can she bought for him, and they stopped here more than once for gas. The way she spoke to him, well, it made my blood boil. I wouldn't speak to a dog like that. I couldn't say other in the box, so don't you go calling me as a witness."

"Thanks for the hint," said Hayter pleasantly. "You're right. It wouldn't help Copeland much, I'm afraid. Good-bye."

II

As he walked up the well-scrubbed brick path a large ginger cat emerged from the gooseberry bushes and accompanied Hayter to the door, where it walked round him, rubbing against his ankles, purring, and arching its back while he rang the bell and waited. The whirring of a sewing machine in the room on the right ceased, and Miss Emily Gort came to the door. The cat abandoned him instantly and vanished down the passage. He was aware, at the same time, of the mingled odours of boiled fish and furniture polish. Miss Gort waited for him to declare his business. She was dressed as usual in grey, and the tip of her long nose was faintly pink. He had noticed that no smoke was coming from either of the chimneys. Evidently Miss Gort economised in firing.

He introduced himself, adding that he was trying to collect evidence for the defence in the Copeland case. "You may think it rather strange of me to call on you, the chief witness for the prosecution, but I'm told that you were the late Mrs. Copeland's best friend. It might help us to know a little more of her early life."

"I met her first when I came to live with my aunt," said Emily Gort. "Strays had been left them by a cousin, who bought the place cheap a year or two before the War. She and her mother took paying guests in the summer months."

"All this must have been a great shock to you Miss Gort."

"Yes, indeed."

"When did you first begin to suspect that there had been foul play?"

"Me? I never thought of any such thing. It seemed to me that Mr. Copeland had shown a want of nice feeling in not waiting a full twelvemonth before he married again, and I knew poor Mabel wouldn't like the way he was throwing her money about over those alterations at Strays. It always annoyed her the way he went on about the beauty of its proportions and the chimneys and corbels and all that. She said he thought more of the house than he did of her, and she wasn't so far out, was she."

"I wonder if I might come inside?" suggested Hayter. "I'm afraid you may catch a chill standing in this wind."

She yielded ungraciously, and led the way into I her dreary little sitting-room. Streams of black material billowed over the table from the sewing-machine, and some trick of light gave the mass of dark stuff an uncanny resemblance to the formidable old woman he had left an hour earlier.

"You're making a dress for Mrs. Simmons?"

"Yes. You've been to see her then?" She sat down and the ginger cat, who had followed them into the room, jumped on her lap.

"There's my beautiful. Have you been out catching the dicky birds then? You're too clever for them aren't you, my precious," she murmured as she stroked the soft fur.

Hayter, who disliked cats, looked on stolidly.

"Do you think Copeland committed this crime, Miss Gort?"

"Oh dear," she said plaintively. "I can't bear to talk about it. It's so sad, isn't it. The vicar feels it terribly, though he's wonderfully brave. He regards it as a slur on him, though, as one is thankful to remember, she is not his niece. No real relation. She invited herself to the vicarage and he was too kind-hearted to tell her it was inconvenient. If only he had been firm she wouldn't have come to Teene and this wouldn't have happened."

"You hold the present Mrs. Copeland responsible?"

"Of course. Lydia Hale as she was then. I must say she deceived us all. Very quiet and nothing to look at. Just ordinary. I should never have said she was fast, and I am rather quick in that way, I can generally tell by instinct. And yet she managed in those few days to lead him astray. As I said the other day to Miss Platt, our schoolmistress, you wouldn't have thought it, but she must have been as bold as brass."

"You blame her then?"

"In cases like this," said Miss Gort firmly, "it's always the woman's fault. And yet she'll get off scot free."

He recalled the dumb misery of Lydia Copeland's small pale face.

"Well, hardly that," he said. "She's not exactly enjoying herself, Miss Gort."

She smiled her tight smile at his masculine ignorance. "She's in the public eye, an object of interest. There have been bits about her in the papers. The young wife of the accused man. I wouldn't waste any pity on her."

"Well, you may be right," said Hayter, "especially as we quite expect to get him off."

She looked startled. "You don't mean that? Everyone says the police have an overwhelmingly strong case, and that the verdict is a foregone conclusion."

"Ah, but we've got evidence of a rough-looking man seen lurking in the neighbourhood of Strays. Mrs. Copeland was the sort of person who might speak pretty sharply to a beggar at the door wasn't she? I'm telling you this, Miss Gort, because I know that as a friend of the family you would be very glad if the husband's innocence could be proved."

"You can't prove that he didn't carry on with Miss Hale," she said quickly.

"No. We've got to admit that."

"And one sin leads to another. It's what we teach the children in Sunday school, and it's the truth. We mustn't palter with the truth, Mr. Hayter. Who saw this tramp you speak of?"

"Miss Simmons."

"Oh, Irene." Miss Gort looked down her nose. "That's rather disappointing. I'm afraid you won't find her a very reliable witness."

"Oh we shan't rely on her entirely," said Hayter.

"I rather hoped you might have seen him yourself. You left Strays about six o'clock that evening, didn't you?"

"Yes. But there was nobody in the lane."

She lifted the cat off her lap.

"Is that all you wanted to ask me, Mr. Hayter? I'm rather busy. I promised to give Mrs. Simmons a fitting to-morrow."

"Then I won't take up any more of your time," he said readily.

He allowed himself to be shepherded to the door. It was closed after him so promptly that he was still uttering some comment on the weather when he found himself alone. He thought he heard the whirring of the sewing machine as he went down the path to the gate. He shivered involuntarily. He had been chilled to the bone as he sat in that icy room with his feet in the ground draught that blew under the door. It was past twelve o'clock, and he wanted a few words with Miss Platt. He drove down the hill to the village and called at the school house. Miss Platt came to the door before he rang.

"I saw you coming," she said. "I can't ask you to lunch. I don't have anything but fruit and coffee in the middle of the day."

"I haven't come to cadge, merely to ask one more question."

"Go ahead."

"You told me that when you cycled up the lane past Strays on the evening of the tenth of June you saw Irene Simmons lingering about near the gate."

"Yes."

"Did you see a rough-looking man who might have been a tramp?"

Gertrude Platt stood with her feet well apart and her hands thrust into the pockets of her green cardigan, staring at him. Her strong, plain face betrayed nothing of what she felt.

"Are you asking me to commit perjury for Alan?"

"Certainly not. I simply thought you might be able to corroborate the evidence of Miss Simmons."

"Irene? You've seen her then—and her mother?"

"I called on them this morning."

"And she told you about a tramp who might have walked into the kitchen at Strays and shoved arsenic into Mabel Copeland's cocoa? It's the sort of yarn a kid like Irene might invent, but you don't suppose it would go down with a jury, do you?"

"Stranger things have happened, Miss Platt. But they might not accept her unsupported word."

"They certainly won't," she said. "She's the kind to go to pieces in the witness-box. Can't you see she invented this because she's still in love with Alan and can't bear to think that in a few weeks they'll be burying him with quick-lime. That mother of hers has been driving her too hard. I thought she'd crack before long."

He looked at her curiously. "You're still enjoying the drama, Miss Platt?"

"Why not? I missed my trip to Spain this summer. I thought there was nothing to beat bull fighting, but this is pretty good." She glanced at her wrist watch. "Sorry, Mr. Hayter, but the children will be coming back to school and I haven't made my coffee."

"It wouldn't take you long to answer my question. Just a plain yes or no," he said rather dryly.

She smiled maliciously. "Which question? You must make allowances for our slow country wits."

"I don't have to do that in your case, Miss Platt. I asked if you saw a man in or near the lane leading to Strays when you rode that way the evening Mrs. Copeland died?"

"Oh, that? No, I didn't. I saw Irene. Nobody else. Sorry I have to push you off now. The evenings are my best time for a chat. Come in any time you want to discuss the case. I get quite a kick out of it."

"Thanks," he said, "but my investigations are at an end for the present at any rate. I shall probably be returning to London."

CHAPTER XV
WHAT THE WORLD SAID

I

THE placid course of Mrs. Reid's existence was unaltered. After breakfast she saw the cook, and later she went down the High Street and did some shopping, and changed her novel at the library where that nice girl could always be relied on to warn one against the books that left a nasty taste in the mouth and recommend something light. Some-times a friend, old Miss Tranter or Canon Chapman's sister, called in the afternoon and stayed for a cup of tea. On Tuesdays and Fridays people came in after dinner for bridge, and on Thursdays and Mondays she and John played at the Chapmans' and at Dene House. John was not as fond of cards as she was, but he had always come without any apparent reluctance. The first time he excused himself from accompanying her she had not taken him seriously.

"Nonsense, Johnnie. You're working too hard. It will do you good to come out."

"Sorry, Mother. I've got some office work left over from this afternoon. I'll just run through that and then smoke a pipe and have a read and come round to fetch you at eleven."

"I'm perfectly capable of walking home alone. It's not more than a hundred yards. I can't think why you can't get your work done in office hours. Your father always did. He made a rule about it." John Reid controlled his irritation. He knew the discussion would go on until his mother was satisfied. There was no point in prolonging it. "I had to run over to Strays this afternoon to see Mrs. Copeland. There were several things to be settled and it took longer than I expected."

Mrs. Reid sighed. "Oh dear, how I wish you weren't mixed up in that horrid case. I shall be thankful when it's over."

"Yes."

"You're letting it get on your nerves. I'm sure that can't be right."

So she had left him and gone by herself to Dene House where the Bramshotts had had to ring up several people before they found someone to take John's place, and she had played with less than her usual calm efficiency, and once at least had let her partner down. And this had happened several times, so that now her friends rang up earlier in the day to ask if John would be coming, which was tiresome. And he looked far from well, too. Very white and drawn. Several people had noticed it. He was not strong, of course. It worried her so that she forgot to send her order for bulbs, and sometimes sitting in her charming drawing-room after lunch she would find that she had turned several pages of her novel without any idea of what she had been reading. And she thought of the man and the woman whom she had never seen with something very like hatred.

John had never been quite the same to her since that evening when she had refused to let him bring that Mrs. Copeland to the house. The change was hard to define. He still kissed her when he came into the dining-room to find her at the breakfast table, and at night when she folded her embroidery after a glance at the clock and wished him good night; he was still pleasantly deferential—but he did not talk to her now, he made conversation. In her heart she knew well enough what his verdict was, the harsh verdict of youth. She had been proved lacking in the cardinal gift of charity. He was wrong, of course, quite wrong, and some time, perhaps when it was too late, he would realise how unjust he had been to her. One afternoon when Miss Tranter, coming in unexpectedly, found her crying, she was impelled to confide in her old friend.

"How could I ask that girl here? You've read about her. She may not have known that he was a murderer, but it's obvious that she led him on. It's so strange to me that John should even think of such a thing—but when I declined I could see he was upset, and now he goes over there two or three times a week. Oh, there's no harm in it, Lavinia, please don't think that. John isn't like that. It's just that she's one of those grasping women—"

Little Miss Tranter was deeply interested. She nodded her grey head sagely. "Predatory," she murmured.

"Yes. And John wouldn't be able to see through her. He has such high ideals of women. That's rather my fault perhaps. He's been brought up too much at home. But you know how delicate he was as a boy. We always had to be careful with him."

"He's not looking well now."

"I know. He's taking this wretched affair so much to heart. My poor boy—"

Her fears were not altogether unfounded. At that very moment John was kneeling on the hearthrug in the panelled room at Strays, making toast, while Lydia was taking the cake he had brought with him out of its box and secretly wishing it had been plainer. He had been to the prison and had brought her a message from Alan.

"He thinks those servants you had are still with you. I ought to try and find you someone else. I don't like to think of you all alone here, especially at night," said Reid anxiously.

"Please let him go on thinking it," she said. "I don't want him to worry. And I don't want anyone else at present. I'm managing very well."

He looked unconvinced. "Do you get enough to eat?"

"The baker and the milkman call every day, and I drive over to Trentholme to post my letters and buy groceries and get the tank of the car filled up at a garage there where nobody knows who I am. At least, they haven't found out yet. I simply can't face the Teene people, and thanks to the car I don't have to. I'm so glad Alan taught me to drive this summer."

He had finished the toast and gone back to his seat where he sat watching her.

"I hope you won't hesitate to tell me if there is any single thing I can do to make things easier for you," he said earnestly. "I want you to think of me as a friend. We are friends, aren't we?"

"You've helped me a lot already," she said simply. She was desperately lonely and unhappy. She would have been more than human if she had not caught eagerly at the one proffered hand, if she had not been soothed and comforted by his open adoration. "You're so kind." Her tired eyes filled with tears.

"Don't," he said. "Hayter—he rang me up this morning. He's quite hopeful. He's coming down to-morrow to talk things over, and the day after that I'm to see Sir Hugh Barrymore at his chambers. Everything possible is being done."

He tried hard to speak confidently, but actually he had very little hope of Copeland's acquittal. His own faith in his client's innocence of the crime imputed to him did not rest on any very sure foundation. There were times when he believed, and others when his mind admitted a cold crawling doubt. He felt that in Copeland's place he, too, might have yielded to a dreadful impulse. There was, however, one point in Copeland's favour of which he reminded himself when he heard other people taking his guilt for granted. It seemed, to say the least of it, unlikely that a man so highly strung would have voluntarily returned to the scene of his crime. He meant to suggest to Barrymore that that point should be made. The ground the defence must cover would be full of pitfalls. So many damaging admissions must be made.

"The frightful thing," said Lydia, breaking a long silence, "the frightful thing is that if—if they don't believe him at the trial it will be my fault. I mean they'll say he wanted to get rid of Mabel to marry me because I—because I was going to have a baby. I want to tell you one thing, Mr. Reid. He didn't know about that until he came up to Town after the funeral. I'd kept it to myself because I didn't want to worry him and make him more unhappy than he was already. Do you think it would help if I said that in the witness-box? I—I can make myself do it if it's any use."

Slowly, without looking at her, he shook his head. "I'm afraid not. I'll put it to Barrymore, if you like, but I think he'll agree with me that you had better not be called to give evidence. Or, at any rate, not on those lines."

She sighed. "My aunt who brought me up would have said that a girl who had a—a love affair with a married man was wicked. I can imagine her saying to me, 'You see what it's led to. The wages of sin.'"

"Yes, but there are degrees in sin," said Reid. "In your case there were extenuating circumstances. I can't bear to see you worrying like this. Please, please don't."

Lydia blew her nose and said in a small voice, "Please forgive me. I—somehow I can say things to you that I couldn't to anyone else."

Reid's thin face flushed with pleasure. He wanted to say that whatever happened in the next few weeks he would be there, eager to serve her, but he dared not trust himself to speak just then. He had already stayed longer than he had meant to. He reached for a parcel he had brought with him.

"I've got some new novels here for you. Reading will take your mind off. I'll look in again on—let me see—Thursday. No, don't come to the door. I can let myself out."

He resisted the temptation to lift the hand she gave him to his lips. She might think him silly. He was nervously anxious not to make a fool of himself. These unaccustomed emotional disturbances were having a very unsettling effect on him. He even drove with less than his usual caution, and was nearly involved in a collision with a lorry on his way home to Wainbridge.

He would have gone straight to his room, but his mother had heard him come in and she called to him as he was about to pass the drawing-room door.

"John, is that you, dear?"

Mrs. Reid was wearing the blue lace dress that contrasted so well with her beautiful white hair, and her evening bag lay with her fur coat on one of the chairs. She looked at her son reproachfully as he came in.

"John—I did remind you that we were dining with the Strutts."

"Oh Lord," he said dismayed. "I forgot—"

The Strutts were old clients of the firm. He could not afford to offend them. And this was a formal affair. The old man had married again and they were invited to meet the second wife. He cast a harried glance at the clock. "I'll be ready in five minutes. I've left the car outside. Go down and sit in it."

He was out of the room before she could answer. She put on her coat and picked up her bag. Her hands were trembling. She greatly disliked unpunctuality and being rushed and flurried. John knew that. He was always so steady, so reliable. Now, out at all hours and coming in looking so feverish and hollow-eyed. "It's that woman," she thought, "as if she hadn't done harm enough."

He did not keep her long waiting.

"You didn't have time for a bath," she said.

"No, I'm sorry, Mother."

"It's a good thing you aren't one of those men who have to shave twice a day."

"Oh, for God's sake," he burst out, "don't nag."

She was shocked into silence, and he was equally horrified, but he could not bring himself to apologise. Fortunately it was not far to the Strutts' house and they arrived two minutes before the appointed hour. Reid hardly knew if he was relieved or not to find that there were only four other guests, Dr. Mackintosh and his wife, Mr. Blane, the manager of the local branch of the Southern United Bank, and a Miss Claudia Gill, a sophisticated young woman with scarlet finger-nails and a good deal of bare back, who turned out to be a cousin of the new Mrs. Strutt. Reid, who had taken Mrs. Mackintosh in to dinner, finding that she really wanted to talk to the doctor about her little Betty's tonsils, was obliged to give his attention to Miss Gill, who had declined soup and lighted a cigarette.

"Is this your first visit to Wainbridge, Miss Gill?"

"Yes. Bunny's promised to have me down again in a couple of weeks. For the trial, you know. She tells me you're defending the murderer. I suppose you see quite a lot of him. How perfectly marvellous for you. I do envy you."

"Please don't call him the murderer, Miss Gill."

"Why not?"

"The matter is *sub judice*," he said stiffly.

She gazed at him as though he had been some queer and amusing insect. "You're not peeved? Not really? You don't have to keep on pretending all the time surely? I mean, here among friends it's simply silly when everybody knows he did it."

He reddened. "I'm sorry to contradict a lady, but everybody's knowledge is at fault. I am personally convinced of my client's innocence. And now do you mind if we talk about something else?"

He was painfully aware that the murmur of conversation around the table had ceased. Young Mrs. Strutt leaned forward to address him.

"Oh, don't disappoint us, Mr. Reid. I've heard he's terribly attractive. We've been hoping for some juicy details."

Her husband intervened. "My dear, Mr. Reid can't possibly talk to us about his clients. It simply isn't done."

There was an awkward pause, and then, Mrs. Mackintosh, usually timid and self-effacing, earned Reid's undying gratitude by hurriedly asking him a perfectly futile question with an appearance of earnestness which enabled him to devote his attention to her until they went into the drawing-room to play bridge.

But his troubles were not yet over, for his partner was Claudia Gill, and his play was not improved by her unconcealed anger and contempt at his occasional mistakes. Her rudeness had one unintended effect. Mrs. Reid, playing at the other table, overheard enough to be roused in her son's defence. She said nothing, but during the drive home she glanced more than once, with anxious affection, at his drawn face, and when he had garaged the car and gone upstairs he found her waiting for him on the landing.

"Johnnie, my dear, dear boy. Don't mind that wretched girl. You were quite right, and she was abominable. Don't let this come between us, darling. I shall always be on your side."

"Thank you, Mother." He kissed her with more warmth than he had shown for weeks.

Meanwhile Claudia Gill, mixing a last cocktail after the guests were gone, commented freely to young Mrs. Strutt.

"Gosh, what a crowd. And that rabbity little man, who tried to snub me. Can you imagine him defending a killer? It's too funny. Like a mouse sticking up for a tiger. And how he dare to sit down to bridge when he can't play. Once or twice I felt like throwing the cards I held at him."

Later still, Strutt spoke to his wife. "I wish you'd give your cousin a hint about her behaviour this evening. I don't care to have my guests insulted. Reid's appearance is not impressive, but I've known him since he was a boy and I have a great respect for him. He's quiet and unassuming, but he's no fool. One can see that he feels his heavy responsibility in this case. A man's life may depend on his efforts. He deserves sympathy, not ridicule."

Betty Strutt yawned and resumed the creaming of her face.

"Yes, dear, but I'm too sleepy for sermons."

Her husband suppressed a sigh. After all, if sixty marries twenty-five—

John Reid, after some hesitation, chose the *Browning Letters* from the books on his bedside table and turned on his reading lamp. Alan Copeland, lying awake in his cell, watched the light over his door and thought of a hill top, dark and silent under the stars. At Strays, in the living-room, the air grew colder as the last spark died out of the grey ashes on the hearth. Lydia, worn out, had fallen asleep where she had lain down on the white bear skin before the fire, with a cushion under her head, and she, too, was dreaming of Gey Rounds, but at noon, with the gorse in flower and larks singing overhead.

CHAPTER XVI
DEVIL'S BAIT

Miss Bragge had written to Lydia, a long, rambling letter full of apologies. She had to consider her brother's position, and it was not as if she could really do anything to help. Lydia answered, assuring her that she quite understood and was not at all offended. In fact, though she liked little Miss Bragge and her big, silent slow moving brother well enough, she did not miss them at all. She shrank from meeting people who, however well meaning, would be almost certain to say the wrong thing. Her mind was still like a flayed surface, agonisingly sensitive to the lightest touch. The trap Ramsden had set for her, Alan's arrest, the police court proceedings, were always presenting themselves and having to be pushed away out of sight. Continuous physical exercise was the only way of doing this. Lydia did most of Bessie Welland's work and some of Tom's. She moved from room to room in the empty house, scrubbing, rubbing, polishing the linenfold panelling of which Alan had been so proud, wearing out her body, trying to concentrate her attention wholly on her aching arms and wrists. She left a slate outside the back door for the milkman and the baker, and drove over to Trentholme to buy groceries.

The postman brought letters from complete strangers, some jeering and insulting, others urging her to repent of her sins. There were offers, too, from Press agents. After the second day she took to looking through them to make sure there was no letter from Reid, and burned all the others unread.

Sometimes the front door bell rang. She always went upstairs then and peeped out of a window from which the visitor could be seen. Reid had warned her that some newspapers would be sending representatives who would try to extract a few words from her about the case. He had been quite frank about it.

"Barrymore isn't cheap, Mrs. Copeland. Law costs may easily cripple the estate. It's my job as your lawyer to see that they don't." In his earnestness he had been about to add that Alan was particularly anxious that she should be left comfortably provided for, but he stopped himself in time. "If we get a really good offer for an article or a series of articles later on I shall advise you to accept it, but meanwhile the less they can get out of you the better."

And so, unless the visitor was Reid himself, Lydia went back to her polishing while the bell rang and rang again until the would-be interviewer grew tired of waiting and went away. Once the caller was a woman. Lydia, looking down from the window at the sturdy figure in the rough tweed coat and black beret recognised Gertrude Platt, and moved away on tiptoe. What could Gertrude Platt want to say to her? She was frightened without knowing why, and she trembled as she sat on the end of her bed for what seemed a long time listening for the sound of retreating footsteps and the clang of the iron gate.

Reid drove over the morning after the Strutts' dinner party. Sir Hugh Barrymore had been studying his brief and wanted to talk over the case with the prisoner's solicitor. He had rung up to say that he had an hour free that afternoon if Reid could come to his chambers in the Temple, and he had added that he would like to see Mrs. Copeland.

"I hope you feel equal to it," said Reid anxiously.

"Of course, I won't keep you waiting."

They caught a fast up train at Trentholme Junction and Reid secured an empty first-class compartment. Lydia sat, ignoring the papers he had bought for her, gazing out of the window at the wintry fields and leaden sky. Reid, facing her, tried hard to compose his mind. What sort of a man was Barrymore? It was said that though he spared no pains when his interest was aroused he had been known to give a perfunctory and disappointing performance when his client's case had failed to appeal to his dramatic sense. Carver had wanted Reid to brief Churchman, who was not so brilliant but more reliable. "If Barrymore lets us down I'll never forgive myself." thought Reid.

The waterlogged meadows had given place to suburban back gardens. An acrid yellow fog blurred the outlines of the maze of mean streets. They had lunch in the station restaurant. Reid forced himself to eat, but Lydia soon pushed her plate away.

"I'm sorry, I can't—"

They went to the Temple by the underground, Reid, who seldom came up to London, asking his way more often than he need and fumbling over his change at the ticket office. "Oh dear, the gates have closed. But there's plenty of time."

On the escalator he held Lydia's arm to steady her.

"Careful, my dear." His voice shook slightly, but she did not notice it. She was grateful to him, for she had lost the habit of getting about in London and felt dazed and bewildered by the jostling crowd. Sir Hugh had asked them to come at three and Big Ben was striking the hour as they climbed his stairs.

A clerk took them directly to his room.

"Mrs. Copeland and Mr. Reid, sir."

Barrymore shook hands with them both. "Good of you to be so punctual. I'm very rushed just now, unfortunately." His quick dark eyes noted the country lawyer's drab insignificance and his obvious nervousness, and lingered on Lydia's small pale face framed by her close fitting black hat and the high furred collar of her coat. *"Fons et origo,"* he thought, "they don't often get the chance to sink a thousand ships, but one man—in this case perhaps two—if her solicitor isn't in love with her I'm no judge."

He was a big man himself, rather handsome in a florid fashion and with a deceptive air of good humour which was apt to mislead witnesses under cross-examination. He had the tact which is the crowning gift of the successful advocate who has not only to browbeat opponents but to defer to the Bench and to feel his way with that always more or less unknown quantity, a British jury.

"You must not be afraid of me," he said to Lydia with a smile. "Won't you loosen your coat? It's warm in here."

He waited until they were both seated before he laid his hand on the papers lying on his desk.

"I gather that you think the defence should be a suggestion that the late Mrs. Copeland was poisoned by a hawker who, resenting being driven from the door, and happening to notice the tin of weed killer on the shelf in the garage, came back and put some into the saucepan of cocoa. It's far fetched, you know. How much of it can we prove?"

Reid answered. "Mrs. Copeland was a methodical housekeeper. She always mixed the cocoa for her supper after washing up the tea things, and left it on the table under the kitchen window. It could easily be got at by anyone coming to the back door."

"Who is our witness for that?"

"Her husband."

"That's no good. I mean—we must have corroboration."

"Miss Gort would know that," said Lydia. "She was often there for tea."

Barrymore gave her an approving glance. "The principal witness for the prosecution. Excellent." He made a note. "And the weed killer?"

"The daily woman remembers seeing it on the shelf in the garage."

"Good. We can prove the relative positions of the weed killer and the saucepan. Yes. The hawker now. A rotten job trying to sell stuff nobody wants to hard-faced women at back doors. A man might get very warped and embittered. Lots of them are ex-soldiers. Head wounds, shell-shock. The means to do ill deeds makes ill deeds done. It's a possibility. And there was actually such a man seen near the house about that time?"

Reid cleared his throat. "A girl, Irene Simmons, says she was coming to the farm for eggs and that she saw a man whom she took to be a tramp sitting in the ditch."

Barrymore was flicking over the pages of the typewritten document before him. "I've got Hayter's notes here. Irene Simmons, aged about seventeen, goes about with men. Her mother owns petrol station at the cross-roads, ex-barmaid grown monstrously fat. The girl was chasing Copeland before his wife's death, and the indications are that she is still in love with him. On the other hand the old woman doesn't trouble to hide her virulent hatred of him, and may very well have been the writer of the anonymous letters to the police."

Lydia looked up. "What letters?"

"I have copies of them here. Hayter seems to attach a good deal of importance to them," said Barrymore thoughtfully. "I'm afraid he is mistaken in imagining that he will help our case by discovering who wrote them. And yet there are one or two sentences that suggest a closer acquaintance with the facts than is compatible with innocence. We'll come back to the letters presently. Are we basing our defence on the tramp story? What became of him? Did anyone else see him? Has any attempt been made to find him?"

"After a lapse of eighteen months—" began Reid.

"I know. It's pretty hopeless to get anything definite. We'll do the best we can with him, but a good deal will depend on the impression this girl Irene makes in the witness-box if this story depends entirely on her. You know this young woman, Mrs. Copeland? What do you think of her?"

Lydia hesitated. "I don't want to be unfair. She doesn't bother to be nice to other women, and I haven't seen her to speak to since I stayed with my uncle at the vicarage before—before all this happened. Her mother asked me to tea. Her mother is a horrible old creature. I don't think she would stick at murder if it suited her. Bessie Welland told me she knows a lot about herbal remedies, and that she sells stuff to the villagers. It may be harmless enough but they have to go there at night and be very secret about it."

"That's interesting," said Barrymore. "There may be something in it. She probably thought Copeland would marry her daughter if he was free. Who's Bessie Welland?"

"She and her husband worked for us."

"Oh, of course. That's worth following up, isn't it, Mr. Reid?"

"Certainly, Sir Hugh."

"By her own admission Irene was up at the farm. The schoolmistress rode up the lane on her bicycle between five and six and saw her waiting about near the farm gate. Copeland says that when he came in about seven his wife told him that she had noticed the girl hanging around and that she had gone out to her and told her to be off. She complained that Irene had answered back and been insolent. Suppose that after Mrs. Copeland had gone into the house Irene slipped round to the back door—"

"Do you suggest that the mother and daughter were in it together?" Lydia answered. "The old woman might have prepared the girl's mind—I mean corrupted her. I don't think she'd tell her to do it in so many words. She's very subtle, I think. She's like a great bloated black spider, silent and motionless in the centre of her web. I've only seen her once, but she terrified me then. I've never forgotten her. I haven't liked to feel that she was living little more than a mile from Strays.

Irene and the nephew who works for her have to do what she tells them."

"Dear me," said Barrymore. "I'd like to meet her. I've got Hayter's notes here, but I want him to supplement them. I rang him up this morning and he's coming round. And meanwhile I have some dry legal business to talk over with Mr. Reid. Perhaps you wouldn't mind waiting in the next room, Mrs. Copeland? I'll tell my secretary to get you some tea."

When the two men were alone he turned to Reid. "I had to see her before I could decide if any evidence of hers would help the prisoner. My advice is to keep her right away from the court."

Reid's thin face flushed. "Does that mean that you aren't favourably impressed?" he said stiffly.

"Certainly not. On the contrary. You'll forgive me if I speak plainly. I gather that she's a friend of yours as well as a client."

"I—yes—I think I may say she honours me with her friendship. I have the greatest respect—"

"Quite. I realise that. I've been greatly struck with her myself. She's hardly even pretty in the accepted sense, but she's got the indefinable quality called charm. Is Copeland still in love with her?"

"He is absolutely devoted to her, and she to him."

Barrymore got up and walked about the room, standing a moment to stare out at the fog. "Just so. The overwhelming motive. The carping, nagging, ageing wife—and that girl in the next room. We must not give the jury the chance to see the devil's bait." He swung round as the door opened. "Here's Hayter, I think." He greeted the private enquiry agent cordially, indicated a chair and held out his cigarette case.

"I take it, Hayter, that you agree with Mr. Reid that our best defence is the suggestion that one or more people besides Copeland had motives and the opportunity to get rid of Mabel Copeland?"

Hayter drew at his cigarette. "I thought that before I knew it was true," he said.

"You haven't changed your mind?"

"No, no. I mean that it was obvious strategy, even if there had been nothing in it. When I went down to Wainbridge I took it for granted that Copeland was guilty. Look at the case for the Crown, Sir Hugh. I'm doing my best—you'll do yours—but if we face the facts we've got to admit it's pretty black. But I've been talking to people and watching their reactions and poking here and there, and I'm now convinced that there's a good deal more in this case than meets the eye. I've no proofs as yet—perhaps I never shall have—but if you ask me there are three people in that village who wouldn't stick at murder."

"You mean—"

Hayter thumbed his note book. "The schoolmistress. Name, Gertrude Platt. Aged about forty. Thwarted spinster. Clever and ruthless. Parades the fact that she's getting a kick out of the murder. Was a fellow student of Copeland's at the Slade school fifteen years ago and probably in love with him. Casual inspection of her sitting-room revealed somewhat doubtful taste in art and literature. Picture of dead horse in place of honours is definitely revolting. Admits that she rode up the lane past Strays between five and six the evening Mabel Copeland was taken ill and that she saw Irene Simmons. Denies seeing any tramp or hawker.

"She'd have done it if she wanted to without turning a hair. But the motive isn't very evident. There's absolutely no evidence that she had maintained her interest in Copeland. They seem never to have met except by accident, and then as casual acquaintances. Irene Simmons, on the other hand, was always going up to Strays to buy eggs and lying in wait for him. She was barely sixteen at the time and girls of that age can be very reckless. I'm not sure that the open way in which she chased him isn't in her favour. Mrs. Copeland caught her that evening lingering by the yard gate, and seems to have told her what she thought of her. One can imagine the girl, lashed by the older woman's tongue, waiting until she had gone into the house and then, before her fury had time to cool, taking the tin of weed-killer from the garage and shaking some of its contents into the saucepan by the open window. She could do it and be back in the lane within two minutes."

Barrymore nodded. "And she's the only person who saw the tramp?"

"Yes. As a matter of fact I more or less suggested the possibility that a travelling pedlar had done the job, and she jumped at it."

"H'm. And who is your third suspect?"

"The girl's mother. It's natural, I suppose, that she should have an exaggerated opinion of her daughter's charms. She seems to have expected him to marry her when he was free. From what I heard in the village young Irene has ridden pillion on a good many motorcycles. Copeland's a gentleman, and he would have been a good match for her. The old woman must have counted on it, and she can't contain her spite."

Reid leaned forward. "Mrs. Copeland was just telling us that Mrs. Simmons does a furtive trade in herbal remedies."

"That doesn't surprise me. It's a good point though. Her father had a small herbalist's shop in Plymouth. He hadn't a good name, and it was closed by the police. But she couldn't have done this job on her own. Strays is over a mile from the cross roads and old Mother Simmons weighs a good eighteen stone. She made her nephew take her over to Wainbridge for the police court proceedings and had a whale of a time there, going to the pictures afterwards and having drinks at the King's Head, but everyone agrees that she hadn't been outside her house for four years, and that she can only shuffle from room to room. She may have supplied her girl with the poison, but I don't believe it. That girl might have done it in a rage, but not in cold blood."

"If the old woman couldn't have done it and wasn't in it with the girl what's the use of the point we were going to make of the secret trade in herbal remedies?" asked Barrymore.

"That's the trouble in this case," said Hayter. "Directly you get below the surface there are too many clues. It's a good point, as I said, if we could get over the physical impossibility of getting her from the garage at the cross roads to Strays and back again."

"What about the nephew?"

"He's sweet on his cousin, and she may end by marrying him if she can't get anyone better. I heard that in the village. Yes, he had a motive, the motive of jealousy. He must have known of Irene's infatuation for Copeland. He's a quiet, reserved sort of chap. A dark horse. His aunt may have egged him on to do it. It's just the sort of thing she'd enjoy doing," said Hayter.

Barrymore smiled. "You don't seem to like the ingenious Mrs. Simmons. She's not popular with Mrs. Copeland either. It comes to this, doesn't it? You think she committed the murder, though you've no proof and don't really expect to find any?"

Hayter was silent for a moment, "I can't even say that," he said at last. "I'm not satisfied, very far from it. I've got three of my staff at work. I've a feeling that we've got to go back some way to get a line on the culprit. When we know who wrote the Justice letters—"

"You haven't found that out yet?"

"No. But I shall. You've got the copies I sent you of the photographs supplied me by the Wainbridge police, Sir Hugh?"

"Yes. Nasty stuff," said Barrymore distastefully. "Hell has no fury like a woman scorned, Sir Hugh."

"A woman, eh? I expect you're right. That icy insistence on getting the poor devil under lock and key, and having him hanged by the neck until he's dead. Whether you find the writer or not the letters will be useful in getting sympathy for Copeland. I shall certainly make all possible use of them, but for the present I don't see how we can decide on even the general lines of the defence. Its a pity. Time's getting very short."

"I'm sorry, Sir Hugh."

"I don't really mind," said the great man genially. "I'm pretty good at improvising. Ring me up at once if you get on to anything. If I'm not here my clerk will pass it on." He looked at his watch, and Reid and Hayter took the hint and got to their feet.

"There's just one thing," said Hayter, turning to the lawyer. "Mrs. Copeland came up to Town with you to-day?"

"Yes. Sir Hugh wanted to see her. She's in the next room."

"I don't think she ought to go on living quite alone at Strays, sir."

"She dreads meeting people."

"Very natural. But couldn't you find her rooms at Wainbridge under another name just for the time being? or a nursing home? She looked as if she needed a rest when I saw her."

"Yes, yes, I know. I have tried, but she won't listen."

"I'd try again if I were you," said Hayter, and his pleasant florid face was unusually grave. "Look at those letters. There's a warped mind at the back of all this."

Reid's jaw dropped. "Good God! You don't suppose—"

His perturbation was so extreme that Hayter felt sorry for him.

"I had to warn you," he said. "She may be in some danger."

CHAPTER XVII
BEFORE THE TRIAL

"I'VE mended them very carefully," said Miss Gort as she laid the pile of choirboys' cassocks down on a chair in the vicar's study. "You can hardly see the darns. What I say is do a thing thoroughly if you do it at all. And I would have taken them into the vestry if the door hadn't been locked. I suppose you forgot I would be coming down."

The vicar, who disliked being interrupted, made an effort to suppress his impatience. Why couldn't Emily Gort, an admirable woman and most useful in the parish, have left the mended cassocks with his housekeeper instead of practically forcing her way in when she must have known he was at work? What a pity she was so fond of that peculiarly unbecoming shade of slate grey, he thought vaguely, eyeing the costume that had been Miss Gort's best for the last four years.

Miss Gort, unaware of these strictures, was still talking. "I can't take the girls' Bible class or the choir-practice this week. I hope it won't make too great an upset, but it can't be helped."

"Oh!" He fumbled with his spectacles. "How's that, Miss Gort?"

If Miss Gort found him irritating she concealed her feelings very well. "The trial, Mr. Perry, the trial. It opens to-morrow and

I have had a notice to attend. My expenses will be paid, so I shall stay in Wainbridge until it is over."

"Oh dear," he said. "The—but how can it concern you?"

"I was poor Mabel Copeland's best friend, and I suppose they depend on me to throw some light on her unhappy married life, Mr. Perry. I had to give evidence, you know, at the police court. It was inexpressibly painful."

"Yes, yes, no doubt," he said with the air of one who does not wish to hear. "I didn't know. I didn't read the accounts. I have put the whole miserable affair as far as possible out of my mind."

"Ah!" murmured Miss Gort, "you have a mind above such things. Wonderful."

Mr. Perry made no answer, but looked wistfully at the pile of manuscript on his writing table. He was revising his twentieth chapter. And this time Miss Gort took the hint.

The shouts of the children just out of school and dispersing to their homes were dying away in the distance as she shut the vicarage gate after her. She was walking up the lane when Gertrude Platt came up behind her and, dismounting from her bicycle, joined her.

"Has Mrs. Simmons asked you to tea?"

"Yes."

"I thought she might have. It ought to be rather amusing."

"Hardly that," said Miss Gort repressively. "But one does not like to refuse. She leads such a restricted life, poor soul. It cheers her up to see a friendly face."

"Well," said Miss Platt grimly, "you can put it that way. And there's no use denying they provide a square meal. Plum cake and three kinds of jam." She glanced maliciously at her companion.

"Where shall you stay in Wainbridge?"

"With a friend. Most fortunately she has a nice bed sitting-room which she lets."

"How dull. Why didn't you book a room at the Crown? The Assizes bring a lot of people. It will be quite an experience."

"Ah, you are trying to shock me," said Miss Gort with her tight smile. "You are not as heartless as you try to pretend, Gertrude.

We all know that there was a time when you were fond of that unfortunate man. Long ago, but a woman never really forgets."

It was a very long time, years in fact, since Gertrude Platt had blushed, but she blushed now. A dark tide rose to the roots of her coarse black hair and slowly receded, leaving her pale with fury.

"I'm sorry to have to contradict you," she said sharply, "but I've never cared twopence for Alan in the way you mean. I was sorry for him letting himself be entrapped into marriage by Mabel Leach. I expect the trial to be very good fun, but it's not because I'm looking forward to gloating over the prisoner in the dock. There'll be worse places than the dock while he is being tried, Emily."

The tip of Miss Gort's long nose, already pink with the raw cold of the December evening was twitching now with agitation.

"Oh dear. I didn't mean to upset you. You—you do say such things. What do you mean by worse places?"

Gertrude Platt had regained her self-control. "Never mind," she said brusquely. "You annoyed me. I daresay it was sheer tactlessness. We'll say no more about it. We must not let old Ma Simmons see we've been quarrelling."

They had passed the four gaudy robots of the filling station and had caught a glimpse of Ern Simmons tinkering with a car in the shabby garage. There was a light in the window of the tiny shop, but there was nobody behind the counter. The rich, husky contralto of Mrs. Simmons summoned them to the inner room.

"I thought it was you two," she wheezed as they entered.

"Make the tea, Rene. Take off your coats and draw your chairs up to the table. We've opened another jar of the quince for you, Emily. I know it's your favourite. How's that cat of yours going to get on while you're away?"

"Poor Bobo. I've been quite worried about that," said Miss Gort in her thin little voice. "He's not used to fending for himself. I'm taking him with me in a basket. My friend I'm staying with doesn't mind. She had a lovely tabby who might have objected, but he was run over last summer. Quite providential in a way."

Mrs. Simmons chuckled. "You old maids with your pussies," she said comfortably, "you don't know what real trouble is."

Miss Gort opened her mouth and shut it again without saying anything. She had never before been alluded to in her hearing as an old maid. It gave her an unpleasant shock.

Irene had sat down at the head of the table and was pouring out the tea. Her sullen face was heavily made up, and she was wearing a new green jumper. Gertrude Platt looked at her curiously.

"Well, how do you feel, Irene?"

She answered without raising her eyes. "Rotten."

"Rene's got the wind up," said her mother. "Seems to think they may make harm of her having been up to Strays the evening Mabel got her packet. I said to her, 'If it comes to that so was Gertrude Platt. She went by on her bike,' I said, 'and I daresay she rode back the same way after you'd gone home.' So there's not a pin to choose between you."

"As a matter of fact," said Gertrude coolly, "I rode home by way of Little Holme and Dancing Hill."

"So you say—but can you prove it?"

"Hardly, after all this time."

"There you are. But neither you nor my Rene have any call to worry. They've got Copeland and they aren't likely to let him go. A bird in the hand—" The old woman shook with her silent laughter as her swollen fingers crumbled the rich dark cake on her plate.

"You think the police case is impregnable?" said Miss Platt with the air of one who seeks for information.

Mrs. Simmons looked at her rather hard. "Don't you?"

"Well, that man who was sent here to ask questions, not for the police, for the defence, he looked more like a farmer than a private detective, but I don't think he was quite a fool."

"There wasn't anything for him to find out," said Irene. Her voice sounded oddly brittle.

"Quite right," said Miss Gort. "Of course there wasn't."

Miss Platt declined a slice of cake. "I'm afraid it's rather heavy for me. Well, if you both say so—but you haven't convinced me. I believe we're going to get a big surprise."

Mrs. Simmons' vast face darkened. "They won't get him off? You don't mean that?"

"I wouldn't be altogether surprised."

"He did it, and he ought to swing for it if there's law in England," said the old woman violently.

"Dear me," said Miss Gort, "this is very unsettling. But I'm afraid you're mistaken. The evidence of his guilt is, I fear, of a kind no jury could overlook."

"That remains to be seen," said Gertrude Platt. "By the way, what's become of the second Mrs. Copeland? I heard a rumour that Strays is shut up."

"That's right," said the old woman with relish. "Old Badger, from the farm, told me. He was supplying her with milk up to the beginning of last week. Mr. Reid, of Wainbridge, had been calling most days, and he took her off in his car, but where to Badger couldn't say."

"Reid, Reid and Pearmain were Mabel's solicitors," said Miss Gort. "They attended to all her business affairs."

"She left you something, didn't she, Emily?"

"Five pounds," said Miss Gort succinctly, "and a few bits of jewellery valued for probate at twenty-five shillings and the workbasket that belonged to old Mrs. Leach."

"Well, I never!" Mrs. Simmons sat back on her sofa. "Give me one of my lozenges, Rene, before you clear the table. That wasn't much considering you were her best friend and all. A work basket, too. Coals to Newcastle."

"I daresay it cost a good bit when it was new," said Miss Gort. "It's lined with quilted satin and it's got gilt fittings. Mabel always used it. I remember it standing on the table that last afternoon. She was marking some handkerchiefs."

"That was when she told you about the row they had, and that he said he wished she was dead?" said Mrs. Simmons greedily.

"Well, she said, 'I believe you wish I was dead' and he didn't deny it."

"That's not evidence unless you overheard it," said Gertrude Platt. "Third hand stuff. Tittle tattle."

Miss Gort reddened. "That may be," she said with dignity. "I didn't come out with it until I was asked. I couldn't help knowing how things were going from bad to worse in that house. You may be enjoying all this. You've got some queer tastes if I'm not mistaken. But you mustn't judge others by yourself."

"That's right," said Mrs. Simmons, "you stand up for yourself, dear. You mustn't think of going yet."

Miss Gort was drawing on her grey fabric gloves. "I'm afraid I must. Are you going to the trial, Mrs. Simmons?"

The old woman licked her lips. "I wouldn't miss seeing handsome Alan in the dock for anything. Ern's driving Irene over, and he may as well take me. We've got a car in stock that'll stand my weight though it's not much to look at. Rene's got to go since she was fool enough to pretend she remembered a tramp." Irene had cleared the table and gone into the shop. They could see her through the rather grimy lace curtain that covered the glazed upper half of the door between, leaning over the counter reading a novelette. Or was she actually reading? Gertrude Platt had been watching her for some time and she had not yet turned a page.

"I told her," said her mother. "A nice mess they'll make of her in the witness-box. You can't get round these lawyer chaps by making goo goo eyes at them. But everybody's let off too easy nowadays. I asked Ern why some of the young fellows hadn't been up to Strays to break the windows."

Gertrude smiled. She liked to see people keeping true to her conception of them. "You're a good hater, Mrs. Simmons. What did Ern say?"

Mrs. Simmons snorted her contempt. "He said 'What for?' That's what comes of all this education. Stuff them with botany and what not and take all the spirit out of them."

"It isn't that," explained Gertrude. "There's no feeling against Alan in the village. I don't want to hurt your feelings, Emily, you and Mabel were friends, we know, but no one else could stick her. Well—" She pushed back her chair. "I must be getting home. I've a pile of exercises to correct. Good night."

Left to themselves Miss Gort and Mrs. Simmons looked at one another. Emily Gort licked her lips. "Gertrude's very strange sometimes," she complained. "What did she mean about a surprise at the trial?"

The old woman picked a stray crumb of cake off her lap and chewed it reflectively. "I've been wondering about that, too."

CHAPTER XVIII
THE FIRST DAY

I

THE jury had been sworn in. Alan Copeland looked at them curiously. There were two women, one stout and motherly and one small and anxious-looking. There was an elderly man with a grey Van Dyke beard, whose face was vaguely familiar to him. The rest had the air of prosperous tradesmen, with no marked characteristics. It was difficult to realise that if these strangers willed it he was going to die at the end of a rope.

Lydia, he knew, was not in court. That good fellow Reid had got her into a nursing home in Wainbridge. He had told Reid that she must not be called to give evidence. "Keep her out of this," he said. And Reid agreed. He had seen his defending counsel for the first time the night before in the bleak waiting-room at the prison where such interviews were held. He looked towards him now and his heart sank a little lower. Barrymore's smile, meant to be reassuring, failed of its effect.

Kynaston, the counsel for the Crown, was on his feet, and had begun to outline the case for the prosecution. The Court was silent and attentive. "My Lord, ladies and gentlemen of the jury, the human drama to be unfolded here has no element of novelty. The facts are, I believe, incontestable. In the month of March, a year and a half ago, the prisoner was living with his wife at a house called Strays, on the outskirts of the village of Teene. The wife was in comfortable circumstances. The house was her property and she had an income of about eight hundred a year. Her husband, who was some twelve or fifteen years her junior, was entirely dependant on her. He had tried poultry farming, but the profits were negligible and his wife was expecting him to repay the loan she had made him to buy his stock. It is, one may suppose, a galling thing to be dependant on a wife's bounty, and Mrs. Copeland did nothing to ease the situation. One is reluctant to speak ill of the dead, and especially of one whose faults were so terribly expiated by the manner of her end, but it is generally agreed that her manner to her husband was overbearing. About this time a young girl spent a fortnight in the village. She was a niece of the vicar, and as such she received an invitation to spend an evening at Strays. This was the only meeting between Mrs. Copeland and the person who was destined to supplant her. She did not see the girl again, but Alan Copeland did, and before she returned to her employment in London they were lovers. Three months later, during the night of the 10th of June Mrs. Copeland was very ill. Her husband was alone in the house with her. He fetched a doctor, but she died a few minutes after his arrival. Mrs. Copeland was a hearty eater and had been suffering from digestive troubles due to her love of rich food and aversion to taking exercise. The doctor had no suspicion of foul play and her death was attributed to the breaking of a duodenal ulcer.

"Mrs. Copeland had made a will leaving everything she possessed to her husband. He left the neighbourhood the day after the funeral. He was going to travel about for a few months, but would eventually return to Strays. He did return the following March. He had married again, and his second wife was the girl whom he had first met a year earlier.

"They were not very warmly received. It was generally felt that he might have waited a year before he married again. But it was only some months later that the police, acting on information received, made certain routine enquiries, and learned that the prisoner in the dock had actually married his second wife at a London registrar's office, within two weeks of the first wife's funeral, and that a child had been born the following December at Leamington. These facts certainly strengthened the suspicions that were being entertained as to the nature of the first Mrs. Copeland's illness. They made it obvious that her death must have been greatly desired by two people. An exhumation order was obtained and certain organs were removed for analysis by Sir Ronald Beaton for the Home Office. He will be called presently and he will tell you that over two grains of arsenic, a fatal dose, were found in this unhappy woman's body. A warrant was applied for, and the husband of the deceased was arrested and charged with murder and committed to the Assizes, after he had pleaded not guilty and reserved his defence. I have not yet touched on an important point. How and when was the poison administered to the victim? The late Mrs. Copeland was in the habit of taking a cup of cocoa with some biscuits or sandwiches for her supper, preparing a tray when she washed up the tea things, and leaving it on a table in the kitchen. The cocoa powder and a spoonful of castor sugar were left in the cup, and eventually they would be mixed with boiling milk. On the evening in question there was ample time and opportunity for the accused to add to the ingredients. There was a tin of weed killer on the shelf in the garage into which he had run his car. They had been quarrelling before he went out and he himself admits that the quarrel was resumed on his return. Whether the crime was planned in advance or whether he yielded to an overmastering impulse may never be known. It does not affect the issue. I shall now call Sergeant Ramsden."

Alan shifted wearily from one foot to the other. He himself admitted it was all quite true, true every word of it except for one thing. He was not Mabel's murderer. He had wished her dead often enough. That was almost as bad, perhaps. He did not listen to the police evidence. He had heard it all before when he was brought before the local Bench. Barrymore's cross-examination of this first witness was very brief.

"Did Copeland apply for a passport after his wife's death?"

"Not to my knowledge."

"He made no attempt to leave the country. In fact he returned to the scene of his alleged crime. When you arrested him did he show any surprise?"

"Yes. He was in his studio working on a picture. I told him the charge against him and gave him the usual warning that anything he said might be used against him."

"What did he say?"

"He said 'It's impossible.' And then 'My God! Have you actually dug her up?'"

"Just so. Thank you, Sergeant."

Sir Ronald Beaton followed. He had been present at the exhumation and had taken away certain organs for analysis. The result of that had put the cause of death beyond doubt. On the other hand the assumption of the local practitioner was very natural under the circumstances. Arsenic was one of the constituent parts of the brand of week-killer of which a tin had, he understood, been kept in the garage.

Barrymore rose to cross-examine. "Just one point, Sir Ronald. Do you agree with the prosecution that the poison must have been administered in the cocoa which was drunk by the deceased at about eight o'clock?"

Sir James hesitated. "I would not go as far as that. She became seriously ill, I understand, round about midnight. It must have been taken during the evening, but it is impossible to fix the time exactly."

"It might have been before eight?"

"Yes."

"Some time before? Two or even three hours?"

"That is not so likely, but I can't rule it out."

"Might a poison like arsenic taken through the mouth only begin to take effect after the drinking of some hot liquid, in itself innocuous?"

"There have been such cases."

The judge intervened. "Could you make that point a little clearer Sir Hugh, for the benefit of the jury, and also for mine?"

"Certainly, my Lord. We have heard a great deal about this cup of cocoa. I am suggesting that the cocoa may have been quite harmless and that the arsenic may have been taken previously. The eminent authority in the witness-box agrees that this is possible. You do agree, do you not, Sir Ronald?" Sir Ronald bowed. "I should put it rather differently. A hundred to one chance—but it exists."

"Thank you, Sir Ronald."

The next witness to be called was Mrs. Povey, Lydia's former landlady.

"Do you recognise the prisoner, Mrs. Povey?"

"Yes. He came to my house to see Miss Hale when she was lodging with me. They were married, at the registrar's office a week later. I was one of the witnesses. It seemed a bit sudden, but she was out of a job and he seemed to be comfortably off, and it was plain to see he was over head and ears in love with her."

Sir Hugh Barrymore stood up. "My Lord, it may save time and the calling of superfluous witnesses if I inform the Court now that we do not dispute the facts alleged by the prosecution from the time Alan Copeland left Strays after his wife's death."

"I see," said the judge. "That may enable you to expedite matters, Mr. Kynaston."

"Thank you, my Lord. It will. Do you recall the date of Miss Hale's marriage, Mrs. Povey?"

"I do. It was the 22nd of June, not last summer, the summer before."

"Exactly twelve days after the death of his first wife. That will be all, thank you, Mrs. Povey, unless my learned friend has any questions to ask."

"Oh—none," said Sir Hugh sweetly.

"Then I will call Miss Emily Gort."

Miss Gort did not keep the Court waiting. She stepped briskly into the witness-box and drew off her grey fabric glove to grasp the shabby black bound book proffered by the usher.

"I swear by Almighty God—"

Her pale and rather prominent eyes wandered round the Court room and rested for an instant on the prisoner standing in the dock. She was wearing the slate grey coat and skirt in which the congregation of Teene church were accustomed to see her playing the organ on Sundays and a new grey felt hat which she had bought the day before at Logan's in the High Street for 4s. 11½d.

Her long nose, faintly pink at the tip, was twitching slightly.

"You were on friendly terms with the late Mrs. Copeland?"

"More than that. I was her greatest friend. She gave me her confidence."

"You knew that her married life was unhappy?"

"I knew that. Yes."

"Now I want you to recall in some detail the last occasion—no, the last but one—on which you saw her alive. You had spent the afternoon at Strays and remained to tea?"

"Yes. It was a regular thing. Mabel seldom went out beyond the garden, and she got dull. She liked me to drop in two or three times a week."

"Her health was poor. Did she seem worse than usual?"

"Oh no. About the same. But she was upset about something Mr. Copeland had said to her before he went out."

"Did she tell you what it was?"

"Yes. They were having words, and she said to him 'I daresay you wish I was dead.' And he said, 'I won't contradict you.' I tried to persuade her that he hadn't meant it. She cheered up after a while. I offered to wash up after tea, but she said she'd do it after I'd gone and that it would do her no harm to move about a bit. I knew that was true, she sat about too much, so I didn't press it. She gave me some cakes to take home with me. She often did that. There was always a lot of food in the pantry at Strays, and she knew I hadn't much time for cooking. I left between half past five and six. I had a dress to finish for a customer. I read a chapter as I always do and went to bed soon after nine. I had been asleep a long time when I was awakened by a knocking on my door. I lit a candle and looked at my watch. It was ten minutes past two. I opened my window and called out to know who it was. It was Mr. Copeland.

"He said Mabel was very ill and would I go along to Strays and do what I could for her while he went to fetch the doctor. I said I would, of course, and he went off. I dressed as quickly as I could and hurried off. She was past speech when I got there, but she squeezed my hand. I tried to make her comfortable, and I tried to give her brandy but she couldn't swallow."

"You had no suspicion at the time as to the nature of her illness?"

"No. I was very sorry for Mr. Copeland. He seemed very upset. He was a long time fetching the doctor, but he told me afterwards his car was out of order."

"Did Mrs. Copeland leave you anything in her will?"

"Yes. She left me five pounds and the work-basket that had belonged to her mother."

"You had not expected a larger legacy?"

"Oh, no. I hadn't thought about it. She was often poorly, but I never dreamed of her dying."

"Just so. Now, Miss Gort, I want you to tell us about a curious discovery you made a few days ago."

"I had put the workbasket in my spare room and had not really looked at it at all. One evening about a week ago I had nothing else to do so I brought it down and turned out the contents. It's one of those old-fashioned things with a quilted satin lining and loops under the lid to hold scissors and bodkins and a fancy thimble and a kind of false bottom that can be lifted out. I moved it and saw a bit of paper underneath. It was written on in pencil and I recognised Mabel's hand. It said, '*I feel awful. I believe Alan's poisoned me.*' I—well, it gave me a shock."

"Naturally, Miss Gort. It would. And you felt it your duty to hand it over to the police."

"I felt I must," said Miss Gort regretfully.

"You have no personal a feeling, no animosity towards the accused?"

"None whatever. I was often sorry for him. Mabel was my friend, but I was not blind to her faults. She was sharp-tongued, and she was close with her money. She liked to feel that people were in her power. He had a lot to put up with. I always tried to smooth things over, and I think he knew it. I told her more than once that she tried him too high, but she only laughed."

"Did you at any time suspect that she might have good cause to be jealous of him?"

"No. I've heard since that he was seen coming away from Gey Rounds with Miss Hale, and that he had his arm round her, but I knew nothing of it at the time. That was at Easter. Mabel died in June."

"Just so. That will be all, Miss Gort."

She was turning to leave the witness-box when Barrymore rose to his feet and addressed her with his deceptive air of languor.

"Just a moment, Miss Gort, if you don't mind," he said blandly.

"My learned friend has rather taken the wind out of my sails. He has asked several of the questions I wanted to put to you. You did not suspect foul play at the time of Mrs. Copeland's death?"

"No."

"When did you first begin to suspect it?"

"I never did. I didn't like his marrying less than a year after poor Mabel had gone, but I was willing to be neighbourly. But I soon saw I shouldn't be able to get on with the second Mrs. Copeland so I gave up trying. I wasn't the only one."

"So that his arrest was a complete surprise, a bolt from the blue?"

"Well, a plain clothes policeman had called a few days before and asked a lot of questions. I told him what I have said here. He told me not to mention his visit to anyone. Naturally after that I began to wonder."

"You were horrified?"

"Wouldn't you be? Mabel was my best friend."

"You were horrified. Bewildered too, I daresay?"

"I think I was."

Mr. Kynaston was observing his learned friend with frowning attention. Sir Hugh Barrymore was smiling faintly, purring like a cat that has got at the cream. The judge, too, was alert.

"Now, about this workbasket and the scrap of paper you found in it with the scrawled message. *'I feel awful. I believe Alan's poisoned me.'* You are convinced that it is in the dead woman's writing?"

"Oh yes. I recognised it at once. It was a frightful shock."

"It must have been. It suggests, doesn't it, that on that last evening of her life, after drinking the fatal cup of cocoa, when she was beginning to feel the effects of the poison, the dreadful truth dawned on her and she wrote this message—this terrible accusation—and hid it in the workbasket which she had left to you in her will, hoping that sooner or later you would find it."

Emily Gort was beginning to look tired. There were blotches of red on her face and her thin neck, and her light lashes flickered.

"I suppose so," she said wearily.

"But if she didn't write it? What does that suggest?"

"She must have. Who else could it be? I'm sure I wish I hadn't found it. I've had a lot to go through."

"We appreciate that, Miss Gort," said the silky voice. "I have no other questions to ask."

The judge looked at the clock. "We will adjourn until half past two."

The warder standing by the dock tapped his prisoner on the shoulder. Alan had been watching Miss Gort with fascinated attention. She had not looked again in his direction. He turned obediently and went down the stairs.

Mrs. Simmons, having obtained a good place in the small space allotted to the public at the back of the court room, had meant to stay in it and eat the food she had brought with her, but orders had been given that the court was to be entirely cleared, and she was obliged to go out, grumbling loudly, with the rest of the crowd that had waited doggedly in the streaming rain for admission.

"The stuff's hardly fit to eat, anyway," she said after looking into the bag in which sausage rolls, jam puffs, and pears had been ground into an inextricable mass during the struggle to enter the building. "Come on, Ern, I'll treat you to a posh lunch at the Crown."

"You wouldn't get served there," said her nephew. "That's where the nobs get their grub. P'raps we can find some quiet place farther down the street."

"If we could get hold of Rene—"

"She's all right. There's a room set apart for the witnesses, and any refreshments they like to ask for are sent in."

Mrs. Simmons' progress rather resembled that of a steam roller. People made way for her when they saw her coming. She was wearing her fur coat and purple toque, and her large face was flushed and her beady eyes were bright with excitement. Ern, who had come under protest, had some difficulty in controlling his exasperation. He was ashamed of his aunt, and resented the attention she attracted to them both as she waddled along, leaning heavily on his unwilling arm. To his relief they found an unoccupied table in a fourth-rate eating room in a side street. The place was empty when they entered it, but gradually filled up as they sat there with people who had been unable to get into any other place. Mrs. Simmons ordered plates of ham, rolls and butter, and a pot of tea. "Hot and strong, miss, if you please."

The slatternly girl who took her order minced away on her high-heeled trodden-over slippers. The old woman looked after her tolerantly. "It's a hell of a life," she remarked. "I served in a fried fish and chips shop once for three months. It's your feet gives out mostly. D'you call this ham, dearie? I've half a mind to send it on to Madame Tussaud's. They could show it in the Chamber of Horrors."

The girl tossed her head and walked away. Mrs. Simmons sighed as she stirred her tea.

"You're tired, Aunt Bella," said Ern hopefully. "Better not go back, I can drive you home and fetch Rene later."

"Don't be a fool, Ern. Why, it's only just started. Come on, we'd best be going now. Look, there's Gertrude Platt."

Miss Platt, who had been seated at a neighbouring table making her lunch of coffee and biscuits, stopped on her way to the pay desk to speak to them.

"I saw you working your way to the front," she said smiling. "I was in the gallery."

"Ah, that's the best place, but I can't manage the stairs. What do you think of it so far?"

The schoolmistress shrugged her shoulders. She was looking tired and heavy-eyed. "I don't pretend to understand what Alan's counsel is trying to do. But I suppose there really isn't anything. It's hopeless." Her mask of amused indifference had slipped for a moment. Her strong mouth twitched. "It seems a waste. He can paint. And he's worth fifty of Mabel. She ought to have been murdered years ago." She left them with a curt nod, and went on to pay her bill at the desk.

Mrs. Simmons finished her tea. "It's surprising the number of women have made fools of themselves over that fellow," she said reflectively.

III

The Court was filling up again. Mrs. Reid, standing at her drawing-room window, watched the people who had been lunching at the Crown returning to the Town Hall. The members of the Bar who were on that Circuit, the Press, the curious public who found interest and amusement in seeing a man fight a losing battle for his life. Mrs. Reid had not discussed the subject with her son since the night of the Strutts' dinner party, they both avoided it, but friends had not been lacking to inform her that he had got that woman—the murderer's wife—into Greylands nursing home, and that he had ordered flowers to be sent to her daily from Merrion's, in the High Street. "It seems a pity," said the friends, "because, even if she didn't know he'd killed the other woman for her sake, she can't be a nice girl, can she?"

Mrs. Reid always made the same reply. "You don't understand. There's nothing personal about it. Copeland is his client. He promised to look after her." But when she looked at John's face while they sat at dinner laboriously making conversation she knew that her friends were right. Well, it would soon be over now. Everybody said it wouldn't last more than two days.

"But I suppose he'll appeal," she thought. "They always do. Afterwards I must persuade John to come away with me for a change. A cruise, perhaps."

If only she could roll back the years and have him a little boy again playing with his trains in this very room. She sighed and went back to the fireside and her novel.

I

MR. KYNASTON had called the last of the witnesses for the Crown. The evidence of Mrs. Butt had established the fact that when she left Strays at about three o'clock, after washing up the dinner things and wiping over the kitchen floor, Mrs. Copeland had seemed to be in her usual health. She had heard raised voices in the sitting-room before she left, but had thought little of it.

"She was always telling him off. I was sorry for him. We all was. I often said I wouldn't have spoken to a dog the way she spoke to him when she was in one of her tempers."

One of the junior members of the Bar whispered to a friend.

"If I were Barrymore I'd try for a verdict of justifiable homicide. It looks like the only chance." And, indeed, as the December day wore on the prisoner's prospects seemed to darken with it. The very circumstances that he was obviously liked by many of the witnesses and that they gave their evidence with reluctance told against him. Dr. Anderson, in spite of his evident desire to say as little as possible, was obliged to admit that he had found Mrs. Copeland a difficult and troublesome patient, and that her manner to her husband had made a disagreeable impression on him. He had not had the least suspicion of arsenical poisoning. Mrs. Copeland had suffered from gastritis, and, to put it quite plainly, she habitually over-ate herself.

Barrymore only asked one question of the doctor.

"You attributed her death to the breaking of a duodenal ulcer. The symptoms in such a case would bear a close resemblance to those of poisoning by arsenic?"

"Yes."

"Thank you."

From the evidence of Abraham Holt, an ironmonger of 72 High Street, Wainbridge, it appeared that Alan Copeland had bought a tin of a certain make of weed killer from him, on the

19th of April, or about three months before his wife's death. The witness knew Mr. Copeland as an occasional customer. He had sold him several rolls of wire netting for his chicken runs. He warned Mr. Copeland to be careful with the weed killer, and he had replied that he did not like the stuff, but that his wife wanted him to use it on the garden paths. Tom Welland, whose replies had to be dragged out of him, remembered seeing the tin on a shelf in the garage. It had been opened, but he did not know how much had been used. Mr. Copeland had told him not to touch it. He put in a few hours' work at Strays every week helping Mr. Copeland with the garden. He never saw much of Mrs. Copeland. A year later when Mr. Copeland came back to Strays he had entered his service with his wife.

"We left when Mr. Copeland was taken off by the police," he added. "We didn't want to be mixed up in any trouble, but Bessie and me've been sorry about it ever since." He looked towards the dock. "I hope you'll forgive us, sir."

The prisoner answered, "That's all right, Tom." And Welland created a painful sensation in the Court by bursting out crying.

"I am sure this witness's loyalty to his old employer does him credit," said Mr. Kynaston smoothly. "I could call more witnesses, but it is hardly necessary. Those you have heard have established the existence of a motive for this crime, of which the prisoner stands accused, of the means and the opportunity. I can, if my Lord and the jury wish, call witnesses to prove that the accused kept up a regular correspondence with the young woman who was to be his second wife during the weeks that elapsed between her leaving Teene and Mabel Copeland's death. Her letters to him were addressed to the Post Office, Wainbridge, and he fetched them every Wednesday."

The judge looked at Barrymore. "Is that disputed?"

"No, my Lord."

"Then we will take the correspondence for granted. Will you open for the defence, Sir Hugh?"

Barrymore was already on his feet. There was a perceptible increase of tension in the Court as he turned over the papers on the table before him, and some members of the jury leaned forward in their seats.

"My Lord, ladies and gentlemen of the jury, I have no complaint to make against my learned friend. He has been scrupulously fair in his indictment of my unfortunate client. It is all perfectly true. Alan Copeland was on bad terms with his wife, he did fall in love with another woman who returned his affection, and she became his mistress, and he married her as soon as he could after the death of the woman who for years had made his life a misery. Does it follow that he murdered her? It does not. Three years ago an uncle of mine, a bachelor, died, leaving me five thousand pounds which enabled me to do several things which I had long wanted to do. Did I murder him? Certainly not. But I had the motive. We all at one time or another profit by a fellow creature's death. The police prosecution, in this case, have made one cardinal mistake. They have concentrated their attention on my client to the exclusion of everything else. From the evidence they have produced it is clear that Mabel Copeland was close-fisted, sharp-tongued, prone to find fault. It is very unlikely that the husband of such a woman would be her only enemy. My Lord, there were other people with motives, who had the opportunity and access to the means. I have a plan of Strays here. Everyone who came to the back door could see the tin of weed killer in the garage. On the last day of her life her husband left the house at about half past two. He had a crate of poultry to be sent off from Wainbridge and afterwards he called on several customers. He returned a little before seven. What proof is there that the crime had not been already committed? Miss Gort had come to tea with her friend and had left at about six o'clock. What happened in the hour that intervened while Mrs. Copeland was alone in the house? That is one of the questions which the prosecution have left in the air. There is another point to which I want to call your attention. You must have been struck by the lack of any personal ill-feeling towards the accused in all the witnesses whose painful duty it has been to give evidence against him. And yet—and yet, as I shall presently show, Alan Copeland has a bitter and unrelenting enemy, a secret enemy who strikes in the dark, an enemy who has betrayed a very remarkable inside knowledge of the circumstances of Mabel Copeland's death. My Lord, members of the jury, I shall come back to this later. I shall say no more now. I call Alan Copeland."

The eyes of everyone in the court followed Alan as he left the dock for the witness-box. His tan had faded during the weeks he had spent in prison. He looked pale and his dark eyes were sunken. He took the book from the usher and repeated the words of the oath after him in a clear, resonant voice.

Barrymore took him through the statement he had made to the police. "You had quarrelled with your wife on the last afternoon of her life. What was the quarrel about?"

"She wanted me to give up my attempt to make a little money by poultry farming. She was right in a way. I worked very hard and the profits didn't amount to more than a few shillings a week. But I needed those few shillings."

"It had nothing to do with Miss Hale?"

"Nothing whatever. She did not know about Miss Hale."

"Why did you leave Strays so soon after her death?"

"I was free. I wanted to marry Miss Hale. When our child died there seemed no reason why we should not come back to Strays."

"You did not feel that the house had unpleasant associations?"

"It was a beautiful old house that had been messed about and spoilt. I had always wanted to restore it. Mabel wouldn't have minded. I used to talk to her about it, and she said I might be right but she couldn't be bothered having workmen turning the place upside down. I want to say here that the people who have given evidence here have not done justice to Mabel. She had her good points. We weren't always quarrelling. Her health made her irritable."

"Did you at any time before your arrest suspect that she had not died a natural death?"

"I had not the least suspicion."

"When you came in that last evening Mrs. Copeland was in the sitting-room?"

"Yes. She complained that I was late. I told her I had had trouble with the car, which was true, and she said it was my own fault, that I was a bad driver, and that I need not think she would buy me another. I didn't say anything. The less I said the better when she was in one of her difficult moods. She said that a girl from the village had been hanging about by the yard gate and that she had gone out and driven her away. I'm afraid I rather lost my temper then because I couldn't afford to lose customers. I knew the girl had come to buy eggs."

"There was no harm in it?"

"None whatever."

"What happened then?"

"Mabel said she felt ill and that she would have her supper and go straight up to bed. She went into the kitchen to warm her cocoa. I went back to the garage to see if I could patch up the car, but she wouldn't budge. When I went back to the house Mabel had gone up to her room. I read until ten and then I went up too."

"You did not occupy the same room?"

"No. I was across the landing. I went to sleep and awoke about one o'clock to hear her calling out. I went to her."

"Did she seem glad to see you?"

"Yes. She was evidently in great pain. I was shocked by her appearance. I got her a fresh nightgown and clean sheets and did what I could for her. It was pretty ghastly. After a bit I told her I must fetch the doctor. She didn't want me to leave her."

"What did she say?"

"She said, 'He can't do more than you're doing.' She said, 'You're sweet to me Alan, and I've been hard on you. Forgive me.' I said that was all right. I didn't like leaving her either in that state, but I thought the doctor might be able to do something for her."

"Did you give her anything to drink?"

"Yes. She asked for water and I gave her some, but she couldn't keep it down."

"She took it readily?"

"She tried to, poor soul."

"You have heard in this Court about the words she wrote on a bit of paper and hid in her work-basket. *I believe Alan's poisoned me.* It is rather strange, isn't it, that she did not shrink from you if she really thought that?"

"She didn't shrink from me. That's all I can say."

"Did you at any time give her arsenic in any shape or form?"

"Never, so help me God. Never."

"I have no more questions to ask of this witness, my Lord."

Mr. Kynaston rose. "You had no private means when you married your first wife, Mr. Copeland?"

"None."

"She did not make you an allowance?"

"No."

"Just doled out a pound or two now and then."

"Well—yes."

"How old are you?"

"Thirty-five."

"Rather humiliating for a man of your age. You said just now in answer to my learned friend that you badly needed the few shillings you made by the sale of poultry and eggs. What did you mean by that?"

"I wanted to start painting again. I wanted to buy materials."

"Did you know that your wife had made a will in your favour?"

"Yes."

"Did she ever threaten to change it?"

"No. She didn't talk about her will. She didn't care to think about dying."

"But you knew she might change it?"

"I suppose so."

"Thank you. That's what I wanted to get at." Alan made a movement to leave the box, but Kynaston stopped him. "No, no. I haven't quite finished with you, Mr. Copeland. Miss Hale wrote to you every week. She had lost her job, she was in trouble. Do you really expect this Court to believe that you merely wanted a few shillings to buy painting materials?"

"I didn't know she—she was in trouble."

"She had not told you?"

"No. She knew my position, that I was dependent on Mabel. She didn't want to worry me."

"She must be a very unusual young woman."

"She is. I didn't know until I went up to London after—after the funeral and saw her."

"What was your object in keeping up this correspondence, Mr. Copeland? Had you any plans for the future?"

"No."

"You just drifted. I see." Kynaston raised his voice, dropping his conversational tone. "Mr. Copeland, I put it to you that Miss Hale told you of her unhappy position and begged you to help her somehow, and that you faced the situation. You were in desperate need of not a few shillings but of a considerable sum of money."

"No."

Beads of sweat had broken out on Alan's forehead and upper lip. He kept his strained eyes fixed on the face of his tormentor. The silence in the Court was such that his hurried breathing was audible.

Kynaston slightly shrugged his shoulders. "Very well. We shall have to draw our own conclusions. I have no further questions to ask you."

Alan stood motionless until a warder touched him on the arm. Then he turned and went back to the dock, moving stiffly like an automaton.

"I call Irene Simmons."

Irene was dressed for the occasion in a new black coat with a leopard skin collar, and a scarlet beret that matched her lips was tilted at a coquettish angle over her black curls. She smiled at she glanced towards the back of the Court where her mother and Ern, she knew, were watching her, and the ease of her manner verged on insolence, but a close observer might have noted the whitened knuckles of the ungloved hands that gripped the rail and an effect of breathlessness in her replies.

"You live near Strays, Miss Simmons?"

"Yes. My mother owns the petrol station at the cross roads."

"Mr. Copeland got his petrol there and came there for repairs?"

"He used to. Yes."

"And in the days when he ran a poultry farm you got eggs from him?"

"Yes."

"Do you remember going up to Strays for eggs the evening of the 10th of June—not last summer, the year before?"

"Yes. I could see Mr. Copeland was out because the garage doors were open and the car was gone. I thought he might be back soon so I waited about."

"Why didn't you go to the door and ask Mrs. Copeland for what you wanted?"

"She wouldn't help Mr. Copeland in his business. She wanted him to give it up."

"You knew her well?"

"I didn't know her at all. Nobody in the village was good enough for her except the vicar and Miss Gort."

"Did you see Miss Gort there?"

"I saw her in the distance as I came up the lane. She was taking the short cut across the fields to her house. I supposed she'd been having tea with Mrs. Copeland. She was often there."

"Did you see anyone else?"

"Miss Platt passed me, riding her bike. She just said 'Hullo, Irene,' and I said 'Hallo,' and that I was going for eggs."

"Anyone else?"

Irene moistened her lips. "I saw a ragged-looking man farther up the lane. He was sitting in the ditch doing something to his feet. I thought someone in the village had given him a pair of old shoes and he was trying them on."

"You were waiting for Mr. Copeland. How did you pass your time?"

"I lit a cigarette. I was leaning on the yard gate and looking down the lane. It gave me a start when Mrs. Copeland came up behind me."

"What did she say to you?"

"She was very rude."

"What did she say? I'm sorry if this gives you pain, Miss Simmons."

Irene tossed her head. "Oh, I don't mind. She said I was to stop running after her husband. I said, run, I didn't have to run. It was he who did the running, I said."

"Was that true, Miss Simmons?"

"Well, no, it wasn't. He was civil to me and I had a bit of a pash for him, like girls get for film stars and that. There wasn't any harm in it. But she'd asked for it, so she got it."

There was a ripple of laughter in the Court which was quickly suppressed. Everyone wanted to hear what else this witness had to say.

"Did the conversation continue on those lines?"

"She said I was shameless, and I said if I was to be insulted I'd have to get my eggs elsewhere, and she said, 'Please do!' and I said, 'I suppose you're trying to ruin the poor man's business now.' Then she started calling me this and that, so I said 'I thought you were supposed to be a lady, but you aren't even lady like,' I said, so I thought maybe I'd said enough, and I walked away down the lane, and when I got home I told Mum I hadn't been able to get any eggs, and the next morning we heard Mrs. Copeland had died in the night."

"Was the tramp still sitting in the ditch when you left?"

"I can't say. I turned in the other direction, you see. He was farther up the lane and I went down the hill to get home."

"Thank you, Miss Simmons."

Barrymore sat down and Kynaston rose briskly. "About the time, Miss Simmons. About how long were you in the lane?"

"About half an hour or a bit over. It was after seven when I got home. I know that because Mum told me off for being late for supper."

"And you saw nothing of the accused that evening?"

"He passed me in the lane. If he'd come just a minute sooner he'd have found us at it hammer and tongs. I was glad he hadn't. It would have been awkward for him, and it wasn't his fault."

"Just a minute? As close as that? Thank you very much," said Mr. Kynaston blandly.

Irene threw him a frightened look. What had she said to afford him so much satisfaction? All these thin-lipped shrewd-eyed men who did not stare at her greedily like children in a sweet shop baffled and alarmed her. She was used to finding older men indulgent and easily amused. Her cheap, brittle prettiness was beginning to wilt in this dry, legal atmosphere. Her scarlet underlip drooped like that of a frightened child. She was thankful to get out of the box. She struggled through the crowd and went to the ladies' room. The attendant had promised her a cup of tea. She sat there crying, and her tears made runnels in the powder on her plump cheeks.

The prisoner's prospects had not improved in the last few minutes. The Judge glanced at his haggard face and directed that he should remain seated in the dock. There was a moment of bustle and activity while a chair was being lifted over the rail and the almost unbearable tension of the last few minutes relaxed. Barrymore glanced at the jury, but their faces told him nothing. The thin woman was blowing her nose. Had she been moved to tears or was she merely suffering from a cold? He wondered if, after all, he ought to have called Lydia Copeland. He might have been able to overcome her husband's objections. With a life at stake—

"I call Matthew Hellyer."

A well-known figure stepped into the box. There was a stir of renewed interest in the Court. It was surely unusual for the superintendent of the local police to be called to give evidence for the defence. But the Superintendent seemed quite at his ease. He looked towards Barrymore when he had been sworn.

"When was your attention first drawn to the circumstances of Mabel Copeland's death, Superintendent?"

"Last April."

"As long ago as that. And by whom?"

"I can't tell you that. A letter came addressed to me and making certain allegations. It was signed Justice, and the sender had taken pains that his or her writing shouldn't be recognised."

"You paid no attention to that letter?"

"No. But others came at intervals of a few weeks. There were five or six altogether."

"You have these letters in your possession?"

"We only kept the last three."

"You were beginning to take them seriously?"

"We made some enquiries and traced the movements of the accused from the time he left this neighbourhood the day after his wife's funeral. We then obtained an order for her exhumation."

"Did you make any attempt to identify the sender of these letters?"

"No. It didn't seem necessary as we were able to obtain sufficient evidence for our purpose without. Anonymous letters in themselves do not carry any weight."

"But in this case they served as pointers?"

"Yes."

"I have here photographic enlargements of three letters, dated respectively the 28th of August, the 8th of September and the 4th of October. Will you look at them please and tell the Court if you recognise them?"

"Certainly. These photographs were taken at your request by one of my men, Constable Henderson, who has retained the negatives."

The judge intervened. "May we know the contents of these letters, Sir Hugh?"

"Certainly, my lord. The first is as follows.

"'28 August.

"'Alan Copeland poisoned his wife. Is he going to get away with it? It's up to you, Mr. Policeman.

"'Justice.'

"The second and last but one of the series came only eleven days later.

"'8 September.

"'The wicked shall flourish like a green bay tree. That stands for the fine gentleman at Strays with his new wife and his posh car. Police are no use.

"'Justice.'

"Then comes the last.

"'4 October.

"'Are you waiting for another murder before you make a move? He did it. Alan Copeland. He looks one thing and means another. Look in the grave.

"'JUSTICE!'

"I have here, my lord, photographs of the envelopes in which these precious missives reached the Wainbridge Police Station. The address in each case is written in black ink and the letters are printed. They have, however, certain characteristics in common. I am calling an expert witness presently to point them out to you. The letters themselves are composed of single letters, words, and, most fortunately for our purpose, sentences, cut out of various newspapers and periodicals."

The judge said. "Pass them up to me, please." There was a profound silence in the Court while he adjusted his glasses and examined the photographs closely. They were then passed down to the jury and finally returned to the keeping of Barrymore's clerk.

Barrymore resumed. "How did these letters strike you, Superintendent? Would you say they came from an enemy of the accused?"

"That's one reason why we didn't move at once, Sir Hugh. They sounded a bit too much like a personal vendetta, if you know what I mean. Too full of spite."

"Have you come across anybody in the course of your investigations who might have sent these letters?"

The Superintendent hesitated before he turned to the judge. "Need I answer that, my Lord?"

"No. Unless you have evidence. What you think is not evidence."

"Thank you, my Lord."

The Superintendent left the box while Barrymore and John Reid held a whispered consultation.

"Mr. Holt hasn't arrived. He missed the train and is coming by car. One of my clerks has just brought his wire from my office."

"That's awkward." He stood up. "My Lord, I crave your indulgence. My next witness, Mr. Gavin Holt, has been detained. He may be here at any moment, but meanwhile—"

"The case for the defence is taking a somewhat unusual course, Sir Hugh."

"My Lord, we are fighting for this man's life."

"Yes, yes, we all appreciate that. Is there no other witness you can call?"

"My Lord—" Barrymore half turned as Reid, who had been out of the Court, and returned, touched his arm. His face betrayed his relief. "Mr. Holt is here."

The handwriting expert was a man of about fifty, with a close clipped grey beard and a dry, precise manner. He was a specialist, and evidently took little interest in anything outside his own subject. He was not moved by the case as a whole, and it was noticeable that he scarcely glanced at the prisoner in the dock.

"Do you recognise these photographs, Mr. Holt?"

"Yes. I have been working on them for the last fortnight. They were submitted to me for examination and analysis by the firm of Reid, Reid and Pearmain. At the same time I was given a list of daily papers and weekly and monthly periodicals taken by various persons who lived in the same neighbourhood as the prisoner at the time the alleged crime was committed."

"Did you arrive at any result, Mr. Holt?"

"Certainly. It will be noted that in the first letter, dated the eighth of August, the name Alan Copeland is formed out of nine separate cuttings, that is to say, eight single letters and to conclude, the word land. The signature *Justice* is in five pieces, four separate letters and the word *ice*. The rest of the missive is in pieces with one word, except *Mr. Policeman*, an unusual combination which, however, I found in a serial story running in a certain monthly. This same serial provided a cutting with three words in the next letter. *His posh car*, and it also provides the conclusion of the third letter, the three words *in the grave*. This discovery pointed to a person whom I have classified as A, and the other words and letters, with one exception, were undoubtedly taken from a daily paper. The exception bothered me. It was the word *Strays*, occurring in the second letter. I found it eventually in a charitable appeal in another paper on my list, not one of those taken by A. I was able to make exact copies of all three letters out of back numbers of these periodicals of the month preceding each of the relevant dates. To make assurance doubly sure, I then attempted to make similar copies with the remainder of the material at my disposal, but without success. The phrases *Mr. Policeman* and *his posh car* only occurred in the serial running in the magazine taken by A. I found another *in the grave*, but in that case the paper was obviously of a better quality. The varying quality and texture of the paper is very perceptible even in the photographs."

"My Lord, I would ask that the names of the periodicals from which the sender of these letters made cuttings should not be made public until I have called corroborative evidence. May this witness write them down and give them to you for safe keeping for the present?"

"This is all somewhat irregular, Sir Hugh, but if Mr. Kynaston has no objection—"

Mr. Kynaston answered stiffly. "None whatever. All this, I understand, occurred some months after the murder had been committed. If your Lordship does not mind the introduction of irrelevant matter it is not for me to complain."

The judge smiled bleakly. "You must pardon my vulgar curiosity, Mr. Kynaston."

Mr. Holt had been given a sheet of paper and had produced his fountain pen. He wrote something down, and the paper was passed up to the judge who glanced at it before he laid it down on the ledge before him.

"That will be all, Mr. Holt, unless Mr. Kynaston wants to cross-examine."

Mr. Kynaston shook his head and Mr. Holt left the box.

The next witness was Benjamin Cattermole, a poorly-dressed, middle-aged man with a badly-scarred face and a perceptible limp, who drew himself up when he entered the box and saluted with a pathetic attempt at military smartness. There were several scraps of ribbon sewn to the lapel of his shabby coat.

"You live at Teene, Mr. Cattermole?" said Barrymore after the usual preliminaries.

"Yes, sir. In the cottage beyond the schoolhouse."

"How do you earn your living?"

"Odd jobs, sir. I do a bit of gardening for the vicar and that, and I've got the newspaper round."

"You deliver papers in the district?"

"That's right, sir. I get them down from Wainbridge. The guard on the 7.50 down train chucks the roll out at the level crossing and I or my daughter are there to pick it up. Then I goes my round on my old tricycle, starting with the school-house and the vicarage and through the village to the crossroads and along by Strays and Fairview to the quarry and home again."

"Now I have a list here of some of your customers and the papers they take. I'm going to read them out to you and you must tell the Court if I am right."

"Very good, sir."

"The vicar takes the *Daily Telegraph*, the *Spectator* and the *Church Times*. Miss Platt also takes the *Telegraph* with the *New Statesman*, the *Sunday Times*, and *Cornhill*. Mrs. Simmons at the cross roads garage takes the *Daily Mail* and the *Weekly Dispatch* and a monthly publication called *Buttercup Novels*."

"That's right, sir. But it's Miss Irene takes the *Buttercup Novels*."

"At Strays Mr. Copeland had the *Telegraph* and the *Sunday Times*. Miss Gort takes the *Daily Express* and *Plummer's Monthly*, which is a woman's magazine specialising in fashions, cooking and household hints and light fiction."

"That's about it," said Cattermole. "Then Mr. Bragge, at the quarry, takes the *News Chronicle*."

"Only one *Church Times* on your list, Cattermole?"

"That's the vicar, but he passes his copy on to Miss Gort when he's done with it."

The judge adjusted his spectacles. "How do you know that?"

"He hands them over to me, my Lord, to take along to her."

"I see. And does she reciprocate with *Plummer's Monthly*?"

Cattermole grinned. "Oh no, my Lord. The vicar's a very learned gentleman."

"Thank you, Cattermole," said Barrymore pleasantly. He looked at Kynaston, who shook his head, and the witness left the box.

The jury had been whispering together and now the foreman stood up. "We would like to know what papers Mr. Holt used to make his copies of the Justice letters, my Lord."

"Certainly." The judge picked up the paper that had been lying on the ledge before him. "The *Daily Express* and *Plummer's Monthly*. But the one word Strays came from the *Church Times*."

"My Lord," said Barrymore. "I ask your leave to recall a witness."

Kynaston had risen. His face was flushed. "If my learned friend is referring to Miss Gort I was about to make the same request. I think this lady should be given an opportunity to vindicate herself."

"I agree. But she will be Sir Hugh's witness now. You may cross-examine her if you wish."

"Call Miss Emily Gort."

CHAPTER XX
REPRESSIONS AND ALL THAT

I

THE short December day was drawing to its close. The Court room had grown dark suddenly and the lights had been lit. As Miss Gort entered the witness-box her shadow, grotesquely enlarged, ran up the wall behind her and seemed to lurk there like a dusky familiar. The lean, spinsterish figure was as neat as ever, the grey felt hat firmly fixed to the abundant coils of string-coloured hair with two black-headed pins. She laid her grey fabric gloves down carefully on the ledge before her and blew her nose with a refined absence of vigour, diffusing a faint aroma of eau de cologne.

"I swear by Almighty God—"

Barrymore adjusted his gown over his shoulders. "When you gave evidence here this morning, Miss Gort, you told the Court that you had no ill-feeling regarding the accused. Do you wish to modify that statement?"

"No."

"You and he were always on friendly terms?"

"Certainly."

"He never offended you in any way?"

"No."

"You have told us that at the time of Mabel Copeland's death you had no suspicion of foul play?"

For the first time she seemed to hesitate. "I—no."

"You were with the dying woman while her husband went to fetch the doctor. The idea that she might have been poisoned did not cross your mind then?"

"No."

"You have a good deal of experience of illness, Miss Gort?"

"Not more than most people."

"You nursed your aunt through her last illness, did you not?"

"Yes. But that's a long time ago."

"Thirteen years. A trying time for you, and Mrs. Copeland's must have reminded you of it."

"It wasn't at all the same."

"You surprise me. The doctor who attended her sold his practice and left the neighbourhood nine years ago, but he is still living in another part of the country. According to him, Miss Gort, your aunt died as the result of the breaking of a duodenal ulcer after a period of ill-health due to gastric trouble. That was the diagnosis in the case of Mrs. Copeland. A mistake, in her case, as we now know. Surely there was some similarity in the symptoms?"

"I don't know." Miss Gort's voice, always rather thin, sounded oddly brittle. "I'm not a trained nurse. I do my best to help when I'm asked, and this is the return I get."

"Have you during the last few months sent letters signed Justice to the Wainbridge police station urging the authorities to arrest Alan Copeland for the murder of his wife?"

"I have not!"

"Be careful, Miss Gort. Perjury is an indictable offence."

"How dare you speak to me like that." Her pale face was stubborn, her pale eyes as hard as flints.

Mr. Kynaston stood up. "My Lord, I protest. This witness is a lady of unblemished character. These are foul insinuations—"

"I agree," said the Judge, "but the evidence we have heard regarding these letters justifies the counsel for the defence in pressing this matter a little further. I will see that he does not go too far."

Mr. Kynaston sat down looking dissatisfied.

"Miss Gort, I have here a copy of *Plummer's Monthly* for last August. A part of one page has been cut out—a part of the serial with the sentence *his posh car* which appears in one of these anonymous letters. I am prepared to call witnesses to prove that you gave this copy with several others to a sick child in the parish."

"It wasn't cut when I gave it. I know nothing about it."

"You still deny that you were the sender of these letters?"

"I do."

"The addresses on the envelopes were written in printed characters, but the writer betrays certain idiosyncrasies in placing the dot of the i, and in the shape of the commas. Would it surprise you to hear that these same characteristics occur in the scrawled pencil message that you found in Mrs. Copeland's work basket?"

Mr. Kynaston rose again. "My Lord, I object."

Sir Hugh smiled. "I will not insist on an answer. I have no further questions to ask this witness."

"Your turn, Mr. Kynaston."

"I will not prolong Miss Gort's ordeal, my Lord. I, for one, am perfectly satisfied with her denials. But, in any case, the identity of Justice is beside the point. I will deal with this attempt to draw a red herring over the trail more fully when the time comes."

"Are you calling any more witnesses, Sir Hugh?"

"The mother of the child to whom the magazine was given. She can swear that she noticed the cut at once."

"I think not, Sir Hugh. I have allowed you a good deal of licence. I am here to try the prisoner in the dock. You must not allow that fact to escape your memory too often. It is growing late. There will hardly be time for you to make your speech in defence of your client to-night. I shall adjourn the Court until to-morrow."

II

In Wainbridge that night the Copeland trial was the one topic of conversation. In public bars, in clubs, those who had been successful in pushing their way into the very limited space reserved for the public in the Court room at the Town Hall were sure of an audience, and a special edition of the *Wainbridge Echo* with a verbatim account of the proceedings up to date, was sold out in less than an hour. Opinions were sharply divided on the line taken by the defence. The landlord of the Crown, helping his staff in the bar during the rush hour, voiced the conclusions of a majority when he said.

"This fuss about the letters. Mr. Kynaston was right when he called it a red herring. That Gort woman's a spiteful old maid, the very spit of an old aunt of my wife's that used to plague her life out, but anyone can see she's as sharp as a needle, and maybe she did get an inkling and did send those letters and don't choose to admit it. What then? It don't prove that Copeland didn't shove arsenic into that cup of cocoa."

"I don't care," said the barmaid. "He didn't do it. I happened to be coming round by the Passage, see, at the back of the Town Hall, this morning, when he was getting out of the car that had brought him from the prison. He was surrounded by police, but I got a good view of him. I only wish I was on the jury. I'd stick out for Not Guilty whatever they said."

There was a general laugh.

"You see how it is," said the landlord. "All the ladies fall for him. I can't think how it is. I can't see anything out of the way about the chap myself. I used to know him pretty well. He supplied us with poultry now and again. Nice manners, he had. Very quiet and retiring. Everybody knew that wife of his led him a life. He did her in. That's as plain as pikestaff, whatever the defence may say, but I don't fancy anybody blames him over-much. A double Scotch for you, sir? A double Scotch, Doris, for this gentleman."

When Ern Simmons, hampered by the bulky old woman who clung like some huge black parasite to his unwilling arm, reached the public car park where he had left his aged Ford he found his cousin there before them.

"That you at last, Mum? What an age you've been," she said fretfully.

The old woman made no reply. She had been unusually silent and subdued since they struggled out with the crowd pouring out of the Town Hall into the raw cold of the December night. Her nephew surmised that she was more exhausted by the effort she had made than she cared to admit. He and Irene between them hoisted her into the back of the car and the girl came to sit beside him.

"You all right, kid?"

"Yes, thank you, Ern."

The narrow High Street was jammed with cars all trying to get away at once. In the Crown and the King's Head every window was lit up and waiters hired for the occasion could be seen hurrying to and fro.

"They've got the jury at the King's Head." said Ern, pulling up to allow a stream of people to go over a crossing. "They moved the table out of the billiard room so they can have their meals there. Nobody's allowed to speak to them, not until they've brought in their verdict."

Irene caught her breath. "Ern—it sounded all right, what I said, didn't it? About the tramp, I mean."

They were on the outskirts of the town now in a tree-shaded avenue of the residential district, and the road was clear. Ern accelerated. "It sounded all right," he said, "don't you worry, Rene. You've done your best."

"I tried. But why did that Mr. Kynaston look so pleased just at the end?" she asked anxiously.

"I don't know. They're too sharp for me. I hope I don't have to go to any more trials," he said.

But by this time Mrs. Simmons was sufficiently revived to intervene by giving her daughter a sharp prod in the back.

"What are you two whispering about?" she demanded. "Speak up so's I can hear."

"Nothing much, Aunt Bella," said her nephew.

Irene merely scowled and relapsed into her usual sulky silence.

Superintendent Hellyer was in his office, with Sergeant Ramsden in attendance, clearing up arrears of his routine work, when the Chief Constable came in.

"What do you think of this new development, Hellyer?" Colonel Meadows looked worried. "I thought it was an absolutely clear case. The evidence seemed almost as damning as that against Armstrong."

"Well—hardly that, sir," said Hellyer. "If I remember rightly packets of arsenic were found in Armstrong's waistcoat pocket. We've been hampered by the time that has intervened. I haven't the slightest doubt of the man's guilt myself."

Colonel Meadows was fidgeting round the room in a manner that was very discomposing to the nerves of his subordinates.

"Those damned letters. There's no doubt the defence has succeeded in discrediting that witness. Did you suspect her of being the sender, Superintendent?"

Hellyer shook his head. "As a matter of fact I thought it was a person who hasn't been called by either side. Ma Simmons. She's never been in trouble, she's too clever for that, but she's a nasty piece of work, and she's had her knife into Copeland for not marrying her daughter."

"Then you think the defence have been barking up the wrong tree?"

"I don't say that, sir. They may be right. I shouldn't be surprised. The Gort woman's one of these ultra prim and proper old maids. They let off steam sometimes in queer ways."

"Repressions and all that," said the Chief Constable.

"That's right, sir. We'll know to-morrow when Sir Hugh Barrymore makes his speech for the defence whether he's actually suggesting that she wrote the message she says she found in the work-basket as well as the letters—"

"You take it very calmly, Hellyer, I must say," fumed his Chief.

"Well, don't you see, sir, even if it's true it's only a side issue. All these women seem to have been more or less in love with Copeland. They all thought they'd have a chance when his wife died and turned sour when they were disappointed. Miss Gort may be Justice. How does that prove that he didn't poison his wife?"

The Colonel picked up a paper weight, gazed at it abstractedly and put it down again. "It doesn't of course. But there's another fallacy somewhere. You know well enough, Hellyer, that counsel for the defence got as near as he dared to making a more serious accusation."

"Yes," said Hellyer, wondering when his superior officer would stop talking and allow him to lock his desk and go home, "but ask yourself, sir, if any person who'd got away with an unsuspected murder would be mutt enough to rake it all up months afterwards in order to accuse somebody else of it?"

The Colonel sighed. "No. No, I suppose it doesn't make sense, and anyhow it's too late. We've set the machine in motion. We can't stop it. But if it crushed an innocent man, Superintendent—Oh Lord! Is that clock right? Good night."

Neither of the men he had left behind him spoke until they heard his car starting. Then Ramsden said "He's badly rattled."

"We're all on edge, I expect," said Hellyer rather absently.

He avoided meeting Ramsden's eye. He was reviewing certain very unpleasant contingencies.

Barrymore had accepted an invitation to dine with Reid. During the meal they had discussed the merits of the modern

Dutch School of painting and a recent production of *Hamlet* at the Old Vic. His host had given Barrymore a hint that the subject that occupied their thoughts must not be mentioned in the presence of his mother, and Barrymore, having seen the young lawyer and his client's wife together, had guessed why. After Mrs. Reid had left them to their coffee and cigarettes Reid spoke impulsively.

"Are you satisfied so far? Has it gone as well as you hoped?"

"On the whole, yes. We are lucky to have Lord Scarlett. Some judges would have pulled me up sooner. But I don't know how he's reacting. He's got a poker face."

"Well, we've got two strings to our bow."

"How do you mean?"

"Our defence is that it needn't have been Copeland. We're suggesting alternatives. If it wasn't Emily Gort it might have been the tramp."

Barrymore sipped his coffee and set down the cup. "I'm afraid not. Wait until you hear Kynaston to-morrow. That girl didn't realise it, but she gave away the whole case. Kynaston was on to it at once, damn him. I'm forewarned, that's one thing."

Reid cleared his throat nervously. "I thought Copeland showed up well in the box."

"Well enough, poor devil. But that won't help much. Everybody's been sorry for him from the first. His wife gave him hell, and the more we rub that in the sorrier people are—and the stronger becomes his motive for getting rid of her. A horrid predicament. And that second marriage so soon after her death does look bad." He looked at his watch. "Sorry. I must be off. I always try to get a minimum of eight hours' sleep on these occasions. I won't disturb Mrs. Reid. Will you say goodnight to her for me?"

John Reid went with him to the door and then, alone in the hall, struggled with an almost overpowering desire to ring up the nursing home and enquire after Lydia. He knew she had been very restless earlier in the day and that she had been given a mild narcotic. She should be sleeping now, poor girl. He picked up the receiver and stood for a moment, hesitant, his sensitive face working a little before he put it down again without dialling the number. His mother, he knew, would be listening, waiting for him to come upstairs.

He was right. Mrs. Reid had left the drawing-room ajar. Surely, she thought, John would come in to say good night. She sat trying to work at her embroidery until she heard him go by to his room. Because of a murderess, she thought bitterly. Her eyes filled with tears, but she blinked them away resolutely. He had been such a docile, sweet-tempered little boy, such a good son always until that—that woman led him away.

CHAPTER XXI
THE VERDICT

I

THE Court was packed again the next morning. It had been rumoured that the trial was expected to end that day. Counsels' speeches would occupy the time before the lunch interval. A queue had begun to form while it was still dark, and several hundred people failed to gain admittance. Some went away but a good number seemed prepared to wait all day in the raw cold and the occasional showers of rain. All the newsagents displayed posters. "Copeland Case; Amazing Allegations." "Copeland Trial; Who is Justice?"

Extra police had been drafted in to keep the roads clear for traffic. Superintendent Hellyer appeared to have been shaken out of his habitual imperturbability. He had cut himself while shaving and he was unusually curt with his subordinates. The jury without exception, looked pale and worried. The prisoner, directly after he had been brought up the stairs from the cells had leant over the dock rail to speak to his solicitor.

"Reid—how is she?"

"I rang up the home ten minutes ago, Copeland. I knew you'd be asking that. They are keeping her under morphia. Not right under. She's just drowsy."

"I'm glad—thank you."

There was no time for more before the Court rose at the Judge's entrance. Those who had seats settled down again as Barrymore began to speak.

"My Lord, members of the jury, more than once in the course of my experience at the Bar I have heard prosecutors say that they are not concerned with motive. In this case we seem to have heard more about the motive than anything else. The argument, so far as my finite brain could grasp it, has been that this man had good reasons for getting rid of his wife and that this fact constitutes evidence that he did actually murder her. It is suggested that he put weed killer from a tin in the garage into her cup of cocoa. No evidence has been adduced. The analysis of certain organs eighteen months later proved the presence of arsenic and nothing else. It may have been administered in tea or on bread and butter, in fish or meat paste sandwiches. Or, if the prosecution guessed right, what proof is there that Alan Copeland's was the hand that mixed the arsenic with the cocoa powder and sugar in that cup left standing within easy reach of the open window? You may have wondered at my choice of witnesses for the defence. I was anxious to show that if Alan Copeland had the opportunity so had several other people. I would like you to assume now for the sake of my argument that Copeland is innocent. He is innocent, and yet the fact remains that at some time during that afternoon and evening Mabel Copeland swallowed a fatal dose of poison. I am not going to suggest that she took it herself. In spite of her incessant complaining and her habit of self-pity she was not a suicidal type, and, in spite of the alleged message scribbled on the paper found in her work-basket I think you will agree that she died in ignorance of what had happened to her. There are cases where the victim is confined to bed and food and medicines are administered by one person, where it is comparatively easy to say who must be guilty. But Mrs. Copeland was not bedridden, she was not shut away. On this last afternoon of her life her friend, Miss Emily Gort, had tea with her and left about six o'clock. Irene Simmons saw her walking home across the fields. The evidence of Irene covers the hour between Miss Gort's departure and Alan Copeland's return. Irene told us that she saw a tramp in the lane. I hope I shall not disappoint my learned friend, the counsel for the Crown, when I say that the defence attach no importance to the tramp's being there at that time. He may or may not have called at the back door earlier in the afternoon. I think you will agree with me that the fact that he lingered in the neighbourhood showed that his conscience was clear. I am in a difficult position. As this very human tragedy has been unfolded I have been faced and I think that you may have been faced also with a certain alternative solution of the mystery of Mabel Copeland's death. I have been reminded, and I think you also may have been reminded, of the sin of Judas—the betrayal of a friend. I am here to defend the innocent and not to accuse the guilty nor to hint at a motive which, however, may occur to those who have realised that my unfortunate client is one of those men who through no fault of their own and to their great embarrassment, are run after by women. I will say nothing more on this head. I will only remind you that according to the medical evidence the time at which arsenic begins to take effect varies, and that the action may be delayed. Mabel Copeland complained of feeling unwell when she went up to bed at nine o'clock. Her husband had come in at seven and they had a prolonged conversation before he went back to the garage to tinker with his car and she prepared her supper. If the poison had been taken some time previously the hot cocoa would bring on the initial symptoms. I have said my say. Alan Copeland's life is in your hands. You know the worst of him. He and the unhappy girl who loved him have had to suffer bitterly for their moral lapse. Because of that, because of his natural wish to regularise her position as soon as possible suspicion fell on him and he stands before you in the dock. Of the dreadful crime imputed to him he is innocent as you or I. I speak now not as an advocate in the court but as a man. I am not asking for mercy, my Lord, and members of the jury, but for justice. Alan Copeland is innocent."

Barrymore sat down, and buried his face in his hands. There was a silence so profound that the scraping of Kynaston's chair on the bare boards as he rose jarred unbearably on frayed nerves.

"I should like to be the first to congratulate Sir Hugh on a remarkable oratorical effort. I confess that I was moved. The appeal to your compassion was masterly. After such eloquence plain common sense must fall like a cold douche on overheated imaginations. But I must return, however reluctantly, to the plain facts of this painful case. The wife of the accused was some years his senior. She was bad tempered and addicted to petty tyrannies. He was financially dependent on her and she never let him forget it. He bore her exactions with exemplary patience and, so far as we know, he was never unfaithful to her until two years ago—I beg your pardon, it is less than two years, eighteen months—when he fell violently in love with a young girl who was staying in the village. He kept up a secret correspondence with this girl after her return to London. The letters that passed between them have not been preserved, but we know that she lost her job—she was a cashier in a draper's shop in North London—and that she discovered that she was, if I may use the consecrated phrase, in trouble. This was early in June. A few days later the first Mrs. Copeland died suddenly. Immediately after the funeral her husband hurried up to London to join the other woman. In less than a fortnight they were married and on their way to North Wales for their honeymoon. All this is undisputed. The counsel for the prisoner has twitted me with making much of the motive. How can that be avoided? It is there, so painfully, so terribly inevitable. He has chosen to dwell on the anonymous letters that were received by the police, the first of them nearly a year after the crime was committed. I agree with him that the wording of these letters indicates spite on the part of the sender. I like them as little as you do. The role of the informer is not in any sense admirable, yet I must urge some defence. Many people are too timid or too inhibited to approach the police openly, though they may have knowledge which should be communicated if justice is to be done. These letters set the police on the track of a crime which might otherwise have gone unpunished. I will take a leaf out of my learned friend's book. I will ask you to assume, for the sake of argument, that the witness, Emily Gort, did send these letters, and that she even went so far as to fake the message found in the work-basket. It may be so. How does that help the defence? This woman, leading a narrow and restricted life, has lost her best friend, the person who, whatever her faults, was invariably kind and generous to her. At first she is unsuspicious, but when Copeland came back with his second wife she began to put two and two together. She concocts the anonymous letters, and here in the witness-box she lacks the courage to admit it. What then? It is the duty of every citizen to assist the police. She did not take the best way, but she is a lonely woman, with no one to help or advise. As to the paper found in the work-basket I say nothing. The prosecution has not relied on it and it is no part of my case. You may, if you wish, discount all of Miss Gort's evidence. The prisoner, giving evidence on his own behalf, has admitted that he and his wife were quarrelling a few hours before she died; we know that he was deeply involved with another woman, that he was in desperate need of money, that he longed to be free. He was going to and fro to the garage trying to repair his car, and the tin of weed killer was there on the shelf. 'The means to do ill deeds makes ill deeds done.' It has been suggested that his return to Strays, the house that was the scene of the crime, is evidence of his innocence. It might equally well prove the callousness that is one of the characteristics of a certain type. I would ask you to confine your attention to those few weeks that led up to the fatal crisis and those that followed, and to dismiss all other considerations as irrelevant."

Mr. Kynaston's dry, deliberate voice ceased. He rested for a moment and drank a glass of water before he resumed.

The thin jurywoman shifted uneasily and stole a glance at her stout friend. Mrs. Williams and she had agreed last night when they were talking over the case, sitting with their knitting a little apart from their fellows. They had been strangers two days ago. Mrs. Williams was the widow of an insurance agent and lived in a neat little semi-detached house in River Road.

Miss Barham kept the wool shop in Church Passage. Neither had served on a jury before. "I'd made up my mind," thought little Miss Barham resentfully, "and now this man is trying to upset it again. I suppose we really ought to hear the Judge before we decide."

Mr. Justice Scarlett began his summing up after the lunch interval. He began with a patient and painstaking review of the evidence and went on to a general consideration of the case.

"One thing is certain. This woman was murdered by arsenic which was placed in her food or drink a few hours before her death. The police have suggested that the cup of cocoa she drank for her supper was the vehicle. But you have heard the medical evidence. It is not beyond the bounds of possibility that the poison was taken some three or four hours earlier. I think you must keep that possibility in mind. Could she have committed suicide? I think you may rule that out. The instances in which suicides have chosen to end their lives by arsenic are very rare. And if you accept the evidence of her husband you must assume that she did not know what was the matter with her. His evidence is, of course, of great importance, and I observed that you listened to it with the utmost attention. So did I. And I am bound to say that I was favourably impressed. On the other hand this is one of those difficult and anxious cases in which it has to be admitted that great provocation has been given, where it is possible that a person with no criminal tendencies has drifted and has finally been overwhelmed by a sudden impulse to break free at all costs from an unendurable situation. If that is your conclusion it will be open to you to urge the existence of extenuating circumstances, though I cannot hold out much hope that such a plea would receive attention. The defence, very rightly, though in somewhat irregular manner, has presented you with an alternative ending to this tragedy of an unhappy marriage. Some other person, not in custody, may have committed this crime. You are here to decide on Alan Copeland's guilt or innocence, and for no other purpose. It is not for you to point to another and say "It is quite as likely that he—or she—did it." But no one can prevent you from drawing your own conclusions as to the actual rather than the ostensible motives of some of the witnesses, or perhaps I should say of one witness you have heard giving evidence in this Court. Members of the jury, you will now retire to consider your verdict. I shall be in my room, and if you are in any difficulty and require my advice I shall be ready to give it."

II

The jury sat round a table with their foreman, a retired schoolmaster, at the head. The murmur of conversation died down as he raised his voice to gain their attention.

"Now, ladies and gentlemen, have we got to talk this over among ourselves, or are we agreed? I will ask all those who believe Alan Copeland to be guilty of murder to hold up a hand." He looked round the table, counting. "One, two, three, four . . . seven. Dear me. Our verdict, you know, must be unanimous."

An elderly man on his left spoke. "I think that those who don't agree should be asked to give their reasons."

"An excellent suggestion. You are one of the five, sir. Will you begin?"

"Well, I can't make a speech about it, but I'll say this. I flatter myself I can generally tell when a chap is lying. I thought Copeland had done it until I heard him in the witness-box. He was telling the truth all right. It all happened as he said."

"I see. And now you, sir?"

The stout man in the horn-rimmed spectacles shook his head. "I'm no good at arguing. To tell the truth I haven't been able to make up my mind, and Copeland's going to have the benefit of the doubt."

The foreman looked at the third dissident, a little man with a reddish moustache. "And what about you, Mr. Flynn?"

"I don't approve of capital punishment."

"Then you ought not to be on this jury." The foreman spoke coldly. Flynn was well known locally as a trouble maker and a thorn in the side of the Borough Council.

Flynn grinned. "You can't hoof me out now."

The foreman turned to Miss Barham. "I have left the ladies to the last," he said. "What are your reasons, madam?"

Miss Barham looked at him timidly. She was unused to giving her opinions. Her customers expected her to agree with them, and, in any case, they seldom talked of anything but the weather. She wished herself back in her snug little shop with the bright coloured wools and her little old dog curled up asleep in his basket under the counter. He pined when she was away even for a few hours.

"He didn't do it," she said firmly. "It was Miss Gort."

Mr. Flynn chuckled. "Trust a woman to see through another woman. Not that I agree with you, madam. My favourite in the murder stakes is the filly. The fair Irene."

"Order," said the foreman. "We'll keep to the point if we can, Mr. Flynn. The only question before us is that of Copeland's guilt or innocence. And you, Mrs. Williams?"

"I agree with Miss Barham."

The foreman sighed. "We must go on talking it over, I suppose."

"I'm not very happy about Miss Gort's part in the drama myself," said a man who had not spoken before. He was one of the seven who were prepared to bring in a verdict of guilty.

Miss Barham forgot her shyness and leaned forward to speak to him. "Don't you see, she hoped he'd marry her. She only began to send those letters when he came back with his second wife. She was bursting with spite."

"I grant you that. But you remember what Kynaston said. It doesn't prove Copeland didn't poison his wife."

Miss Barham looked about her earnestly. "Aren't you all forgetting what Sir Hugh got out of her when she was recalled about how she nursed her aunt through her last illness? That doctor thought it was a duodenal ulcer. She left Miss Gort all she had to leave. Don't you see? Sir Hugh couldn't press it, but he hoped we should notice, and ask ourselves if that was something more than a coincidence. Murderers, and especially poisoners, don't stick at one crime. If they get away with it they try again, and they seldom vary their methods."

"Good Lord!" the foreman gazed at her with mingled surprise and interest. He knew something of little Miss Barham. His wife got her wools from the shop in Church Passage. "I didn't know you were a student of criminology. Well, gentlemen, you have heard Miss Barham's theory. It's worth considering."

The Judge had gone to his room. The prisoner had been taken down to the cells. In the crowded Court room there was a subdued murmur of conversation. Barrymore had gone out to smoke a surreptitious cigarette. He whispered to John Reid on his return.

"I looked out of a window. The market square's packed with people. In spite of the rain. I wonder how long they're prepared to wait."

Reid was drawing rings on the sheet of foolscap on the table before him. One ring inside the other until there was only room for a dot in the middle. The dot represented a man. Any man. In the fell clutch of circumstance. . . .

"They're a long time," he said. "I thought they'd be back before this."

"How is Copeland standing it? Have you been to see him?"

"I've just come back. He's fairly steady. Is there a chance for him or not, Barrymore?"

"I can't say. One never knows with juries. Over two hours now. All right, Reid. There's someone over there I want to speak to." He came back a little later. "I hear they sent to the Judge to ask if they could give a majority verdict. There was a considerable diversity of opinion at first, but only two were still holding out."

"For Copeland or against him?"

"I don't know. It's just a rumour. In any case the Judge would have to tell them they must convert the minority or admit that they disagree and that would mean a new trial. Look out. They'll be coming now. They're bringing Copeland back." Alan was coming up the stairs from the cells. He had been given a cup of tea and a cigarette and one of his warders had offered to play draughts with him while they waited. They had broken off in the middle of a game. He moved forward to the front of the dock and stood there gripping the rail with both hands.

The Judge had returned. Alan wondered which of the officials standing behind him was holding a square of black cloth in readiness. The jury were coming in now. The Judge was saying something. Alan couldn't distinguish the words. There was a roaring in his ears. The foreman of the jury was speaking.

"Not guilty, my Lord."

"That is unanimous?"

"Yes, my Lord."

The Judge bowed his head. "It is a verdict in which I concur. Alan Copeland, you have been tried and found not guilty of the crime of murder. You leave this court a free man."

"Thank you, my Lord. I—" Barrymore and Reid were trying to force their way through the crowd. Pandemonium had broken out as the Judge and his attendants left the Court. The cheers from the public gallery had been heard in the square outside and taken up there.

CHAPTER XXII
THEY HAD BEEN WARNED

BARRYMORE had to clutch his gown to prevent it being torn off his back as he was caught in the rush of people making for one of the doors out of the Court room. His hand was still aching from the grip Reid had given it. "Splendid effort. Magnificent!" Reid could hardly get the words out.

Barrymore had smiled. He was inclined to agree, but he only said, "Thanks to your spade work, my dear fellow. Sorry I can't stop to shake hands with our client. I've got to catch a train. I promised to take the chair at a meeting if I could get away in time."

They were separated by the pressure of the crowd. Reid edging his way round one of the pillars supporting the gallery cannoned into the burly figure of Superintendent Hellyer.

"I was just coming for you, sir. We've got Mr. Copeland below. I've advised him to let the crowds disperse before he attempts to leave the building. He'll be wanting to thank you. Come this way."

He unlocked a door and Reid followed him along a passage encumbered with buckets and brooms and down a short flight of stairs to a basement room where Alan Copeland was pacing to and fro. He stopped as they entered and held out his hand to the lawyer.

"I'm eternally grateful. I owe you my life," he said huskily.

He looked past Reid into the passage. "Where's Barrymore?"

"He had to catch a train. I was to tell you—"

The Superintendent cleared his throat. "I wouldn't like you to think I'm not as pleased as anyone at the verdict. I—we all make mistakes."

Alan's weary face lit up. "Thanks. That's very decent of you. I don't blame the police for arresting me. Appearances were damnably against me."

There was a knock at the door. Helyer opened it and a constable gave him a note.

"For you, Mr. Reid. Its marked Immediate."

Helyer, watching him as he read it, saw his face change.

"Anything wrong, sir?"

"It's from Hayter. He had to get back to Town, too. He—he says he warned me before there might be danger and that we had better look out."

Helyer stared. "What does he mean?"

Alan threw the cigarette he had just lit into the fire.

"Danger to whom? Danger from what?"

Reid licked his lips. "He warned us before—because of the letters signed Justice. I think he felt they weren't quite sane. Look here, Superintendent, what are you doing about Emily Gort?"

"That will depend on the Chief Constable, Mr. Reid. There will have to be a conference. We don't want to slip up a second time."

"That means that so far you've done nothing. She's still at large," said Reid impatiently.

Helyer stiffened. "Certainly. We can't rush a thing like that."

"Emily Gort," said Alan slowly. "Mabel was good to her. She made use of her. Bullied her, too, of course. Do you really believe she poisoned Mabel? I can't take it in somehow."

"She'd had some practice," said Reid grimly.

"That's only guess work, sir," the Superintendent reproved him.

"It's up to you to prove it, Hellyer. But meanwhile, for God's sake, don't neglect this warning—"

"What do you want us to do, Mr. Reid—"

"Can't you discuss that later?" said Alan. "The crowds must have cleared off by now. I want to go to my wife. You'll come with me, Reid? She'll want to see you, I know."

"If you'll wait here a minute," said Helyer, "I'll see if the road is clear. Mrs. Copeland is at Greylands, isn't she? You'll take him in your car, Mr. Reid?"

He came back very soon. "I'm taking you myself," he said curtly. "We shall get there quicker. Come along."

Reid glanced at his set face and said nothing. It was apparent to him that during his short absence from the room Helyer had heard something that had changed his attitude. He hurried them out to the waiting car and spoke to the driver before he got in after them.

"Greylands. The nursing home in River Road. As quick as you can make it, Evans."

Alan seemed unaware of the growing tension. He was looking out of the window as the car leapt forward, looking eagerly at the lighted shop fronts, the red and green and amber of the jars in the chemist's shop glowing through the wintry darkness, with the child-like enjoyment of a convalescent to whom everything in the world he had expected to leave seems fresh and new.

They had left the maze of narrow streets in the centre of the town. The constable on duty in the Carfax had stopped the stream of traffic to let them pass. Evans turned the car into the quiet road that led to the river and stopped at the gate of the nursing home. Alan was the first to get out.

Reid took the opportunity to speak to the Superintendent.

"What's wrong, Hellyer?"

"One of my men got her a taxi. She gave this address."

Reid's heart seemed to miss a beat. "Miss Gort?" He knew now what he feared, and the knowledge turned him cold.

Evans, at a word from the Superintendent, joined them, and they hurried after Alan, who was already half-way up the drive. There were two doctors' cars drawn up before the entrance and the windows were all lit up. Alan had to ring twice before the door was opened by a stout woman in a print dress.

"It's not my business to answer the bell, but the staff are all busy. Got to have an operation at short notice. What do you want? These aren't the visiting hours."

Reid intervened before Alan could speak. The matron had stipulated that Lydia's name should not be mentioned. Some of the other patients might have objected to her presence.

"We have come to see the lady in number seven," he explained. "This is her husband."

The cook's mind worked slowly. "I don't know," she began. "She's got one visitor now. Very pushing she was, too. I couldn't keep her out. A middle-aged person dressed in grey."

They left her staring as they brushed past and ran down the hall. Again Alan was first, taking the stairs three at a time, but the others were close behind, and Reid called to him, "The first on the right across the landing."

Alan knew now why the others had been so silent on the way, why the car had been driven at such reckless speed. He had experienced fear, but never such fear as this.

He burst into the quiet room.

The curtains were drawn. A fire burned in the grate. The shade of the lamp on the night table was tilted so that the light fell on the neat, sparse figure bending over the bed, with its right arm uplifted over the terrified white face on the pillow. Alan sprang forward and thrust her aside. The lifted arm had struck downward with all the force of a passion long repressed, but he had spoiled its aim.

"Alan, oh Alan!" Lydia clung to him desperately. "Don't let her. She said—"

He held her close. "It's all right, my darling! All right now."

Reid was looking at one of Miss Gort's long steel hat pins buried almost up to its head in the mattress.

He left the room, closing the door after him very gently.

The Superintendent and Evans were waiting for him on the landing with Miss Gort between them.

Her felt hat had slipped to one side during the struggle. There were patches of angry red on her face and throat, and her light eyes glittered.

Helyer looked at Reid gravely.

"Is Mrs. Copeland any the worse?"

"No. Thank God we were in time. She had a hat pin in her hand, Hellyer. She struck to kill."

The Superintendent nodded. "We'll get along to the station. Now, miss!"

His prisoner said nothing but she jerked furiously at the steel bracelets on her lean wrists.

"That will do," he said sharply. "We don't want any trouble here."

Miss Gort, who had always been so lady-like, spat in his face. Evans held her while the Superintendent wiped his cheek with his handkerchief. It was something less than human that they carried down the stairs between them.

Reid waited until he heard the closing of the front door before he went down to the hall. He had still to see the matron and arrange with her that Alan should remain there that night. Half an hour later he started on his homeward way. The long-drawn-out suspense was at an end and his strained nerves relaxed. He had done what he set out to do, and if Lydia had not one thought to spare for him to-night he could not blame her. His was not a selfish love and he could be happy in her happiness. These violent delights, and violent ends were not for him. His more sober existence had its compensations.

And as for that other. "Mad, quite mad, poor thing. God help her."

The rain had ceased. He looked up, as he paused before crossing the road, and saw a star shining through a rift in the clouds. He thought it might be the planet Venus. "The fault, dear Brutus, is not in our stars."

THE END

Printed in Great Britain
by Amazon